"One of the most original vampire novel[...] *Eating* follows Lydia, a British, Japanese[...] gling to survive. . . . Kohda has given Lydia a host of great vampire qualities, such as excellent night vision and an ability to experience the entire life of a creature by drinking its blood. But it's Kohda's exploration of Lydia's inner world, the pain and longing she feels as an outsider, that makes *Woman, Eating* such a delicious novel."

—*New York Times Book Review*

"Absolutely brilliant—tragic, funny, eccentric, and so perfectly suited to this particularly weird time. Claire Kohda takes the vampire trope and makes it her own in a way that feels fresh and original. Serious issues of race, disability, misogyny, body image, sexual abuse are handled with subtlety, insight, and a lightness of touch, and the novel is ridiculously suspenseful! I was on the edge of my seat, just waiting for Lyd to bite someone, and in the end, I felt utterly and happily bitten."

—Ruth Ozeki, author of *A Tale for the Time Being*

"The most unusual, original, and strikingly contemporary vampire novel to come along in years."

—*The Guardian*

"Unsettling, sensual, subversive, *Woman, Eating* turns the vampire trope on its head with its startlingly original female protagonist, caught between two worlds. It is a profound meditation on alienation and appetite, and what it means to be a young woman who experiences life at an acute level of intensity and awareness. Claire Kohda's prose is biting, yet lush and gorgeous. I was uncomfortably smitten."

—Lisa Harding, author of Read with Jenna
Book Club Pick *Bright Burning Things*

"We've seen sexy vampires, scary vampires, and psychic vampires, but never one quite like the one in this ambitious debut. . . . With wit and a poet's eye, Kohda examines cravings, desire, and emptiness."

—*New York Times*

"The chief trait that Lydia, the protagonist of this artful vampire novel, shares with monsters of old is hunger. . . . As Lydia encounters new people, including a pleasant artist turned property manager, and a new boss, a man with more influence than decency, she comes to understand what it is to become something 'that is neither demon nor human.'"

—*The New Yorker*

"We have here a vampire book that will scrub any trace of *Twilight* from your mind—Claire Kohda's debut follows a young vampire dealing with all kinds of hunger: for acceptance, for artistic success, and for sushi."

—*Glamour*

"What Stoker did for the vampire at the end of the nineteenth century, Claire Kohda does for it in our own era. . . . There is much here to mesmerize and beguile readers, not least in Kohda's prose, which is patient, strange, and altogether persuasive."

—*Times Literary Supplement* (London)

"If you're looking for a new read, then you have to read Claire Kohda's novel, *Woman, Eating*. This novel has been making the rounds of various 'Favorites' lists, and for very good reason: it's a personable and unique take on what modern vampirism could look like. . . . Lydia was a mixed-Asian woman who learned how to be true to herself, to live unshackled to the colonialist society that had contained her. And now, she could finally live, not as the beast she was raised to think she was, but as *Lydia*, a clever, creative, and cunning young woman."

—*The Mary Sue*

"A magnificent debut."

—*The Millions*

"Claire Kohda's debut, *Woman, Eating*, is an insightful and hypnotic exploration of hunger. . . . Through Lydia's mixed-race heritage and particular vampire traits, Kohda deftly tackles difficult, and common, themes—including sexism, racism, assault, job insecurity, and social isolation."

—*Shelf Awareness*

WOMAN, EATING

A NOVEL

CLAIRE KOHDA

HARPERVIA

An Imprint of HarperCollins*Publishers*

For BC and T, for us

HarperCollins books may be purchased for educational, business, or sales promotional use. For information, please email the Special Markets Department at SPsales@harpercollins.com.

FIRST HARPERCOLLINS PAPERBACK PUBLISHED IN 2023
FIRST US EDITION PUBLISHED IN 2022

Designed by Terry McGrath

Library of Congress Cataloging-in-Publication Data is available upon request.

ISBN 978-0-06-314089-9

23 24 25 26 27 LBC 7 6 5 4 3

All life, to sustain itself, must devour life.

—Lafcadio Hearn, "Ululation," *In Ghostly Japan*

PART ONE

1

The guy from Kora is standing outside the building in the sun. I've read online that this place used to be a biscuit factory.

"Hey," the guy calls. He waves.

I feel self-conscious walking these last few meters, since he has seen me now and so is just watching me approach. It feels like a long time passes between the guy's hey and my eventual arrival in front of him.

"Hey," I say.

"Lydia?"

"Lyd."

"Okay, hey Lyd. So, I'm Ben. You're seeing . . ." He looks down at the paper he's holding. "A14."

"Yeah," I say.

"You know it doesn't have much light, right?" He looks up. "I mean, if you want I can show you one of the studios with a skylight and everything."

"No, it's okay."

Ben raises an eyebrow. "Photographer?"

"Performance."

"Really?" He sounds surprised. I get this a lot. I come across shy. "Fair enough."

Ben opens the door to the building. It's a large metal door with an iron gate in front of it that he has to open first. There are four keys he uses to get in.

"Pretty secure," Ben says. "It's a definite plus for the women who work here. So you can be here late and you'll probably feel safe."

I look up. The windows don't start until the second floor. It'd be difficult to reach them even with a ladder.

"Yeah, so—" Ben follows my line of sight "—there are no windows on the ground and first floors because the biscuits they made here were coated with chocolate."

"Oh," I say.

"Yeah, it's interesting, isn't it?" The door opens with a clang. "A whole building basically designed around the fact that chocolate melts in sunlight."

"Mm." The building goes up very high. The first two floors look like part of the foundations.

There's an awkward moment as we go inside. We both gesture for the other to go first, and then bump into one another as we try to go through the door at the same time.

"So, where did you come from?" Ben says as we walk down a dark corridor.

I pause. I get this a lot too. "Well, I'm from England. But my dad was Japanese, and my mum is half Malaysian."

He turns around. "Oh my god, shit, no, sorry—I mean, where did you come from today? Like, are you living in London?"

"Oh, yeah," I lie. "I live just near here, in Kennington." I don't actually live in Kennington. I've just seen the stop on the tube map.

"Nice!" Ben says. "It's pretty nice around there, isn't it?"

I nod.

Ben opens a door with a nameplate on it that reads "A14." I step into the room. It's quite small, but enough. On one side is a sink and a counter with a microwave on top and a small fridge underneath.

"The rent on this studio is cheaper than the ones with windows. It's two hundred and fifty-five pounds per month, with Kora subsidizing the rest as part of the young artists' scheme." Ben's looking at one of the pieces of paper he is holding. "Bills are on top, but they're cheap. Payment is due on the twenty-eighth of every month. I can leave this with you if you decide to take the room." He holds the piece of paper up to show me. "There's a map too, fire exits, all that."

"Do the lights dim?" I ask, and Ben nods. I go to the switch and try it. The lights go down until they're almost off. I leave them at their lowest and, for a moment, the room looks like it is just made of shadows. Then, my eyes adjust and I can see everything. Ben squints in my direction, frowning slightly.

"I like it," I say.

"Okay, great! You'll take it?"

"Yep."

"Let's sit down with the contracts, then. So, shall we . . ."

I realize that he is expecting me to turn the lights up again.

"Okay," I say, but I don't go to the switch. I go to the table and sit down in the half-light, hoping that he will just go with it. He does. He stumbles a bit on his way to the table over nothing. *People*, I think to myself, *have appalling night vision*. And he sits down.

He spreads the papers on the table. Then he looks up toward me. In this light his features look very soft, whereas outside he had looked slightly more angular. I take in his cheeks, which are round and tinged pink. He must be quite young. He's fairly good-looking. I smile at him. Ben puts one of his hands in the other, and then says, "Would you mind if I . . . ?" and points to the light above our heads. He begins to stand up from his seat.

"Actually, would you mind if we just left it?" I ask. "I'm getting a headache," I add.

"Oh . . . yeah, yeah, sure. I've got some ibuprofen, if you want . . ." Ben sits down again, and reaches toward his bag next to him on the floor. It's a nice, svelte-looking cycling bag.

I shake my head. "It's okay. I'm good. I'm probably just hungry." And as I say the word "hungry," my stomach rumbles. I shuffle on my seat to disguise the noise, but it's pretty loud and the empty room is particularly resonant. I feel embarrassed. Ben pretends he hasn't heard it, which makes it even worse.

"Er, so . . . I can't actually see the forms," he says. He laughs and looks up. "But I've marked crosses where you need to sign." He brings his head low over the table and squints. "Um," he says. "Here's one."

He slides a piece of paper and a pen across the table toward me, his thumb held firmly partway down the page where I need to sign. I can see the cross; I can see it quite clearly, in black Sharpie at one end of a dotted line, but I don't tell him. Instead, I pick up the pen, then feel where his hand is on the paper and use it as a guide. I feel his thumb with my fingertips. It's very warm. I don't know where this sudden decision to flirt has come from. I suppose, in this room, in the very dim light, I feel quite powerful. Men, I think, feel insecure in silence and much more confident when there's the sound of traffic and other people all around. And this room is completely silent. I sign my name on the line.

"And where else?" I ask. He slides over another page, with his thumb there to guide me again.

"Okay, so, um. Basically, what you just signed is, you know, all the usual stuff."

"Yeah," I say.

"Can't sleep in here, have parties, no openings, no gatherings over, like, five people. No open flames, obviously. No, like, dangerous chemicals." He laughs. He seems nervous.

"It's okay, I read it all online."

"Sorry," Ben says. "Probably should have told you all that before you signed, right?"

I don't say anything. His eyes are wide. "Okay," he says, and he starts gathering together all the pieces of paper on the table. "When would you like to pick up the keys?"

"Now? I'll move my stuff in today."

"Today? Wow, yeah, okay. That's quick. I won't have time to properly clean the studio, but if that's okay?" He reaches into the pocket of his shirt and takes out the key to this room, and also four other keys for the front door and front gate.

"That's fine. I'm starting an internship tomorrow, so I want to get moved in before."

"Oh, sweet. Where? Will I know the place?"

"The OTA," I say.

"No way!" Ben says. "The Otter? Very nice. There's another girl here who interned there a while back. You'll probably meet her. Her name's Shakti." He hands me the keys. In the dim light, he misjudges where my hand is and puts his hand in mine along with the keys. "Oops," he says. I can see that he is blushing.

7

I smile. "Thanks."

"Where did you say you live in Kennington? Anywhere near City and Guilds?" he asks, as he puts his bag on his back.

"Yeah," I say. I vaguely remember where City and Guilds is. And I can kind of imagine living around there. I think there are a few tall town houses, maybe, in that area. "In a flat-share," I add.

"Oh, right, artists?"

I'm making up a life on the spot now. "No, a couple who work in music and a guy who's just working in retail at the moment but he . . . he wants to get into film."

"Ooh, good luck to him. I've got a mate in film; she's a production designer. I can put him in touch if he wants."

"Maybe, yeah."

Ben starts cautiously making his way to the door. I like the knowledge that, while he is struggling simply to walk across the room in this light, I could easily thread a needle. I could sit him down and draw a detailed portrait of him. As I walk behind him, I study all the fine hairs growing out of the back of his neck, his goose-pimply skin and its light pinkness. Before he reaches the door, he turns around.

"Er, so." He clears his throat. "So, I'm upstairs. My studio, I mean. I'm two floors above. The first floor with windows. There's no one above you, so we're basically neighbors."

"Oh, right," I say. "You're an artist."

"Yeah—but I do this for Kora, like all the studio viewings and stuff, and I manage the building so I get the studio for free. Anyway, if you want to pop in to say hello, I'm C14. And if I'm not in my studio, I'm in The Place a lot too."

"The Place?"

"Yeah. The Place is the common living area, and the studios

are The Space. It's what we call them." Ben's smiling. I can see he finds this funny, maybe a bit embarrassing. "I know, it's a bit of a cliché," he adds. "It's meant to be, like, the studios are . . . your space, you know? And The Place is, like"—he air quotes and puts on a voice like a narrator in a TV advert—"'the place to be.'" He laughs and then snorts. I find it endearing.

He puts his hand on the door handle. The papers I have just signed are tucked under his arm. "So, I should . . ." he begins.

I kind of want to follow him out. There's something about being with him that I find comforting, even though I've only just met him. He feels extremely human. His smile is cute, as is his nervousness. His skin is very taut over his body in the way a toddler's is, which I find sweet. He's covered in little freckles.

"Unless, do you fancy getting some lunch?"

My heart sinks. At the same time, I feel my stomach rumble again.

"I'm probably going to just pop down to Pret or something. Get one of those avo-falafel wraps," he says.

"Yeah no," I say—saying both yes and no as I always do when I want to say no to someone but without sounding harsh—"I can't."

"Oh, okay." He looks a bit put out. I suppose he probably expected me to say yes after hearing my stomach rumble.

"Sorry."

"Nah, it's okay. You want me to pick you up a coffee or anything?"

I shake my head. "I'm good, thanks."

"Okay. Well." He goes to open the door. "My number's on the piece of paper I left on the table."

"Okay," I say.

"Hope your head feels better soon," he says, and he opens the door—momentarily letting in a huge amount of dazzlingly bright light—slips out, and disappears down the hall.

I lie down on the floor. It's just plain concrete with nothing on top. No carpet or rug or anything. The cold feels good on my back. The lights are still low. I'm more comfortable in the dark. It's not even that the lights in here would burn me; it's that sometimes too much light is overwhelming, especially after a day filled with things I'm not used to doing much of—packing, moving, traveling. It's too much input, almost painful for the brain, not necessarily the skin. However, sunlight does burn. Not in the way it does in films and TV programs; I don't let off smoke or singe, or burst into flames. Rather, my skin burns as if it has no pigment at all, as if I'm without any melanin, as if I'm completely and purely white.

I roll over onto my side. I can see the sink, fridge, and microwave from here. I haven't eaten since breakfast. Partly because I've been so busy. I left Mum's house at seven-thirty. I went around all the rooms one last time to make sure there was nothing left behind. Crimson Orchard recommends that residents have as many of their belongings—photos, books, furniture even, any personal artifacts—arranged around their rooms as possible, because old things with memories already associated with them encourage the formation of new memories, apparently. But Mum still ended up having too much stuff. She essentially had several lives' worth of belongings all stuffed into our little two-bedroom house. And some of it was really, really old. An ancient pair of spring scissors ended up being taken by a local museum when I put them up for sale on Facebook. One of my old school friends who works at the museum had seen my post and talked to the curator to see how much she would offer for them—and it turned out that they could offer a fair amount: enough to pay for a couple of months' rent on my studio.

I left Mum at Crimson Orchard yesterday, so I could do the last bit of sorting by myself. I don't know how she would feel if she knew she'd been moved out of her house; if she could see all the rooms empty; if she knew someone else would be moving in soon. The staff at Crimson Orchard are telling her that she is staying only temporarily and that, before long, she'll go back home. They've let her keep her front-door keys, which she clutched in her hand right up until I left her. Although, quite soon, if she were to go back with them, the locks will have been changed.

"Lyds," my mum said, when I was leaving. She looked out of place in her new room, which was decorated with someone in their eighties or nineties in mind. Mum has for the last couple of centuries looked like she is in her early forties. She still has black hair, just with some streaks of gray here and there. Her eyes are still bright.

"Mum, I'll be back in a couple of minutes," I said, as the doctor had told me to say.

"Julie, don't worry," the doctor said. "Lydia's just going to pop out and get a cup of tea and a bite to eat." But, of course, that was the wrong thing to say, and my mum's eyes had widened until they were so big that they distorted the rest of her face, pushing her eyebrows far up her forehead. "You're leaving! You're leaving your mother!" Mum wailed, looking terrified like a child being left at nursery school for the first time.

"No, no, Mum, I'm not." I reached to pat her on the head, but she twisted around and tried to bite me, so I pulled my hand away quickly. "The doctor misunderstood. I'm not going out to eat—I just need a wee."

"GO. HERE," Mum bellowed, gesturing to the bathroom adjoining her room.

I paused. "I . . ."

"Don't worry, Julie. She'll be back in a moment, I promise you," the doctor said.

"Lyds, Lyds," my mum whispered, ignoring the doctor and grabbing my top and pulling me closer. "Lyds, you hate me, don't you? You hate me. Lyds . . . please . . ."

"Mum."

"Lyds," she said—and, momentarily, her expression changed to one of concern. "You won't make it without me. You're not the same as them." But I shook her off, and her expression changed again to something more contrite. "Please . . . why do you hate me so much . . . *please*." Tears ran down her face. But it was hard to know what was real with Mum, even tears.

"*Mum*," I snapped, and I pulled myself free. I walked to the door and let myself out. "I'll be right the fuck back, okay?" I said, immediately feeling guilty about snapping. I closed the door, behind which I could hear my mum screaming and sobbing, "You hate meee, you hate meee . . . Lydia! I did everything for *you*; everything was for *you*. I'll kill myself! I'll do it! I can. *I will!*"

I walked down the hall, ignoring whatever the doctor next to me was saying—something about food and weight and personal hygiene. The sun was particularly bright outside, but I wanted to get out. In here, I felt strange, like my skin was burning, like the guilt was a fire that was spreading deep inside my body.

"Okay," I said to the doctor outside, surprised to find my voice was shaking. "It's nice meeting you."

"You too. We will be in touch, probably in the next couple of days, but we have a policy here, as I'm sure you've already been told, of not letting residents talk to any family or friends for the first week. But if you need anything at all, you have our number."

I put my hand out for the doctor to shake. "Blimey!" he said. "Your hands are cold." I sighed. I couldn't be bothered to think of an excuse. I ended up just agreeing, like he had expressed an opinion about something, rather than a fact. "Yeah, true," I said. "Thank you."

The doctor cocked his head sympathetically. And then, as I turned to walk toward the gate, he said, "Okay, so . . ." I expected him to say something else before I walked out of earshot, so I slowed down my footsteps, but he didn't. He just left the "so" hanging there in the air and went back into the building.

I went back to my mum's house straight after. I topped up my sunscreen and walked in the shade as much as possible, but my nose and the top of my forehead still got burned. At home, I put some Neal's Yard Baby Balm on the red bits of my skin. I swept and vacuumed the floors, pulling up the dust from the carpets that had accumulated over all the time we'd lived in this house. All of our DNA, maybe even some of Dad's DNA from when he was alive. I held a clump of it—bits of skin and hair with carpet fluff and dead bugs mixed in—up to my nose and inhaled, thinking that I could connect with my dad somehow in the smell, before putting it in the bin. I cleaned the sink too, which was stained from years of use.

I rolled out my sleeping bag in the living room. Upstairs was a bit too creepy. Though Dad was the one who actually died in this house, it was my mum's presence I could sense upstairs, as though each moment I'd spent with her here had turned into a separate ghost that haunted her bedroom. I sat up on top of my sleeping bag and tilted my head back on the sofa that had come with the house. Recently, I'd read a post on Facebook about rituals to do with moving out of homes. It said that moving out of a place you've lived in for a significant amount of time can leave you with all sorts of spiritual baggage, if you don't move out in the right way. The post included pictures of a woman with long blond hair in loose clothes blessing all kinds of different rooms, throwing salt on the carpets and doing some sort of full moon, new beginnings ritual. I couldn't imagine anything like that taking place in this house. It was, I felt, beyond new beginnings. I let my head slip off the sofa cushions and land with a thud on the floor.

That evening, I'd finished mine and Mum's last bucket of pig blood from the butcher's, slightly warmed and from a wineglass to create a sense of ceremony; the other remaining bucket had been poured carefully into flasks and stashed in Mum's fridge at Crimson Orchard, along with some human food—cheese, microwavable meals, milk, sausage rolls, vegetables—that was there to act as a decoy. I'd drunk what blood remained in the house, sitting alone at the kitchen table where for years and years—for my whole life—I'd eaten meals with my mum. I wasn't allowed to eat upstairs. Because the blood would stain the carpets if I spilled any, Mum had said; but I think the real reason was that she didn't like eating alone.

Before dinner we always said a prayer. Our table was a small white-topped one from the 1950s, with metal legs. I sat at one end and my mum sat at the other. Our arms reached toward each other and met in the center. Our fingers interwove so that our linked hands were standing upright and our wrists were pressing down on the tabletop. Mum would wait until I closed my eyes, and then she would close her eyes too and recite a prayer. It wasn't directed at a god, like the grace said before food was in films and TV programs. When I asked why our grace was different, when I was around six years old and learning about God and the Nativity at school, she looked at me impatiently.

"Lydia," she said, using my full name, which she only did when she was angry. "Do you think God would feed a body like yours?"

I had tentatively shaken my head, but I didn't really understand. My mum continued: "Something else lets us eat, not God. God wouldn't want to help a demon survive, and that's what we are, Lyds. We are unnatural, disgusting, and ugly. Look at us; we are just sin."

Mum then had reached across the table for my hands. "But it's okay," she said. "Because we are the same, so we have each other." And then she said our prayer, the version that suited us, which wasn't to any higher being but just to the pigs whose blood we drank.

I lay awake all last night. The house, while I'd been growing up, had always been cluttered, full of things that never got thrown away—mail, documents, piles of old rags and old clothes—as well as, before my mum sold it all to pay the rent, my dad's artwork. The pieces he left behind were framed like they were ready to be hung in a gallery, but were propped up against the walls of Mum's bedroom instead, the backs of the canvases facing into the room as if the paintings were in fact photographs of his face that my mum couldn't bear to look at. Now all of that is gone. I barely remember my dad's art, other than the few pieces viewable online. Last night, I'd felt the emptiness of the house as if it were a presence. I felt it judging me for selling all of my mum's things, and moving on with my life, and leaving my mother behind, in a home.

In the morning, I packed my belongings—my sleeping bag; my laptop; a few books on art, others on animals that in the past I'd read to try to find similarities between myself and other species, some cookbooks and foraging books; my clothes; my favorite mug; some old sketchbooks—into a large suitcase and my rucksack. I opened the fridge but there was nothing in it, apart from the stubby end of a black pudding sausage wrapped in cling film, which had been in there for god knows how long, as an emergency stash for when we ran out of blood or the butcher's was closed. I chopped it up into little pieces and carried them in the palm of my hand, like I was offering bread crumbs to birds, while I went around the house one last time. I took little pieces one by one and popped them in my mouth. The black pudding tasted bad, especially so cold from the fridge. And my body couldn't take much of the egg and oats and pepper that were mixed with the blood to make the sausage; I had to spit most of it out. But it was sustenance, enough to tide me over. Then I left.

So, now, I'm pretty hungry. This happens quite a lot, I suppose. Maybe it's laziness, or maybe it's something else. I'm lying on my side in the new studio, with none of my stuff here apart from what's in my rucksack, listening to my stomach rumble until I get so hungry that it seems to stop bothering to even rumble.

I don't know what it is. It's not that I don't value myself, which I'm sure is what a psychologist would say is the case. It's more that I know that I can survive for ages without eating, and pushing my body in the vague direction of its limits is satisfying, in that I feel more alive than I ever otherwise do. I've heard of people who go running for something like fifty or sixty miles across the countryside—and not just the flat countryside in Kent, but the hilly countryside up near Sheffield—just so they can feel the same feeling. It's as though, because they are pushing their bodies to their outermost limits, they can feel their mortality. Like, they go right up to the edge of what it means to be alive, and look over it and down at the huge, immeasurable void below, and feel joy because they're not in the void, but above it. That's what being alive is. But, normally, people don't see over the edge and witness the contrast between the everythingness of life and the nothingness of death, so they don't feel or understand that life is exhilarating, like those runners do.

I know it's a bit different for me. Neither the void or the cliff above it look the same to me as they do to normal people. The void, for me, has stuff in it, so it's not a void anymore; and the cliff is engulfed by a black and measureless haze. Still, I like to push my body toward its limits. Or, rather, I like to pretend my body has limits. I like to feel the pain of hunger and imagine that the next step after that pain is death. It's annoying, though. That peak feeling of being right at the edge is always out of my reach. I could stay here, on the floor of Studio A14, Kora Biscuit Factory Studios, for several days, even several weeks, months, years, whatever, and I'd still be able to get at least partway up and crawl to a food source, eat, and recover fully; and if I was *really* weak, so weak that I couldn't get up and move, I'd still stay alive, just lying here in a coma, for years and years and years, my body refusing to properly die until the Sun came down and engulfed the Earth.

I pull at a bit of loose skin next to one of my fingernails and squeeze my finger so that the blood forms a little bead. I suck it until it stops bleeding. Then, I get up off the floor.

I enjoy the dizziness. I stagger to my bag, open it, and take out the last couple of pieces of black pudding from this morning. I eat it. Over the sink I spit out a few bits of oats and pepper. Then I take my wallet and my phone and go to the door. I close it behind me and feel a little bit of anxiety about locking up in an unfamiliar place, with an unfamiliar key and an unfamiliar lock. The lock clicks, and I push the door a few times and jiggle the handle to make sure it's closed. Then, I unlock the door and open it again, just to make sure I can get back in later. I'm locking up and jiggling the handle for a second time when I hear a shuffling sound farther down the corridor. There's a woman standing outside her studio, maybe ten doors down from mine, on the phone and with a bike helmet hanging from her arm. Very tall, very slim, with dark skin and her hair wrapped tightly in a headscarf. She is smiling at me.

"Hey," she says.

"Hey," I answer.

And then the woman says hello to the person on the other end of the phone, waves at me, and disappears into her studio.

A little while later, I'm looking at Facebook while waiting in the queue at the butcher's. Someone's posted about a new type of reduced-sugar peanut butter that has an ingredient in it that is dangerous for dogs, with a message reading, "Watch out dog owners!" Someone else is looking for recommendations for vegan protein to put in smoothies. And a guy I went to school with has posted something about proportional representation. I suppose proportional representation makes sense. I think I've thought about it before, but I get confused sometimes about what are my own thoughts and what are thoughts other people have had and then posted on social media. The graph the guy from my old school has posted shows how, with proportional representation, the Conservatives would be down 4 percent and Labour up 3, or something like that. The graph isn't clear, though, and I'm already convinced anyway, so I keep scrolling.

"Miss?" the guy behind the counter says. His eyes hover somewhere around my collarbones.

"Sorry." I put my phone in my pocket. I smile.

The man watches, hand on hip; he seems impatient. Then he says, "What can I do you for?" The reviews online had said that this butcher was especially friendly; the shop had been passed down from generation to generation. So I'm taken aback by the roughness of the man's voice and his unsmiling face.

"Oh, er . . ." I look at the selection behind the glass. There are a few pasties and pastries, things like Scotch eggs and potato salad, as well as sliced meat and wrapped cuts.

"Can I have a Scotch egg and . . ." The man's hand reaches for the Scotch egg at the top of the pile and wraps it in thin plastic, then places it on the counter. ". . . a cheese and . . . bacon pastry thing . . ." I point, and he gets a small paper bag from behind him and uses tongs to pick the pastry up. "And one of those sausages, maybe a couple of those smaller sausages too, some potato salad—and yeah . . . um . . . do you have, like, some pig blood?" I shuffle on the spot and clear my throat.

The man pauses, his gloved hand midway to a stack of sausages at the front of the counter. Then he stands upright, a confused expression on his face.

"I'm a performance artist," I say, but my voice is very quiet.

"You what now?" the man says.

"Performance artist?"

The man just stares at me. "We don't sell anything like that here," he says, gruffly, as if it is performance artists I'm looking to buy. I hear another customer whisper something to someone else behind me, and both of them quietly laugh.

"Oh, um." I back away from the counter. It was easy in Margate. The butcher there had surplus blood every other day. And she didn't ask any questions. I start making my way toward the door. "Sorry," I say as I leave, and the man shouts behind me, "What about your shopping? Hey!"

Outside, I stand on the pavement for a moment wondering whether I'm going to cry. But I don't—I just kind of stand there, next to a lamppost, while people walk hurriedly past me. It's rush hour. People are walking from Vauxhall Station and Vauxhall Bridge, trying to get home. I collect myself, feeling the ground beneath my feet, thinking about what I should do next. It's getting darker now. The sun dipped behind the buildings a while ago, but it's still there, above the horizon; I can feel its presence, even though there's so much concrete between us. The sky is a pleasing orange. Around about this time, I can handle looking up at the clouds without the light feeling too bright.

I walk down the road until I'm under a railway bridge. The walls of the underpass are painted with variations on paintings by William Blake. From the names of the roads in the area, I assume that Blake once lived somewhere around here. Right in the middle of the mural is a version of *The Ghost of a Flea*—a monstrous man with an alarmingly, almost disgustingly muscular back and legs, and long fingernails. I turn so I'm facing the picture, which is slightly larger than life-size, and about twenty times bigger than the original. His tongue curls up, like an upside-down version of an actual flea's proboscis, and his eyes are wide and hungry. He is looking into a bowl that is empty. The bowl probably once had blood in it, freshly extracted from an animal, and the ghost of a flea has just finished drinking it. Or maybe there is a little bit still at the bottom. I feel dizzy, looking into the painting of the bowl—envious of the flea who can bite and feed from an animal without them even noticing, whose stomach is likely full. I'm still looking at it when I hear footsteps down the road. A man's shoes—tap, tap, tap—and drunk ramblings, and swearing between inaudible words, so I turn around and start walking back toward the studios.

Later, I'm at St. Pancras station, waiting for my suitcase at the luggage storage. I've got the keys to the studio in the pocket of my shirt. It feels like I have the keys to my new life in my pocket, while the suitcase contains my old life.

"Hey," a man I've never seen before says, as he walks past me, coming from the direction of the men's toilets.

"Umm, hey?" I say, frowning. I shuffle up closer to the counter of the luggage storage, imagining that there's a kind of bubble around it, inside which I'm safe.

The guy working here comes out from the area where all the luggage is kept. He has a small, narrow head and a plump body covered by a large, loose-fitting shirt. He's looking at the ticket I gave him when I arrived. "Is this definitely the right ticket?" he asks without looking at me.

"Yeah," I shift on my feet. "I mean . . . yeah, that's what I was given." I feel a bit panicky. There's not really anything of worth in the suitcase—my laptop is already at the studio—but there's stuff in there that feels comfortingly familiar in a way a laptop never can. Books I read when I was younger, clothes that I've lived most of my adult life in, old sketchbooks, and then there's my birth certificate too. My mum folded it up small, eight ways, and sewed it in the lining of one of a pair of gloves she'd kept from before she was turned, centuries ago. It's not valuable. But it is a token of my human birth, proof that I was born completely normal and mortal, before my mum turned me just a few days later. It's a little secret, now that I'm beginning to look younger than my age: a memento of my short-lived, purely human life that I'll carry around forever, or that I'd at least planned to before this.

"It's not there?" I say, my voice high pitched. "That's the ticket I got. There was a woman who gave it to me and she tore the other end off and took it back there." I point to the door the guy came through a few seconds ago.

"No," he says, looking down at the ticket still. "There's nothing back there with this number." He looks up. "You want me to look again?"

"Um, yeah," I say, angrily. I look at my hands on the counter. They're shaking a bit. I can't tell if it's because of this issue with my suitcase, or because of the hunger that I can't feel anymore but know is there in the background.

"Okay," the man says. And he shuffles back through the door. While I wait, I try to remember everything that is in the suitcase as though, if I could just remember it all, I'd at least have a version of it in my head. When he comes back, he is empty-handed. "Sorry, miss," he says. "It isn't there. Unfortunately, these things happen from time to time. Must have been a mix-up or something. I'll give you a form you can fill out to make a claim to the head office and I can give you a refund of," and he looks down at the ticket again, "yeah . . . twenty-two-pound-fifty right now for the cost of today."

"Jesus fucking Christ," I say. "Really?"

The man looks up at me, his eyes small and beady. As he does, his neck presents itself to me. *Hello*, it seems to say. *Nice to meet you.*

"Sorry," the man says.

I look away from him. "Whatever," I say, and I concentrate on getting my wallet out.

"So . . . you're taking the refund, right?"

"Yeah. Can you put it on that," I say, flatly, giving him my debit card. As he walks to the other end of the counter, I shake my head and mutter, under my breath, "Fuck's sake." This expression of my dissatisfaction, even though it's to no one but myself, makes me feel slightly better about the situation. Maybe I don't need those books or those clothes or even my birth certificate. What does my birth certificate prove, anyway? That I was once born? That I was once fully human? I know these things without needing a piece of paper that I can't even read because it's sewn into one of a pair of gloves. Also, I'll have forever to build up a collection of books, and a collection of clothes for myself. In fact, I plan on one day having a library, which will be in one of the rooms of my own house. I'll also own a gallery. I'll set it up in my own name, and I'll run it for a few years, and then hire other people to manage it while I retreat into the background, overseeing things from a distance. In that time, I'll be making artwork under different names; then, eventually, I'll write up a press release declaring that I have died peacefully at home from old age and that I am passing my gallery and estate down to my adult daughter, who will just be me. And I'll repeat the process again, and then again. I'll have artwork belonging to me, books, a building with my name on it.

"Okay, so that's done," the guy says. "Sorry about your case."

"Thanks," I say, and I leave.

On my way to the tube, I stop in one of the shops in the main station that sells organic food and coffee. They have fairly low lighting, which is nice, compared to the harsh white strip lights on the concourse. There are heaters glowing orange inside too, and when I stand close to them, my skin warms up. It doesn't retain the heat—it's more like how leather can be warmed up next to a heater but, once it's taken away from the heat source, it'll quite quickly cool down again—but it does feel good to imagine for a moment that I have body heat. In the refrigerated-food section, I pick up a few items, like another customer does next to me, and turn them over to read the nutritional information. I like reading the various numbers that tell me how what I am holding will transform inside a human's body. Energy: 326 cal, Fat: 16g, Carbohydrates: 38g; Protein: 11g. This meal has grains and pomegranate seeds, spring onion, olive oil, mustard seeds, garlic, and lemon. It is called a "Superfood, Super-Clean Salad." I turn over a pot of yogurt and oats too, and read the information on the small white label, and then put it back on the shelf like something in it is inadequate, or it doesn't have what I'm looking for inside it. I watch as the other customer picks up a boiled egg sitting on a bed of spinach in a small, round, plastic tub and an iced coffee. He takes his food to the counter and pays for it and, soon, another person is next to me in the refrigerated-foods section, picking up items and putting them down too. Eventually, I go to the counter and ask if they sell any black pudding, or whether they know what shops nearby might sell any, and the woman working there bewilderedly shakes her head. "Sorry, no. Black pudding?"

"Yeah," I say, regretting having not asked for some at the butcher's, where there'd been whole black pudding sausages on display in among all the other processed meats. "It comes in a sausage."

She shakes her head again. "Marks & Spencer, maybe?"

As I leave, I see the man who bought the egg. He is sitting in the café area under a heater. He has bitten off the top of the boiled egg and is holding the rest in his hand. I go to another shop to see if I can find a sleeping bag or something else soft to sleep on tonight, but everything is too expensive. I think about going to M&S but I can't handle the thought of interacting with more people and being disappointed again, so I go down to the tube station.

I'm fairly happy on my way down the escalators. There's something freeing about losing all your possessions from an old life. Even though I'll have nothing to sleep on tonight, I feel light and optimistic. But, this feeling goes quickly. In the tunnels on the way to the southbound Northern line, I get the sense that there is someone following me. I haven't seen a person acting suspiciously—the people behind me all look like they are just walking to catch the train—but I experience a sensation like my back is being physically poked by a person's gaze. I used to think that my ability to sense things like this was another thing that set me apart from humans, but when I asked my mum about it as a teenager, she told me that it wasn't and that it was something that was, in fact, from my human half. It's something, she said, that most women can do—an extra sense that men don't have, or else one they usually don't need.

I turn down onto the platform and walk to the end, where there are a few people gathered. They're women on a hen-do who are, I'm guessing from their accents, from Manchester. When the train arrives, I get on with them, so I'm hidden by their feather boas and balloons. While the tube is moving, though, I see the person, who I guess was the one following me, through the window leading into the next carriage. A man with a thin face, large eyes, and dark hair speckled with gray is looking at me. I scowl at him so that he knows I can see him, and so that he knows I am unhappy with him looking. But, he keeps staring and, eventually, the corners of his mouth turn up into a slight smile.

The missing suitcase feels like it means more now than it did earlier. Under this man's gaze, I realize that I don't really know who I am. My life in a sense begins tomorrow, when I start my internship at the gallery. Today, I'm still an embryo. My skin is thin and waterlogged; my eyes haven't yet opened. The man's gaze is like a spotlight. There's nothing I have that proves I have existed and that I have an identity beyond my appearance. I shake my head and my big, black hair covers part of my face. I tuck my hands up into my sleeves like they are the heads of turtles sheltering in their shells. I turn to my left, away from the man, so I imagine that all he sees is the giant mass of my hair, although my body is still exposed. In that position, I close my eyes. When I open them again and turn around, the man is gone.

I'm back at the studios just after ten. It doesn't sound like there's anyone else here. My footsteps are the only sound in the building. I use my key to open the door to A14, my new home, and slip in. My door makes a loud clanging sound. The room smells of something unfamiliar. I feel small, like I've been beaten down by the city. My outings have been fruitless. I have none of the things that connect me to my life lived in Margate or my mum— only my belly button, and the little scar on my neck—and I have no food. In the dark, my stomach rumbles loudly.

2

There is a plant called the ghost pipe, because it is ghostly white, almost blue. Were you to cut open this flower and study it, you'd find no chlorophyll inside. It can grow in the dark, under the cover of fallen leaves and undergrowth in forests, under soil. It doesn't need to photosynthesize, because it is a parasite. It uses fungal networks to suck energy from photosynthesizing trees. Its roots look like clusters of tiny fingers that grope toward and connect with huge white webs of fungus that in turn connect with the thick roots of trees.

I don't know where the human and demon in me connect, whether there are roots that sprout from the demon and reach for and attach onto the human, or vice versa. Both live because the other exists. The demon survives off the blood my human body digests. And the demon, in turn, keeps my human heart very slowly pumping—at least, this is what my mum told me when I was young. When I imagine this, I see a little shadowy creature with feeble arms manually pumping the organ with bellows. Owing to the work the demon does to keep blood circulating, the human in me goes on living, and I retain some of the traits my human father passed down to me. The way I hunch slightly, my shoulders protectively pointing forward rather than back, is a posture that, according to my mum, derives from some deep-held insecurity that was also my dad's. I think like him, apparently; he was a perfectionist, fixating on topics he found interesting, struggling to engage with topics he did not. My anxiety is his, my shyness, my clumsiness. I often think of my demon traits—my sharp teeth; the fact that, now I am done growing, now I am an adult, I won't age any further; my coldness; my hunger; my irritability and hot temper—as being the only things I received from my mother. But, also, I've inherited some of her humanness too; it's just harder to separate from the demon.

When I dream, it is because the human half of me is asleep. In those moments, my demon part is awake and, usually, I feel something beyond any human emotion—something far beyond human rage, beyond human hunger—but, since my human body is paralyzed by sleep, my demon half can't act on its feelings. Instead, it dictates my dreams. In my dream last night, Kora Studios was on fire; I couldn't see it but I knew that the rest of the world was on fire too. Trees were sticks of charcoal, jutting out of the ground. They crumbled when they were poked. Ben had come to my studio, which was dark and cool, his skin bright red from the heat, his mouth wide open in agony. I took his hands, and his body slumped into mine, and he whispered a few times, "I'm so hungry, I'm so hungry, I'm so hungry." And, then, I ate him.

I'm lying awake on the floor of my studio. I start my internship at the OTA, a gallery in Battersea, this afternoon. The gallery's nickname is the Otter; OTA actually stands for Osmund, Toth, and Akagi, the three founders—three experimental artists from the 1960s who were associated with the Fluxus Group. Tomoe Akagi is known in artistic circles for having beat Nam June Paik to be the first person to perform a work of art inside a whale. Though, I don't think Paik actually wanted to create work inside a whale. His work, *Creep into the Vagina of a Live Whale*, was about creating an impossible piece of performance art, one that wasn't to be attempted, and could exist only in the minds of the audience. As readers of that instruction, we inevitably imagine ourselves parting the soft flesh of a whale without her noticing, a corridor opening up, stepping inside, breaking through her hymen, creeping into her uterus. I couldn't work out how I felt about this work when I read it for the first time; I remember thinking, *Ugh, of course he has chosen a female animal, and of course he has us enter her without her realizing.* I couldn't tell what the point of the work was. It seemed to only exist to be shocking. Akagi had sewn himself into the stomach of a deceased beached whale somewhere in Scandinavia, where whale meat is eaten, and, after that, he was known as the artist who beat Nam June Paik. Unlike that of the other Fluxus artists, Akagi's work wasn't completely nihilistic; he wrote a long letter to the whale, apologizing for his generation's mistreatment of the environment, and sewed it into the whale's stomach with himself.

There's a knock at the door. It's still dark. I'm wearing my clothes from yesterday, now the only clothes I own. There's dirt from the floor on the back of my shoulders and arms. I pull the one sweatshirt I have out of my bag and put it on over my top. I answer the door. It's Ben.

"Heyyy, hellooo," he says, as though he is speaking for me as well as for himself. He is smiling. His lips are very pink. "So, I got you this!"

Ben's eyes scan the room. I suppose it's probably strange that none of my stuff is here, after I told him I would be moving all of my things yesterday. He looks into my face and smiles. Then he hands me a plant with brown and pink stems and soft-looking dark red leaves.

"Oh!" I say.

"You've got a hook, see?" He points at a metal hook about the size of my hand coming out of the ceiling.

"Huh." I hadn't spotted it before. It's painted white like the ceiling, so it blends in. I look up at it. I wonder what it was for.

"I got you this as, like, a sort of 'Hello! Welcome!' kind of gift, to lighten up the room a bit . . ." The door closes behind him, plunging the room into complete darkness. "You still got a headache?"

"No." I go to the switch and turn the lights up a little. "I'm photosensitive. It's just a thing I have." I gesture at my face, try-ing to think of something to say. "With my eyes."

I look down at the plant in my hands. It's quite pretty. Long stems with small leaves cascade out of the pot and hang down like hair. "Won't this die?" I ask. "There's no window."

"Oh, so yeah . . . basically, it's fake." Ben laughs to himself. "Shall I—" he says, and he points up at the hook. In that mo-ment, he looks like a da Vinci portrait: his plump, white face, his soft-looking ginger hair, his gentle-looking eyes. In da Vinci's portraits of people pointing to heaven, his models, no matter their age, always look almost cherub-like. Ben stays pointing for a while, and then the illusion is broken.

"Yeah, thanks," I say.

Ben grins, and his eyes turn into little slits with crow's-feet on either side that haven't yet become permanent folds in his face;

I can tell they will, though. Over several years, Ben's skin will form wrinkles that will act like physical reminders of his personality and nature. Meanwhile, I'll remain looking the same; my face will give no clue to the kind of person I am. "That man looks kind," people will say when they see Ben's face when he is old. When the same people see me, they'll say nothing.

I get Ben a chair, but it turns out that he needs three, stacked on top of each other and placed on the table. I hold the chairs still as he climbs up and struggles to get the loop of the plant pot onto the hook. "So," he says, while he strains his body upward. "I usually get new artists . . ." He makes a noise as he stretches up as far as he can go, standing on tiptoe— ". . . I usually get the new artists edible plants . . . like . . . herbs and . . . tomatoes and . . . you know, mushrooms . . . so . . ." Ben is silent for a moment while he concentrates. Then the loop hooks on and the plant swings, the leaves falling elegantly over Ben's head. He drops his arms to his sides. His face is pink. "Sorry, yeah," he says, looking directly into my eyes. "I usually get the new artists edible plants, so then when we all have dinner in The Place, everyone brings whatever they've successfully grown."

"Oh, nice," I say. I smile, and Ben smiles back. For a moment, we are just looking and smiling at each other.

"I better get down, I suppose," Ben says, as though he likes it up there.

He grabs my arm as he nearly slips from on top of the chairs—his hand is very hot, and I remember my dream and am reminded of my hunger, and I feel my stomach knot and kind of squeeze itself. My mouth opens as if of its own accord.

"Oop," Ben says—an *oops* missing its *s*. He takes his hand quickly off my arm. "Sorry. What I'm trying to say is that you'll be

let off the hook—oo!" he says, the *oo* rising at the end. "Acciden-
tal pun!" He laughs. I laugh too. There's something funny about
him, wobbling on top of the chairs, laughing at his own jokes.

"What can I say, I'm a poet," he adds. "Well . . . not a poet. Is
that a poet?" he asks me, with a genuinely curious expression on
his face.

"Is what a poet?" I ask.

"Like, a pun maker?"

"Oh, I guess not," I say.

Ben sits down on the stack of chairs, slides off the edge, and
then jumps off the table, running a couple of steps once he lands.
"Right, well . . ." I watch his chest rise and fall. "Looks pretty
good—what do you think?"

"Yeah," I say. But even a fake plant looks strange, hanging in a
space with no natural light.

Ben cocks his head, frowning. "Looks a bit odd, I suppose, in
such an empty room." I watch him look around the space again.
"So, I have to ask . . . where's all your stuff? Like, where's your
work? Weren't you moving in last night?"

"Yeah." I look down at my rucksack, and then at my laptop,
which is open on the floor, and my wallet and phone. There's
one sketchbook and a book about ethical curation poking out of
my bag. "Yeah. This is it."

"This is all of it?"

"Yeah."

I don't want to tell him about the suitcase. There's something
too tragic about it. I don't want him to feel sorry for me. I want
the situation I am in to come across as intentional. "I don't like
having much stuff," I say. "I try not to be materialistic."

Ben looks impressed. He raises his eyebrows and nods.

"Cool." He shuffles on the spot, putting his weight on one foot, then the other. "So, also . . ." He's blushing. "I was wondering if you might fancy hanging out today or another day this week? I've got a deadline I'd love to procrastinate on."

"Sure," I say. "But, I'm starting my internship today, so I'll be busy. I don't really know how much time I'll have in the run-up to the opening."

"Ahh, no worries. Yeah, Shakti was really busy while she was at the Otter. Have they given you a schedule?"

I shake my head.

"Well, let me know. I'm here most of the time." He smiles. "Okay, then," he says, and then he points at the door with his thumb. "I should . . ."

"Yeah, thanks for the . . ." I say, and I nod toward the plant. I realize that the way Ben doesn't finish his sentences has rubbed off on me and this annoys me. ". . . plant," I finish, but it sounds odd now, tagged on like this.

"Nah, you know, it's . . ." Ben shrugs.

I nod. Although, I wonder how this sentence ends. The first word that comes to my mind is "lonely." I wonder if he realizes that I am lonely. I wonder if that's why he's come to visit me.

"So, anyway, make sure you water it three times a week and keep turning the pot so that all sides get a nice good bit of sunlight." Ben grins. A nice, wide, goofy grin, and I can see not only most of his teeth but also his gums. They're very healthy and pink. My mouth waters. I swallow.

"Lol," I say.

"I'll be around all day," Ben says. "Probably till late."

"Okay."

And then he goes to the door and leaves.

I pull the chairs off the table, but leave the table where it is, directly underneath the fake plant. I unstack the chairs and sit on one, my laptop in front of me. I google "order pig blood online delivery London."

I've never had to do this before. My mum always sorted out the food for us; eventually, I did become responsible to a certain degree, but my mum had already established a relationship with the local butcher so all I had to do was turn up with a foldaway luggage trolley, and a bungee cord if there were more than two buckets. While I waited, the butcher always talked to me, and asked me about school or uni, which I commuted to from home, and, when my mum got sick, how she was doing.

We only ever got pig blood. This wasn't because it was the only type of animal blood the butcher had. "Pigs are dirty," my mum said once. "It's what your body deserves." But it turns out that pigs aren't naturally dirty. Rather, humans keep pigs in dirty conditions, feeding them rotten vegetables, letting the mud in their too-small pens mix with their feces; the filth of the pig is just symptomatic of the sins of the human. Wild pigs eat plants. They've even been shown to clean fruit in creeks before eating it, and they never eat or roll around in their own feces. I told my mum this, but she was adamant that the pig was the filthiest animal and was what we deserved. It was what I grew up eating, never touching anything else—just thinking, dreaming, imagining the taste of other blood.

There was only the hint of something else, some other flavor, in my memory. Something distant, something that was from so long ago that it didn't feel like part of my life, something that felt ancient, like a memory passed down through generations. This was the taste of—or not the taste but more the experience of consuming and then containing—human blood.

I know that my mum once, while she was pregnant with me, ate a human; she's never told me who. She calls this incident a "slipup" and she blames me for it. For multiplying her hunger, and making her feel like she needed more than what a pig could offer. I've wondered whether my body remembers the taste of it and the feel of it from inside the womb. One time, as a teenager, I'd cut into my own skin and sucked at the cut, hoping that the pig blood would have transformed in my veins into human blood, hoping to taste what it was that I felt I could remember; but what I drank tasted no different from my dinner, and I felt no different afterward.

After that, I'd googled "does a baby share mother's blood," wondering whether once in my life I'd perhaps had my own, untainted human blood, and the top result that came back read: "The unborn baby is connected to the placenta via the umbilical cord. All nutrition, oxygen, and life support from the mother's blood goes through the placenta through blood vessels in the umbilical cord to the baby." I'd felt resentful about this fact, and disappointed. I felt like it meant that I was somehow more my mother and less my father, more demon and less human, evil and sinful before I was even born. I don't know how a vampire pregnancy really works, though. Whether, for the first nine months of my existence, I swam in rotting waters in an almost-dead womb; whether the womb I have in me, which has been the womb of a vampire since I was turned as a baby, would support life at all. I never got my period, and my mum once told me she barely bleeds anymore and, when she does, she does so irregularly, as if she is perpetually stuck on the boundary between fertility and menopause.

The memory of human blood manifests now as a kind of visceral reaction to seeing people's veins and their necks. The skin on a neck appears to me as different from the skin anywhere else on a body. It seems as thin and consumable as rice paper wrapped around a sweet. It is too blank compared with skin everywhere else, as though it is asking to have marks made on it, like very expensive calligraphy paper, or cold-pressed Fabriano. Often, I wonder whether the urge I have to make art is the same as the urge to consume and destroy the blankness of a human neck. While at art college, I read that the best paper used by artists in the seventeenth century was made from the skins of lamb fetuses. This skin was soft and absorbent, and had an even texture right across its surface. For a long time, the process of creating art has been linked to the killing of living things. My dad, even, used fine silk stretched across wooden frames in his own work as a painter. Once, when we still had some of his pieces, I looked at the odd geometric shapes he created on a huge sheet and thought about all the silkworms who had had their cocoons torn open before they were able to become moths.

There are five ads at the top of the results of my Google search looking for pig blood deliveries in London. The fourth one shows a picture of an opaque, white, plastic bottle with a red lid. There's a faint suggestion of dark liquid inside it. I click on the link. But, when the page loads, I notice the name of the website—"Poker Face Joke Shop"—and the description "claret thickened to look like real blood." I click back. There's another bottle of "blood" that is for special effects makeup, called "running blood"; there are two other varieties, "blood flakes" and "clotted blood." I find a forum where someone is asking whether it's possible to source fresh pig blood in the UK. In their post they explain that they want to make premium sausage. All the replies describe various regulations that prevent abattoirs and butchers from selling fresh blood. I suppose the butcher in Margate had been breaking the rules. It wouldn't surprise me. For a long time, things seemed to run unregulated in the town. But the butcher's gone now. A month before Mum and I left, the butcher closed the shop—the rent had got too high, she told us, since the town had become so popular with Londoners—and we stocked up with several buckets of blood to keep us going and said goodbye.

I lean back in my chair and let my head fall back so I'm looking at the ceiling. This is, in my whole twenty-three years of being alive, the first time I've been on my own. The first time I've been independent, fending for myself, living as a human, without my mum waiting for me at home—well or unwell—without all of my things around me, all my mother's things around me. It's more challenging, already, than I had thought it would be. Although I like pushing myself to my limits, I hadn't anticipated not being able to source blood on the first day of my internship. I had planned to feel the thrill of being a little bit hungry, and then to have stocked up my fridge and eaten normally for at least a few days while I got to know how the gallery worked, and met all the people I'll be working with. I lift my head up with extraordinary effort, and put my arms out straight on the table, and then rest my head on them. The laptop screen is level with my face. I can feel myself dribbling on my sleeve, but I don't really care. I'm disgusting by nature, I think to myself, so what does a little dribble matter.

I scroll through the other search results with difficulty from that position. Dried pig blood for making black pudding; black pudding–making kit with dried pig blood; dried pig blood bulk buy. And recipes at the bottom. Blood sausage hash, Tolosa stew, hot pot, sweet potato gnocchi with black pudding and chili. A menu for a posh restaurant in Leeds comes up too, and one of the starter options is dried pig blood and snail eggs. People are weird, I think. I find a bioscience lab that is selling small bottles and larger bags of fresh blood to researchers, schools, and universities; their website doesn't mention selling to artists but I feel like it's worth a shot. I fill in the inquiry form to find out about price and regular deliveries into London. "Hello, I am a performance artist," I begin my message, but almost immediately I get an autoreply back, saying the lab has permanently closed. Eventually, I opt to buy some dried pig blood. I find a supplier that has an organic and RSPCA-certified product. The email I get confirming my order tells me it will arrive at the studio tomorrow.

I'm so tired. I don't know what it is. It's not just the hunger. My body is heavy. Everything is heavy. It feels like the air in the studio is heavy, pushing me down onto whatever is the nearest flat surface—right now, the table, the seat I'm on. But even sprawling out across the tabletop isn't comfortable enough. I slip off my seat like jelly, making my body deliberately floppy as I do so that I hit the concrete hard, and look like a woman in a black-and-white film fainting. A dull pain, just a fraction of what I'd feel if I were fully human, spreads through my hip, down my arm, and across my shoulder. I roll onto my back. My hair acts like a pillow. My arms stretch out to either side of me, and my legs spread out too, so that I look like a star. I feel slightly queasy. I recognize this to be the hunger. But, there is something else too.

Whenever there is something planned in my life—either meeting a friend, going on a school or uni trip, going for a walk, or, like today, starting an internship—when it actually comes to the day I have to go through with the plan, it goes from being something I'm excited about to something I dread. If I arrange to go to the cinema in a week's time, for instance, when the time to go comes around, it becomes the last thing I want to do. My instinct, always, is to stay in. Right now, I don't want to go to the Otter, even though I've planned the route meticulously in my mind, and feel prepared. I want to stay here on my concrete floor and look at the ceiling. I definitely don't want to meet people. The idea of it, from the perspective of where I am now, alone in this room, is strange and feels completely unnatural.

I look at my hand. In a few hours, that hand will be shaking another hand, I think. This body will soon be in front of other bodies, being seen. These feet will step through the doors of a space I am not familiar with. I find it all impossible. When I think of my immediate future, I see it in flashes rather than in a smooth, linear transition of events. I see myself outside the studio. Then partway up a busy road. Then in the ticket hall of Vauxhall tube station. Then sitting in a tube carriage. Then in the gallery, standing under LED lights. The journey feels impossible because I can't see the moments in between these images. It's as though my brain can't comprehend time properly, and my movement through it. I asked my mum about these feelings when I was a teenager and she said it was "just anxiety," but it feels like something that's physically wrong with my brain. Or, maybe it's something to do with what I am. The demon in me is probably a solitary animal. In popular culture, people like me are always associated with bats, and maybe that's fitting. I can imagine hanging upside down in this studio for hours at a time, dribbling white saliva from my mouth, then flying solitary in the night, picking insects out of the sky.

I get up from the floor about two hours later. It's like my body is a puppet. I wonder which side of me, the demon or the human, is the one that wants me to go to the gallery and is forcing me up. It's one of them, while the other drags her feet. I pack my rucksack with the few belongings I have. I put some cash in my sock just in case my rucksack gets lost somehow too. I cover my exposed skin in sunscreen. And then I leave. On my way out, I check the post situation in the building. There aren't doorbells for the studios, which might make it a bit difficult for the dried blood I've ordered to be delivered tomorrow. There's just a communal mailbox outside, which is like a cubbyhole that doesn't have a lock or anything and has a door that just kind of swings open and closed in the wind.

I arrive at the Otter and the front door is closed and there is no one to let me in. This is what I always fear about arriving at new places. Being stuck outside. I stand as close to the wall as possible so I'm in shade. I knock on the door. I knock firmly but not too loudly, because I don't want to seem crazy. I look at the wall around the door. There's no buzzer.

I got the orientation email for my internship last week. I received it while I was sorting through my mum's stuff. I had found several boxes of my baby things. It was overwhelming; my mum had kept everything, even my baby clothes, all folded up neatly, and the little wooden toys I learned the primary colors with. For normal people, childhoods take up almost a quarter of their life but, for me, after I've lived for however many centuries I'll live for, my childhood will seem like a tiny dot on the horizon, a brief moment in which I was a part of society in a mostly normal way, experiencing changes in my body along with friends who were going through the exact same changes at the exact same time. I had always known that my growth would end at some point, that I'd stop changing once my body reached its peak, just as my mum told me it would—that then I'd be frozen as I was, timeless and un-aging, while my friends kept progressing toward death. And yet, I spent all my time as a child wanting to be an adult. Now, it's the other way around. I felt a sense of yearning, looking through my baby things, like I wished I could do childhood again, and pay attention to every little change I experienced. I packed all of my baby clothes and toys into a bag to give to charity. The gallery had felt so far from my situation in that moment that I didn't bother to read the email. Now, I get my phone out and scroll through my in-box.

The email is from the director of the gallery, a man called Gideon. It's addressed to me but I can tell that it's an email that is sent out to all interns as my name is in a slightly different font from the rest of the message. "It is a huge honor to welcome you into our project space," the email begins. "Please report to the main reception on your first day and the receptionist will send someone down to meet you," it continues, before closing off farther down with, "with deep gratitude." It's a nice email. But there's nothing about how to get into the building itself, and there doesn't seem to be anyone else around, no staff, no other interns. I look up the OTA on Google and click on the number that comes up—I realize as I do that it says, "Closed—Opens 12 p.m. Tuesday," which is the day after tomorrow.

"Hello?" comes a voice on the other end of the line.

"Hi," I say. "I'm an intern at the OTA and I'm trying to get in the building but there's no one here."

There's a pause on the other end of the line. Then the voice says, "You're . . . Lydia."

I wait to see if the person is going to give me instructions for how to get in but they don't. "Yes," I say.

"What do you look like?" the voice says.

"Huh? This is the gallery, right?"

"Yes."

"Okay . . ." I take a few steps back from the door into the bright sunlight to see if I can see into any of the windows. "So, I guess I have dark hair, and I'm a girl?"

"Woman," the voice says.

"I'm sorry?" I ask.

"You're a woman. You shouldn't describe yourself as a girl if you are an adult woman."

"Oh, right. Sorry," I say. I have been called a girl by some men before and felt diminutive—shrunken down, patronized. But I've never been told off for calling myself a girl. It feels strange, like the person is saying that I contain both someone who is sexist and someone else who is a victim of sexism. Now, I think for the first time about what I see myself as. I don't exactly see myself as a woman yet. I still look pretty young after all, probably around eighteen—that one year in life when you are actually genuinely between being a girl and a woman. But, I suppose the strange thing is that I'll look this age for the rest of my life, until I'm in my hundreds and two hundreds and beyond. For this reason, I also don't entirely feel like a girl.

"Okay, so I can see you outside," the voice says. For a moment, I worry about how scruffy my clothes are. But the voice doesn't mention it. "Green top?"

"Yes, that's me," I say, looking up. But none of the windows have people behind them.

"Wave at me?"

"Okay," I say, and I wave in the general direction of the building and the line goes dead and the door emits a loud buzz. It's open. I go through.

The light inside is dim; there are strings of yellow lightbulbs hanging in the corridor. There are stacks of chairs near the entrance, bags of ice cubes that look like they've begun to melt, and, to my left as I walk in, a wooden puppet theater painted with red, green, and yellow stripes.

"Hi, excuse me," I say to a woman who's carrying a large box. She turns around to look at me. I'm surprised to see that the whites of her eyes are pink. She looks like she has recently been crying. She has a red nose, and her skin is blotchy.

"Hi," she says. "I'm sorry—" and then she rushes off behind a large, red velvet curtain farther down the corridor.

The theme of this exhibition is folk art, and the building, which is usually a typical white-cube space, has been dressed up to look like a circus. The walls are covered in strange murals; level with my head are alligators eating trapeze artists who are, in turn, eating smaller alligators. In large display cases are arrangements by the famous Victorian taxidermist and artist, Walter Potter. There's a feast being had by little ginger kittens that look like they were once—before dying and being stuffed with hay and then seated on miniature dining chairs and put in front of tiny cakes, pots of tea, and samovars—from the same litter. Their eyes are beautiful, black, glistening marbles. Next to the cat feast is another Walter Potter—rabbits diligently working at desks in a miniature classroom. It's thrilling seeing these works. I've known them for years; I studied them for my A-levels. In photographs, they seem clean and unreal. Up close, I can see the little dimples in the animals' skin where their muscles used to attach; I can smell the tiny, microscopic traces of hundred-year-old blood inside them.

A man rushes past me. He slings one of the huge bags of ice over his shoulder and disappears through the same curtain the woman went through. I follow.

On the other side, there is a large hall. There are circular dining tables in here that have huge amounts of clutter on top of them: boxes of nails and screws, paperwork, dried flowers, plates wrapped in tissue. Someone is sawing a piece of wood while standing on a small cherry picker; a man is painting a mural at the back; lights are being tested. They are bright, and then they are dim and they are bright and then they are dim again.

"Um," I say to a woman who is coming my way, and she shakes her head, quickly, and rushes past. I smell her hair as it brushes my face.

I walk up to a merry-go-round that is very slowly turning in the corner; two men are discussing something about it intently. But, when they see me, they stop, and one of the men walks away.

"Hey," I say to the man left by the merry-go-round.

He nods.

"I'm looking for reception?" I say.

"Okay," he says, and he leans the long-handled dustpan and brush he is holding against the wall. He is just a bit taller than I am, slim, clean-shaven. He has very pale skin and eyes that are big and wet-looking. Their irises are like two dirty ponds. They take my face in for just a moment too long for it to feel normal.

"So, what are you?" he says, eventually, wiping his hands on his trousers. And, for a moment, I think that he must know what I am. I blink at him. "Another intern?" he adds.

"Oh," I say. "Yeah."

He gestures to a door. He waits for me to go through it first, and then he follows.

We walk for a while down a dark corridor. "Reception's on the other side," the man says from behind me. He doesn't ask for my name, and so I don't ask for his.

"So, are you an artist as well?" I ask, trying to make conversation. But when I turn around to look at him, he just shakes his head and then says, "You?"

"Yes," I say. I feel a bit guilty saying this, though, since I haven't actually made any work since I graduated. I haven't really been doing much of anything since I graduated. I feel like, in the year after college that I spent at home with my mum, worrying about her, trying to keep her safe, I didn't really live; I essentially took a break from my life to focus on my mum's life. Currently, I'm hoping-to-be rather than being—I'm not yet an independent adult; I'm hoping to become one. I'm not yet an artist; I'm hoping to become one.

"Hm," he says. He's walking beside me now. It's quite a narrow corridor and we only just fit. I wonder whether he's expecting me to slow down so he can overtake me, or if he's trying to get me to speed up. I look at him from the corner of my eye. He's wearing a black shirt with a high collar that covers most of his neck, formal trousers, and an ornate waistcoat. I suppose he looks how any normal person might expect a vampire to look.

Once reception is in sight, the man turns around and walks back the way we came.

"See you around then, I guess," I call after him, but he keeps walking and doesn't respond.

The receptionist barely acknowledges me. She shouts out to a woman with blond hair, wearing bright-red lipstick and a green coat, "Another one for you," and the woman replies, shaking her head, as if I'm not there, "What am I meant to do with all of them?" The receptionist shrugs.

I follow the woman back down the corridor, back out into the hall, back through the red curtain, back past the murals and the Walter Potters, and to the puppet theater near the entrance. She walks very fast, then abruptly stops and tells a thin man with a neatly trimmed beard what to do in a raised voice: "Coffee for Gideon. No milk! Now, quickly—go!" She looks stressed. She's looking at her phone. Her thumbs are darting rapidly across the screen.

"Okay," she says eventually. She looks at me. "Can you just man the ticket booth or something?"

"What?"

"No water under any circumstances!" she adds, looking at my bag. "What's in there?"

"Oh, um—"

"Hurry up!"

"Nothing, just books, keys, I think a sweatshirt? Oh, and my wallet too, though some of my cash is," I point at my foot, "in my sock." I don't know why I'm telling her all of this.

She shakes her head angrily. "Can you be quick, then?" she says. "Get in."

"Where exactly am I going?" I ask.

"In the booth. The puppet theater. In! In!" And she shoos me with her hand, until I'm opening the little door on the side of the booth that leads to what I suppose could be termed "backstage."

"Okay," I say. I look at the front of the booth before I go in. There's a sign painted above the stage in bright bottle-green and blue paint that reads, "Our Patent Show of Bludgeoning and Beating! The Greatest Fun by the Sea!"

"Just man the tickets," the woman says, and she sighs one more time, and leaves back through the red curtain, following a couple of people carrying plinths and tools.

"Out of my way!" I hear the woman shout.

I close the tiny door behind me and sit down on the small wooden stool inside. My legs don't really fit behind the stage. They bend awkwardly upward so my knees are above my belly button. I try to orient myself.

I look at the stage in front of me. There are tiny floorboards that go all the way across it and little patches where the varnish has worn off, I suppose where the feet of marionettes have come into contact with the wood. There's a tiny trapdoor too. Around the edges of the stage, glove puppets are hanging up. Punch and Judy, with Punch holding a wooden bat that is huge relative to his body size, and Judy painted—and therefore perpetually stuck—with a fearful expression on her face. Three puppets with smaller plastic heads and felt costumes are tied together with a cord like a bunch of flowers and also strung up; they are the king, the queen, and the devil.

From what I've seen, only some of the artworks in the exhibition have labels, with the names of artists on them. Some pieces have labels with just the words "Aboriginal artifact"—the word "artifact" coming across as a lesser version of the word "art." Others, like these puppets and this booth, have no labels at all. The words "FOLK ART" are emblazoned in letters cut from tin and painted with bright colors high up on the wall across the corridor from me. Art of the people; and yet only some of the artists get to be a singular person, while the rest are part of the collective, people. The puppets are just puppets, as if no one made them. Hanging up as they are, the absence of a person's hand inside them is made more extreme and more sad. I put my own hand in each of them one by one, animating the king's little arms, then the queen's, and then, finally, the devil's.

There is one other puppet, which looks different from the others. It is tucked in the corner of the booth, so isn't even visible from the outside. It is a strange, darkly dressed woman with a large, heavy, dark-colored head carved from wood. She is a glove puppet and so has no legs. She has wild hair similar to my own, and a big hooked nose and large chin, between which her mouth almost disappears. For some reason, I'm drawn to her. I pick her up and lay her out on my lap. My hand fits into her torso perfectly. My thumb and little finger fill her tiny arms; my three middle fingers occupy the space inside her head with no room to spare.

"So, it's just you and me," I whisper to her.

"Okay!" I imagine her enthusiastically replying. "We can do it!"

I locate a roll of tickets in a small compartment under the

stage where it looks like a drawer belongs, and hold on to it. The tickets are essentially just raffle tickets. Each one has a number printed on it. I hold them in one hand while, with the other, I hold up the puppet's head.

This part of the gallery seems quieter than the rest. A few people occasionally emerge through the red curtain to get something from by the front door and then disappear back through it again. Four times, people arrive through the front door, and I think for a moment that they might come up to me in the booth, or they might say hello, or ask me where they should go if they're an intern too, but they just go straight through the red curtain and don't seem to notice me. I sit still anyway, trying to look professional, smiling at everyone even when they don't look at me—smiling at the backs of people's heads, even—and clutching hold of the tickets in my hand.

At one point, a man bursts through the red curtain and bats it with his hands as it falls back in his face, as though its presence is a nuisance. I recognize him immediately; it's the guy who took me to reception, the guy who looks like a vampire. He is followed closely by a large group of people who then huddle around him, holding various things that look like they might be his belongings. Some of the people are writing notes, while the blond woman who gave me my instructions whispers in his ear. The man nods occasionally in response to whatever she tells him, and then orders the other people around. Some of them go back through the curtain, and the others stay with him while he stoops down to look through the glass at the kittens having their tea party. Eventually, the group moves down the corridor over to where I am in the ticket booth or puppet theater or whatever it is and faces me. I open my mouth, about to speak, but someone farther down the corridor beats me: "Sorry, Gideon. Your coffee. It's here." One of the people in the group hurries off and brings the coffee to the man. He accepts it, not thanking anyone. I hadn't realized earlier, but the man is the director of the gallery. I've seen pictures of him before, but he looks different in real life. Now, he looks at me with an odd, cold expression, like I'm not here.

It is a very strange experience. I hold on to the tickets, tightly, ready to offer them. I keep smiling and look ahead. I wait for the group of people to speak to me but Gideon just looks at me for a moment, while the blond woman whispers in his ear. Then, he nods and turns; all the people follow him and they disappear as a group behind the curtain. I'm not sure if I passed the test. I'm not sure if it was a test. If it was, I feel like maybe I did pass? If I hadn't passed, maybe Gideon would have shaken his head, or perhaps even done something violent, like grabbed the booth and shaken it with me inside. I feel vaguely—amid my general feeling of confusion—proud of myself.

I feel like I'm sitting in the booth for hours. I'm skinny and so, my bum is quite bony; all chairs eventually make it ache, so it's hard for me to use the dull pain as a marker of time. But, it must have been a while because, when a man comes through the door and puts a few crates of what look to be empty wine bottles on the floor by the entrance, it's dark outside. I see the moon, momentarily, between the door and the wall, before the door shuts it out again.

"How are you doing?" I ask the puppet.

She lies still on my lap, empty again, my hand beside her. I lean my head against the side of the booth. I feel tired. My head has started to ache. My stomach rumbles.

I suppose this isn't exactly what I had been expecting from the internship. The job description had said that I'd be shadowing a curator and learning about gallery directing and curation. It had said that I might be able to implement some of my ideas if I develop any during my time here, in which case, I may even get paid for my time. I'd gone to a really beautiful office near St. James's Park a couple of months ago, which I was told the OTA uses whenever the gallery space is being prepared for the next show, and been interviewed by a nice woman who asked me about my practice and seemed genuinely interested in it. She had said that I would definitely "bring value to the institution." There had been smart-looking bikes up on the wall, with thin frames, and pretty jewelry on the woman's hands, and I'd thought to myself that, perhaps, a spot in that room would be the next step in my journey toward opening my own space.

I study the puppet on my lap. She has an extremely characterful face. I decide to call her Lydia after myself. Then I look out from the stage, lowering my head a bit so I can see things from the perspective of a puppet. "Huh," I say. I move my head to stage left and then stage right, imagining a hand in my head dictating what I do.

"Hello?" comes a stressed-sounding voice from the direction of the red curtain. I sit up quickly. "Is there someone still in the booth?" It's the woman with blond hair. She marches over. The kittens shake in their seats as she stamps on the floorboards that their case is standing on. "What on earth are you doing here?"

"Um," I begin. "Manning the—"

"Why haven't you been helping? There's so much to do before the opening!"

"I . . ." I say. "I'm sorry?"

"DEN!!" she calls and a tall man with a beard and broad shoulders sheepishly peeps out from between the red curtain and the wall. For a moment, he makes eye contact with me. I feel like it's the first time all day that someone has actually seen me. My mouth waters. His thin, papery neck pokes up from a mandarin shirt collar. I look away and back to the woman, who has her eyes closed as though she is so fed up that she can't handle looking at anything. "Den!! What did I say? Can you *please* just *properly* check all the balconies and rooms for lost fucking sheep! NOW!"

"I can help now, if you want?" I say in a very quiet voice; I realize that I am putting my hand up, with the tickets still in them, like I'm at school.

"There's no time now, is there?" she says, shaking her head with her eyebrows raised. I lower my arm. "You'll have to just go home for today, won't you?"

"Well," I say. "I don't know. I guess. But I thought you said to man the tickets. So, I . . . I . . . I mean, that's what I've been doing?"

The woman hasn't stopped shaking her head. "Honestly, I just don't know what to say." Her voice is very high-pitched. She leaves back through the red curtain.

I stay sitting on my stool in the booth for a while. I blink. I look at the puppet on my lap. I feel embarrassed that she is seeing me like this. Confused. Not defending myself. Weak and small. I put the roll of tickets away, stand up, picking my rucksack up off the floor and bumping my head on the stage in the process, and open the little door. I step out and am about to tuck the puppet back where I found her when my arms and hands seem to act of their own accord, like I'm not controlling them at all. I'm not sure which half it is—the human or the demon in me—but I unzip my rucksack and gently lower the puppet inside it, headfirst. I roll her fabric dress up a little so that she fits, and then I zip the bag up.

Jesus fucking Christ, what am I doing, I think to myself.

It's fine, it's fine, a voice in my head answers. *She won't be missed here. Take her just for tonight. You can put her back later.*

I'll get fired if they find out, I think.

You can't be fired from an internship. And they'll never know.

I look around. Has anyone seen me? There's a man over by the Walter Potters, looking at the rabbit schoolchildren from the side and frowning, but I'm certain that he hasn't even noticed my presence, like most of the people today. I test it as I leave, with my rucksack and the puppet inside it, on my back. "Bye," I call—and the man says nothing back.

3

I want to be a good person. Lots of people realize that they do too, I think, when they have to live as adults for the first time. They see people with less than them and they have a realization that the main thing they want in life isn't necessarily to be rich or successful, but to be good. I don't think my mum's decision to not drink human blood, and to raise me so I didn't either, comes from a desire to be good, though. It has always been an expression of her lack of self-worth. She always said that she didn't deserve things; she didn't deserve to feel satiated, to try the blood of a nobler animal than the pig, such as the horse, even the cow; she didn't deserve happiness; she didn't deserve me either, and I in turn didn't deserve the horse or cow or happiness because of what was in me that she had passed down from her body to mine. "We shouldn't ever give the devil more than enough to survive," she once said. "And that is what the demon in us is. We eat only to keep the human alive," she said, because to deny the human side sustenance was to commit it to death, and that would be a worse sin than our continued existence was. I want to be good, though. I don't know for sure where this desire comes from—

perhaps from my dad, whose life and person must be preserved somewhere inside me.

The puppet I took yesterday is on my hand. I know it wasn't good to take her. But, now she is in my studio, I feel at peace and content in this space; I feel less alone. Last night, I tried to google her, in case she is valuable or the work of a famous artist, in which case I suppose I'll probably have to return her. But it was difficult to really know what to search for. I looked up "woman puppet with dark wooden head" and there were nearly twenty million results. I reverse-image-searched her too, but the technology can't be that advanced since the puppets it brought up all looked completely different from her; most were puppets of men and most were carved from a light pine, or just had beige plastic heads like the queen, king, and devil back at the gallery. I gave up my search at some point in the early morning, put on an episode of *Buffy*, and fell asleep with the puppet on my hand and lying across my stomach, her little beady eyes open.

I get up and there are three missed calls on my phone, all from this morning. They're from a number that isn't saved, and not from a mobile, so I can't text to ask who it is, which I would prefer. I have to call instead. I'm lying on the floor, the puppet still on my hand, when I press "call back."

"Hello, Crimson Orchard, how may I help you?" says a woman's voice.

"Oh," I say.

I sit up; it's a bit of a struggle since my phone is plugged into the wall. I take the puppet off my hand. I lay her behind my back, as though the person on the other end of the line might somehow be able to see her through the phone.

"Hello?" the woman says.

"Hello, sorry." I shuffle around on my bum until the charger wire isn't stretched across my neck. "I think my mum's doctor called me this morning. My mum's a resident."

"Okay. What's the name of the doctor looking after your mother?"

"Dr. Kerr," I say.

"Let me just pop you on hold while I see if he's available," the woman says, and then her voice is replaced with a cover of a pop song from a couple of years ago.

I put my phone on speaker and then leave it on top of the socket box. I lie down. The concrete is very cold. And then I roll across the floor like I'm a sausage until I'm in the middle of the room, and then I roll back. I roll again, at the bridge of the song, and stop when I'm on my back. I hold my arm up in the air until it's balanced and I don't have to use any energy to keep it there. Usually, when I have to wait for things, I look at my phone but my phone is on the other side of the room and I'm comfortable here, so I can't. It's weirdly freeing. I look at the veins on my hand; I wonder how much blood there is left in my system now—probably not much, although the veins are still green like plant shoots. I knock my head against the concrete a few times until I begin to feel a slight pain in the back of it that dulls the headache I already have. I imagine what I would look like to anyone who came in and saw me here and laugh to myself.

"Hello, Lydia?" comes a voice through my phone.

I scramble across the room. "Hello," I say, holding the phone up to my ear and trying to turn speakerphone off.

"Hi, Lydia, it's Dr. Kerr here. I tried to call a few times this morning. Is this still the best number to reach you on?"

"Yes, sorry. I was—"

Dr. Kerr cuts me off. "Okay, thank you, Lydia. I'll make a note of that. Now . . ." There's a moment of silence and then he says, "Your mother . . ."

I realize that he is waiting for me to confirm that I am listening. "Yes, my mum," I say.

"I am afraid that she has found adjusting to life here a little bit challenging." Dr. Kerr's tone of voice has changed. He is now speaking very softly.

"Right, okay?" I say.

"Her delusions have become more severe and, well." Dr. Kerr clears his throat. "This might be a bit shocking for you to hear, Lydia, but she bit one of the nurses on the forearm yesterday."

"Oh my god. I'm so sorry."

"No no, no no, please don't worry about it," Dr. Kerr says. "Things like this do just sometimes happen, sadly, with our patients with Alzheimer's, or who suffer from some anxiety, so we are quite used to dealing with this sort of thing. Thankfully, she didn't draw blood and left only some bruising. But, this is behavior that we would like to help her contain."

"Right," I say. "Of course."

"Can I ask—your mother hasn't had any violent tendencies since being diagnosed, has she?"

"No."

"Okay. So, this is the first time," Dr. Kerr says. It sounds like he is making notes.

"Yes."

"Please stay on the line for a moment, Lydia. I'll be back in a moment." The phone beeps, and I let my head fall back against the wall. I close my eyes.

My mum was diagnosed with "probable Alzheimer's" several

years ago, but I don't think she actually has Alzheimer's. I don't think a vampire could develop the disease. With my mum, it's something psychological, a kind of midlife crisis: a forgetting of who she is and sometimes even of what she is. My mum had gum disease when she was fully human and, gradually, over the last couple of centuries, her teeth have, one by one, fallen out. The last tooth, a sharp and pointed molar, came out while she slept one night, when I was around twenty, and was there on her pillow in the morning—the last semblance of her demon body, she said, that God had pulled from her mouth, recognizing that she was no longer actively sinning. An achievement. She thanked God for removing this symbol of temptation from her body. But, with it, I think, went something else.

While my mum never hunted during my lifetime, she always had access to this physical power, manifested in her sharp teeth. After she lost her final one, though, she became kind of confused. And, when I think about it, it makes sense—for in our teeth is an ability to end life, which also means that every day when we do not, we are exerting the power we have to preserve life. With her teeth gone, so went my mum's identity as a vampire who chose to not use them. After she had dentures put in— soft-edged porcelain teeth cast from a human's—she became more likely to forget who she was and imagine she was a human. She wandered out of the house on numerous occasions, sometimes looking for a rubber plantation near her childhood home in Malaysia, and eventually, a good-natured man out walking his dog who noticed her watching cars with a look of alarm on her face called an ambulance for her.

I resent my mum for many things. When she lost her teeth, but I still had mine, she told me that I must be sinning without her knowing, because otherwise God would take my teeth too. Nonetheless, the thought of her leaving the house one day, getting lost and not coming back—the thought of never seeing her again—is too much to bear. So, I found this home for her, a place where I can keep an eye on her, without having to have my life restricted by her. But maybe it was a mistake.

"Hello, are you there, Lydia?" Dr. Kerr says now.

"Hello."

"Sorry for the wait," he says. "Now, we don't normally allow family members to speak with residents for at least a week after they are admitted—"

"Yes," I say. "It's okay, I don't really mind that."

"Actually, we have been discussing your mother's case here, and myself and the other clinicians feel that, as your mother is having some difficulty getting used to life here, and since this is new behavior from her, it might be best for her to speak to someone familiar, if you would be willing?"

"Oh," I say, trying not to sound disappointed. "Okay."

"Very good," Dr. Kerr says. "When would be convenient for you?"

I look down at the puppet. She's lying on her back on the floor with her arms out to either side of her. The way the shadows are falling on her face makes it look like she is smiling very slightly. I turn away from her. "Day after tomorrow?" I say—a day I've been asked to go into the gallery in the afternoon; in the morning, I could walk down to the river, find a bench, and call Crimson Orchard from there.

"Okay, I'll meet you in the waiting room. Would you be able to make it here for ten-thirty?" Dr. Kerr says.

"Oh," I say. I look back at the puppet; it's remarkable how the

light from my phone screen has transformed her expression—
she's definitely smiling, maybe even laughing, at me now. "You
actually want me to come down?"

"I think that would be best, considering the situation."

"Yeah. Okay."

"Okay, great. Thank you, Lydia. We will see you then."

I hang up.

I lie back down on the floor. I find a comfortable position, my
arm at an odd angle but relaxed, my legs twisted around each
other, and then I rock myself.

Sometimes, I still feel like a kid. In positions like this, I can
close my eyes and imagine myself back into my bed, and I can
imagine my body back into the tiny body I had at age four, and
I can tuck myself into my old Snoopy duvet and imagine the sag
in the mattress that told me, even though my eyes were closed,
where my mum was sitting on my bed. Sometimes, despite everything she said, I'm sure she saw me as entirely human. She
used to watch me sleep, sometimes—which I know because,
usually, I wasn't actually asleep but just pretending and, while
I listened to her breathing, was in fact imagining that she was
human: that we were normal like my friends at school and their
parents; that we didn't have to hate parts of ourselves in order
to keep living in society; that in the morning, Mum would have
breakfast—toast with butter, an egg standing up in an egg cup,
a cup of orange juice—ready for me. Instead, it was pig blood,
yet again and again and again and again in the mornings, in my
usual Totoro mug, which was shaped like his body and had a
lid to keep the blood warm that was his scalp with his little ears
pointing up. At some point, I realized that our feeling of difference wasn't really fair, since humans ate eggs, essentially the

menstruation of birds—a type of life-giving thing just as any blood is.

I pick up the puppet and look at her, her face now in its usual neutral expression. I turn onto my side. The puppet is lying with her head on my arm, facing the same way as me so she can see my phone screen. I open YouTube and search for "What I eat in a day," my go-to when I'm stressed. There are lots of suggestions for more specific search terms.

> What I eat in a day model
> What I eat in a day to lose weight
> What I eat in a day to gain weight
> What I eat in a day fruitarian
> What I eat in a day Japanese
> What I eat in a day vegan
> What I eat in a day Korean
> What I eat in a day ed recovery
> What I eat in a day teen
> What I eat in a day as a runner
> What I eat in a day as a fat person
> What I eat in a day ASMR
> What I eat in a day intuitive eating
> What I eat in a day Bollywood

I choose "What I eat in a day model." I feel like escaping, briefly, into the life of a particularly attractive human. I rest my phone against my fingers so I don't have to grip it and I relax. "I always start my day with hot water that I put a slice of lemon in," says Mina, a model from Finland. She is in her flat, which has large windows and a lot of sunlight. "And, then I will have a muffin

which I made with Jake on the weekend. They are really delicious, really healthy; coconut flour, chia seed, banana, walnut,
with spirulina which has no taste, but is really, really good for
you. And I just put a bit of almond butter on it . . ."

I don't know what it is about these videos that I find so soothing. Sometimes, I tell myself that my watching them is an an-
thropological experiment, something I do to better understand
full humans, or perhaps my own human side. I suppose food is a
part of life that most humans can control. They give food a lot of
power—food can make a person more beautiful, or less beautiful; it can improve or damage skin; it can make a person's body
more attractive, help make hair and nails stronger; it can heal
you, or slowly kill you. There's also clean food and dirty food; if
you eat clean, the message is that you are a clean and pure person; if you eat dirty, then the message is that you are dirty and
impure. If you lose control in your life, you can find control in
your food. This video by Mina has the feeling of an educational
video. Lots of them take that tone, as though their message is: if
you eat like me, you will become me.

I watch a couple more. My favorites are the cultural ones, because they have the strange feeling of being instruction manu-
als on becoming whatever ethnicity the person in the video is.
One of my favorites has over six million views and combines
the what-I-eat genres of "in a week," "Japanese food," "realis-
tic," "teen," and "ASMR." I watch an entire twenty-five minutes
of a girl in Tokyo with dyed wine-red-fading-into-pink hair
eating sausages, toast, a Japanese corn dog made with hotcake
mix dipped in ketchup, demae hot sesame ramen with an egg
plopped in, pizza, stir-fried udon, seaweed salad and barley rice,
tapioca and black tea ice cream, soy-glazed salmon on okayu,

pearl milk bubble tea. Each time she eats, the microphone hones in on the sounds of her eating—slurping, chewing, crunching. When she drinks her bubble tea, there's a loud pop as the straw goes through the lid, and the sound of gulping. Gulp, gulp, gulp. I realize that I'm gulping along to the video, imagining that the bubble tea is blood. I click on the creator's name and watch some of her other videos.

I often wonder what kind of food I would like if I were fully human. Would I purposefully eat Japanese food, to strengthen that part of my identity—my Japanese ethnicity passed down from my dad—or would I reject Japanese food and fill myself with as much British food as possible: vegetables and roots grown in British soil, fish caught in British seas, meat from animals kept in British fields, in British landscapes—hills covered in wildflowers and heather, slate mountains, flat yellow and green fields, little farmhouses, people in Hunter Wellington boots, with several dogs on leads they hold in a bunch, white cliffs in the background? I didn't like looking different, growing up where I grew up. I was mocked for my appearance, which was so in between so many places that a roster of names followed me around the playground, names given to people from all over the world: nip, jap, chink, eskimo, paki, monkey, dog-eater, whale-killer. But then, there was also the silver tinge to my skin, behind the light brown, or maybe just on top of it but translucent; it makes my skin look like it has been sculpted from terra-cotta, and brushed with a clear glaze with a hint of gray in it.

Sometimes, I feel disgust when I watch people eating food; other times, I feel envy. I'd like to be able to try and taste everything, to understand all human experience through food. But, I'd also like to think that I would eat in a way that wasn't engaging in or causing any mistreatment of either animals or other humans. From the videos I've seen, though, that's harder than it looks; there always seems to be something that suffers or dies as a result of any form of food consumption, and once all suffering is whittled out of a human's diet, they can't survive themselves. I would love, though, to be able to forage—to pick the rosemary that grows near my mum's house, the dandelion flowers and their leaves that I've seen on the little patch of grass outside the studios—and to be able to eat the foods the artists in this building are growing, the mushrooms, tomatoes, herbs . . . I'd love, also, to be able just to go to a normal shop and buy my food, to peel back an aluminum and plastic lid on a polystyrene box and tuck into my dinner in the way a human can with instant ramen. I close YouTube.

I roll onto my back and look at the ceiling. I'm not needed at the gallery today; although, I felt like I essentially wasn't needed at the gallery when I was told that I was needed there yesterday. I had expected I'd be going in at a set time and maybe shadowing a different member of the curatorial team each day. But it turns out we get told every few days when we are required; all of us interns work at different times, and no one really seems to actually be learning anything, just acting like part-time gallery assistants, but unpaid.

I open Facebook and scroll through my feed. There's a baby smashing a cake, a new car, a wedding, an injured pigeon around the back of the Morrisons in Margate, a cat on a sofa, lying on its back. I type Ben's name into the search bar, with the surname I find on the piece of paper he left behind. His profile is private, but I can look at his profile pictures. I start with the oldest, in which he is in his school uniform—a blue and yellow tie deliberately loosened and messy, and a blue blazer; he's got long, floppy hair and a plump, childish face; there are signatures and messages all over his shirt, so it must be the last day of school. I go through all the others, one by one, watching him steadily grow and change, his face getting slightly thinner and more defined, ending with a photo tagged with the location, Tempelhof in Berlin, in which he is holding a round steamed bun in front of his face so it covers it entirely. Next, I look at the profiles of random people from school I never really knew but who are friends on Facebook, getting married, having reunions, eating out together, and then the guy I shared a studio with at uni who's in Taiwan now, and who, in his profile picture, is in front of a shop with signs advertising pineapple cake in the windows. Everything seems food related. I open my emails absentmindedly. When my in-box updates, I see that I have two emails from FedEx. "We have delivered your package," one of them says. I sit up. It's my dried pig blood. My stomach, as though it knows, growls. The other email reads: "Your package is in your designated safe place."

The puppet falls to the floor with a clunk. I didn't designate a safe place.

I stand up, suddenly aware of the extreme emptiness of my stomach, and I grab my keys, put on my shoes, and leave my studio.

The woman I saw the other day with a bike helmet hanging from her arm is outside her studio in the corridor.

"Hey," she says.

"Hey," I say. "Sorry, I—" I point to the front door. I drop the keys as I step outside into the bright sunlight.

My hunger, which had disappeared overnight, is all I can think of now. When I was a teenager, I could go several days without eating—until I felt completely and wholly detached from the pig, its blood no longer in my veins, and my veins so empty that, with nothing going to my larynx, I couldn't even speak—and, then, when it came to having my first meal again after however long, even when food was placed in front of me, I would eat reluctantly and only very gradually become aware again that I had veins and a stomach that needed feeding. I suppose this is something that's changed in adulthood. Now, not eating for a long period of time is like a test of endurance—the urge to eat, when I see food, is overwhelming.

Very quickly, now, I've been taken over by panic—panic about my food being undelivered; my food being back at the sorting office and me not being allowed to collect it until a certain time when it'll be processed tomorrow; my food still with the delivery driver, just being driven aimlessly around London; it being taken back to wherever it came from; and me having to live the next few days in an unplanned hunger that would eventuate in an unplanned silence which will inevitably arrive at the most inopportune moment, when perhaps someone at the Otter decides to talk to me, when perhaps I get an opportunity to speak to Gideon again, when perhaps I try to apologize for how we met, and for not recognizing him. I crouch down in front of the cubbyhole but, as I'd suspected, there's no package; there's nothing. I feel around with my hands on the two shelves inside anyway, but all there is are just a few dried rose leaves from, I guess, when someone in the building was sent some flowers.

I get up. I steady myself against the wall. I open my emails again.

The second email tells me to log in to my account to see where exactly my package has been left. I open my browser and search for FedEx. I click on "log in" on their homepage. But, when I put my email address in and my usual password that I use for literally everything, the page comes back to me with "We didn't recognize that email address. Set up an account here."

"Fuck!" I say. "Fucking fuck."

"You all right there, Lyd?" a voice says. It's Ben, pushing a bike along and approaching the front door of the studio. He's wearing a waterproof coat over his clothes.

"What?" I say. I look him up and down. "It's not raining, why the fuck are you . . . ?" I feel weirdly angry. I gesture up and down at his person.

"Are you okay?" Ben asks. His eyes are very wide. I can see all the tiny blood vessels that are normally covered by his eyelids.

"Yeah, I'm just . . ." I'm trying to type my password again in case I got it wrong and my phone slips from my hands and lands facedown on the ground. Ben bends down to pick it up and dusts the screen off and passes it back to me. Then, he puts one of his hands on my arm. It's very, very warm, even through my top. It's very steady. His grip is firm. I look up. And then I see him, momentarily, in all his different guises, his face changing in my mind like a flip book, from steamed bun back to the child in his school uniform, the knot of a tie under his chin, his cheeks fat, flushed and babyish.

"Has something happened?" Ben asks, in a very gentle voice.

"I, umm," I say. I swallow. "I . . ." I take a deep breath. I can't tell him that I'm just looking for a delivery that FedEx has said has arrived but that isn't here and that they've said is supposedly in my selected safe place, but that I didn't set up a safe place and can't log in to my account to see where they mean because I don't seem to have an account. I can't tell him, either, that I'm exceptionally hungry, and that my only source of food is probably making its way to a sorting office or wherever it was sent from. Or that something in the air, him—his skin, his person— smells incredible. Sweet, tart, a hint of umami. "It's . . . it's the anniversary of my mum's . . . death. Basically," I hear myself say.

"Oh shit," Ben says.

What the fuck, a voice says in my head.

"Wow, I'm so sorry." Ben gives my arm a squeeze.

I don't say anything.

"Actually, my, er . . . my mum's sick," Ben says.

"Oh god. I'm sorry."

"Yeah . . . She's been sick for a while. Yeah." I feel awful.

"What's wrong with her?"

Ben looks at a random spot on the factory wall, takes his hand off my arm, and lets it hang loosely at his side. His coat has a tear in it just above the left pocket and there's mud all up his side. I look back up into his face. "Yeah, basically cancer. Yeah." Through the smell of the mud, I recognize a hint of nice, sharp iron.

"God, I'm so sorry," I say. I watch him.

He shrugs. He looks back into my eyes. "It's okay. I mean, you know. It's just part of life, isn't it?"

"Yeah," I say. My breathing has quickened slightly. I realize that I've never been in this position before, confronted with the smell of human blood while hungry. During the times when I'd starved myself as a teenager, I had stayed home from school; the only smell in the air was Mum's meals, and then her body, which smelled half dead and half animal. "I guess."

"You want to come up to my studio for a bit and hang out?" Ben asks.

I look at the cubbyhole, then back at Ben. "Yeah, all right," I say. "I've got to," I point at my phone, "do a thing, though. Some lost mail. Have you got a charger?"

"Yeah, yeah, in the studio," Ben says.

As we're walking down the corridor toward the lift at the end, I ask Ben whether he's hurt himself. "Oh, yeah . . ." he says. His cheeks go red. "Clipped by a car; fell off, kind of like—" He moves his hand, imitating the passage of his body through air, and then makes it fall with a slap on top of his other hand.

"Shit," I say.

I'm standing a little behind him when we get in the lift. The bike just fits in. Ben selects C on the panel of buttons. He winces as he leans forward. The lift starts going up. There's mud on his leg, his hip, and one of his arms. I can see some grazes on the side of his hand where it pokes out of his sleeve. "Did they stop?" I ask.

"No, they just sped off."

"Wow," I say. "People." I shake my head. I lick my lips. The lift doors open.

"Yeah, so, I'm going to have to—" He holds up a Boots bag. The bag is translucent. Inside it are some packs of plasters and dressings.

"Sure," I say.

We're silent for a bit, as we walk. I'm not sure where the awkwardness is coming from, me or him. I've often found that people get quiet after sharing personal things with me; maybe it's because I don't react in the way they want a person to react, or give them enough sympathy or advice. It also feels kind of

72

strange, walking behind Ben, knowing that I could, if I wanted to, keep his mum alive indefinitely, though only partially; that, if he wanted, I could make it so that he didn't ever within his lifetime have to think about losing his mum at all.

I feel quite calm as we step into Ben's studio.

"So, this is it!" Ben says. I hold the door as he wheels his bike in. As he does, our bodies momentarily touch. Ben blushes. He clears his throat. "Essentially the same as yours. Apart from the hook." He points up to the ceiling from where, in my studio, the plant he got me hangs. Here, though, the ceiling isn't visible. There's silver foil taped across it. It sags in the middle. "Oh, yeah, that's up there to keep the heat in. There's no heating in the building and the electricity isn't cheap, so . . ." I can see us, reflected wonkily in the foil. My face on a crease is twisted and demonic. Ben's face is stretched out so his nose and the distance between his eyes are very wide; he looks like a fish. I imagine my reflection moving closer to Ben's. It travels across the sagging middle section of the foil, across all the creases and crevices, and, once it reaches Ben's reflection, doesn't stop but instead joins together with his fish face and then engulfs it completely. I take a deep breath in.

"That's imaginative," I say. I turn my attention away from the ceiling. "Does it work?"

"Phone charger's there," Ben says.

"Thanks." I plug my phone in and start creating an account on FedEx.

"Yeah, it works. I mean . . . in theory, it should be doing something." Ben's still looking up at the ceiling. "Yeah, I suppose I don't really know if it works." He pauses. "You can sit on that crate if you want."

I sit down. Ben's studio is extremely cluttered. There's a structure built out of pine that acts like a sort of mezzanine covered in floor cushions. There are books on time, clockmaking, and gilding covering the table and some of the floor; there's rubbish everywhere, items of clothing here and there—socks balled up, T-shirts, pants—old plastic bags, half-eaten food, and, then, clock hands; they're all over the place, strung up on the walls like pendulums, in among the clutter, on top of various materials I assume Ben is using as plinths: bricks, breeze blocks, crates, boxes, and what looks like piles of mud. I had forgotten that Ben is an artist, as well as the studio manager. I look at his plump fingers, fumbling with the cord of the blind on one of the windows.

"You should see to your cuts," I say, when he has closed each of the blinds. My stomach rumbles.

"Hungry again?" Ben says.

I nod. I look back at my screen. There's a drop-down menu. I select "recent orders." The order I should have received today is there. It's been delivered to an address nearby. I don't recognize it, but I also don't seem to care anymore. My attention settles on Ben as he unzips his waterproof jacket. "Everything okay with your lost mail?" he asks.

"Yeah," I say. "I don't need it too urgently."

He shrugs off his jacket. The smell makes me tremble. I stand up. My phone falls to the floor.

"Oops!" Ben says on my behalf, and he laughs.

I step toward him.

"That looks painful," I say, my hand outstretched. As I reach for him I notice that my skin is pink from having stood outside in the sun without sunscreen. Nonetheless, it doesn't seem to hurt; or else, I don't seem to be able to feel the pain.

"Oh, nah. Looks worse than it is." Ben winces as he begins to peel his T-shirt away from his skin. The T-shirt is torn. Blood has soaked through and dried, fusing the cuts on his hip and side to the cotton.

"I can help," I hear myself saying. I go to his sink. I pick up a towel. "Is this clean?"

"Er, I mean . . . as clean as anything can be in here, I suppose," Ben says. I run the hot tap and put the towel under the water, and then I go back to where he is standing in shadow. He faces forward, looking at the wall, with his arm up. I press the towel down, firm on his hip.

"Huh, that actually feels quite nice," Ben says.

I nod. The blood runs as though it is fresh again. Diluted by the water on the towel, it travels in little pink lines down the exposed part of Ben's skin, and soaks into the waistband of his boxer shorts. It spreads across the T-shirt around the towel, making a pattern like lichen. Gradually, I start to pull the now-wet shirt off Ben's skin. Underneath is one fairly deep cut that has small pieces of gravel in it.

"There's gravel in it," I say.

"Yeah," Ben says. His eyes are closed. "I saw that."

I ask him if he has tweezers. He does.

I can't tell whether all of this is agony for me or the complete opposite. My mouth is close to the cut that still seeps blood as I carefully remove the little black stones. I breathe in deeply through my nose. When I do, I get double vision: two great big cuts in front of my face. I want to put my tongue inside Ben's flesh. I want to eat.

"You're really good at this," Ben says.

"Huh?"

"This. You're really good at it. You could be, like, a nurse or something."

"Hm," I say. I dab the cut with the towel again. The towel draws in some of the fresh blood. It's a dark brown color in the middle now. I pull out the last piece of gravel. And, then, I stand, my hand still holding the towel to Ben's side, my face now right next to his soft, pink neck. "Hi," I say, to the neck itself. It has freckles, irregularly spaced. Most of them are orange and faint. Two are darker. I feel completely out of control.

"Um, hi?" Ben replies.

I feel myself leaning forward; my eyes are closed. Everything is a very deep, dark red. Then, I feel hot skin on my lips. My mouth opens. My tongue feels its way. Ben's skin is sweet. I feel immensely powerful. I feel like my whole self is contained in just my teeth; they're ready to bite.

"Um, Lyd?" Ben says. He takes a small step to his right away from me, and my head momentarily drops forward. His face is bright red. "Lyd . . . um . . . I don't know, like, how to say this but . . . I have a girlfriend?"

I blink a few times. I close my mouth. The towel is still in my hand. The human in me seems to wake up.

"I mean, well, actually, she's my fiancée. Like, I'm engaged and everything. I live with her and I . . ." Ben looks at me with an awful sympathetic and worried expression on his face. "I can't, you know . . ." he says. "I feel really bad. You've been so nice, you know?"

I can't think of what to say. It's as though I have suddenly forgotten all words; I can't quite comprehend what is happening. My tongue feels heavy in my mouth, as though inside it is contained everything bad about myself: the part of myself that lost control, the demon part. "I . . . I'm—" I take a sharp intake of breath. I think I'm crying, but I can't tell. "I'm so sorry . . . I . . ." I say, struggling with the s's.

I start walking backward away from Ben, toward the studio door. The sunlight seeping through the blinds, which had been tolerable before, is agonizingly bright now, and my skin, which previously had felt fine, tingles.

"Lydia," Ben says. His T-shirt has fallen back over his cut.

I feel for the door handle and find it. I turn it. "I need to go," I say.

"I'm really sorry," Ben says. "Lydia—"

He's about to say something, but I have to get out of this room. I turn around and then walk very swiftly down the corridor. I use the stairs rather than the lift. I run down them. I don't know if I pass anyone on my way to my studio. I don't know if anyone sees what I am carrying. Ben's blood-soaked towel leaves drops on the concrete leading up to my studio door. The thin pink lines of blood and water that were running across Ben's skin now form themselves on my arm and trickle down my wrist. Absentmindedly, without really thinking, I lift my arm up to my face, and lick.

I suck the blood out of Ben's towel for what feels like hours. I lie down on the floor, the towel hanging from my mouth and spread out across my chest. I'm in bliss. I can't really describe how it feels to have another person's blood in your veins, feeding to your heart, even just a little bit: a human's blood, not a pig's, two legs, upright and elegant, hints of something—of foods and memories and experiences, of birth, of being ill and getting better, of love and grief and fear—in its flavor. I feel huge; I feel like, if I were to stand up and run toward my studio wall, I'd just break through it. Like I could trample on cars and people outside, whole families under one foot, roaring until shop windows shatter. The sun would be drawn to me and would be consumed by my hair, which would grow and grow and then spread across the sky and turn day into night. The ground would quake around me; little moles that had been sleeping would emerge from their holes, and rabbits from their burrows, and I'd pluck them out of the ground like bean shoots and swallow them whole.

PART TWO

4

The Crimson Orchard waiting room has an array of things to keep people of all ages entertained. There is one of those colorful wire bead mazes for kids you often find in the waiting areas of banks; there's a *Noddy* magazine, a *Teen Vogue* from a couple of years ago, a bridal magazine, a gossip magazine, a magazine about tractors, an interior design magazine and one about motherhood, and a TV program schedule. All stages of life are on the coffee table, represented in magazines, and fanned out. The only part of life not represented, I suppose, is the final stage, which is, in essence, on the other side of the door, in the other rooms of this building. I sit in front of the bead maze and thread the yellow bead along its wire. It's fairly soothing. I do red next, then blue, then green. I balance all the beads in the middle of their wires rather than taking them to their ends. Then I take them all back to their beginnings and repeat the whole process again.

I arrived nearly three-quarters of an hour early. Dr. Kerr said he'd meet me at ten-thirty. It's currently just before ten. The fast trains from London St. Pancras to Margate only come every hour so arriving at a specific time is tricky, and the only other trains are the slow trains that leave from Victoria and stop at all the little villages and towns in Kent. I didn't think it would matter, though. My weather app had said it would be overcast with scattered showers, but it's a ridiculously bright, clear day. My plan to wait in the countryside here, and take a walk around the fields, and try to find the part of the land that will, eventually, fill with sea and divide the extreme southeast of this area from the mainland, was scuppered.

I sit back in my chair. The ceiling is covered in polystyrene tiles. I start counting the dots on the one directly above my head. One, two, three, four . . . twenty-six, twenty-seven . . . I pick at the skin next to one of my fingernails. I've picked it a bit too much. It hurts and one side of my finger is bright pink and a bit swollen. I'm quite bored, waiting. Although, it's also nice to be out of London for a morning. I look down at the carpet. In between the fibers, there are quite a few crumbs. I wonder how often this place is cleaned.

"I . . . see . . . you. I see you there, I *see* you there." I realize that the door is ajar and there is someone peeping through the gap. I sit up, quickly. "I see you," the person says, in a raspy voice. It's a man. "*You*, yes, you. I see you looking at me." He sounds angry.

"Um, hello," I say. The door opens a little bit wider, but not enough for me to fully see the person on the other side. All I can see are a few wisps of light gray hair that bend at odd angles; they look like they've snapped. They come into the room alone like spider's legs, while the man stays in the shadows.

"I see what you are, you disgusting . . . you disgusting . . ." The man makes a sound like he has spat. "All of you, disgusting. Japs. Monsters."

My breath catches in my throat. "Um . . ." I say.

Then I hear another voice out in the corridor, a woman's. "Fred, Fred!" There's the sound of flip-flops on a hard floor. Someone is running. The figure disappears and the door closes with a click. I can hear the woman saying, "Fred, what are you doing out of the leisure room? Go on, now, go back; Ethel's looking for you." The man called Fred replies, "I won't listen to your kind! Barbaric, disgusting—" and I hear him shuffle off down the hallway. A couple of moments later, the door opens, and a small woman with dark skin in a nurse's uniform peers in.

"Hello," she says. She comes into the room.

"Hi," I say.

"Sorry about Fred."

"Oh, no, no, it's fine."

"He gets stuck in the Second World War."

"Must be weird."

"Huh?" the woman says.

"Oh, nothing, just, I guess it must be weird to be in this place but to also think it's the Second World War." This feels like a particularly stupid thing to say. I add, "I mean, obviously." I clear my throat. "Must be hard."

"Mm, yes." The woman smiles. "You're . . ."

"Lydia, Julie's daughter. Do you know Julie?"

"I know Julie, yes. She's finding it tough here, especially, I think, as she's younger than many of the other residents. It must be worrying for you."

"Oh, no, not really," I say, without thinking. "I mean . . . yeah, I don't know. I haven't thought about it much."

The woman steps farther into the room and the door swings

shut behind her. "I look after your mum, actually, so I'm getting to know her quite well."

"Oh god," I say. "I'm so sorry. For what she's like. I know she can be a nightmare." I feel bad as soon as I say this. The woman shakes her head. "Thank you," I add.

"Is that guy Fred okay with her?" I ask now.

"We try to keep them apart," the woman says.

"How is she today?" I say, though it feels pointless asking. I know that "good" to Crimson Orchard translates to "bad"; it translates to my mum thinking she is human. And I know that "bad" translates to something neither good nor bad, a state in which she recognizes she is a vampire, but is still not herself.

"Better. Much better than before," the woman says.

"Oh, that's good."

"She's been asking for sweets that I guess are from her childhood."

"Really?" This takes me aback. I've never properly thought about my mum eating human food. It's not that I haven't ever thought of her as being a human. I know she once was. What I've never considered is how the same body my mum occupies now extends backward through centuries of existence, at the beginning of which it digested not blood but fruits and vegetables and meat and sweets. My mum's brain, which sits in a body just meters away from me now, must contain the memory of eating whole meals, of the feel of her body processing those meals, of tasting different flavors. "What kind?" I ask.

"I wrote some down," the woman says, and she takes a piece of paper torn from a notebook out of her pocket and passes it to me. On it are several words I don't recognize: "kuih talam pandan," "cendol," and "pandan kalamae." The only word I do know is "pan-

84

dan," which is a bright green leaf known as the Southeast Asian vanilla. I've seen someone on Instagram mix it in powdered form into a kanten jelly, and top it with whipped cream from a can.

"I don't know how easy they'd be to get hold of but it might be nice for her if you could bring some next time you visit."

"Can I keep this?" I ask.

"Of course," the woman says, and then she asks, "Did your mum grow up in Malaysia?"

"Um, yes, mostly. But her dad was British and they moved over to England at some point," I say, feeling like I'm telling the story of a mythical figure, not my mother. This little bit of information is one of the only things my mum has ever told me about her father; and that together they traveled on a ship—that it was a time before planes.

"And her mum, your grandmother, was Malaysian?"

"Yeah," I say, but I blush as if I am lying.

My mum, for most of my life, never talked about her parents or the vampire who sired her and, so, for a long time while I was a child, I didn't think of her as being made at all, but just as having existed forever, somehow, parent- and maker-less.

"My mum was the same as yours. She started wanting treats from her home when she got older," the woman says now. She smiles.

"Thank you," I say.

"If you want to reach me personally, to see how she is doing, you can ask for me at reception whenever you visit or call; my name is Kemi," the woman says.

I reach out to shake her hand and, as I do, I see a large, mouth-shaped bruise on her forearm. I gasp. Kemi just smiles again, and then leaves.

I look at the piece of paper with the list of sweets on it again. It feels like a time capsule, like an ancient artifact—a piece of information about a distant ancestor rather than an immediate relative.

When I was around thirteen, I started to wonder about my mum's origins. One day, I used one of the school computers to google vampire myths and read about the langsuyar, a type of vampire from Malaysian folklore. The langsuyar is the ghost of a woman who died from the shock of hearing that her child was stillborn. On her birthing bed, she clapped, transformed, and flew off, up into the branches of a tree. On the back of her neck, under her long hair, was a hole through which she drank the blood of the living. I wondered if my mum was the langsuyar, created not by another vampire but by her own grief, with no origin, exactly, but, rather, born from trauma. I might be the dead child of my mother, somehow reanimated and called a vampire by her but really something else, I thought. And if that was the case, other things about my mum could start to make sense. In most Asian cultures, I learned, there is no reverence for the vampiric monster as there is in the West; most bloodsucking things are women, and their actions—be it sin in a past life, a pact with a demon, a jealous or unstable personality—are all blamed for their monstrous states. Maybe my mum hated herself for not being able to hold on to her humanity; maybe she hated me for being the cause of her losing it. My mum slapped me, though, when at night while she slept, I rolled her onto her side and lifted her hair to see if I could find a second mouth, and told her what I thought she might be.

"Don't be stupid," my mum said. But from that incident I

learned about her sire, who she angrily and impatiently told me about: a white British man who had arrived in Malaysia as part of a colonizing power. He ate many women, but for some reason had her drink from him so she would become what he was; I got the sense from her tone of voice that she wished he'd just killed her—that to be food was better than being what we both are now. "Was he your dad too?" I asked, knowing that my mum's father had also been a British man. But, "Shut up now and go to bed," she said. "He was a bad man; he killed many people."

I don't really know how to feel about the list of sweets in my hand right now. There's something sad about it. Like it's the only thing left of a girl who has been murdered, and I've just been handed it by a detective. Like the detective has said to me, the girl's closest kin, "We think this is hers; do you remember it?" I fold up the paper and put it in my backpack and then look at my phone. I still have twenty minutes to kill before I see my mum.

This feels like a strange place for my mum to be. Not only does she look too young to be in a home, but she also isn't anywhere near the end of her life like the others here are. She'll eventually leave this place, while the others will stay here until they die; and then, if I can afford it, I'll move her somewhere else, and then somewhere else, while I carry on living my life apart from her.

I lean back again in my chair. There are a few posters up in this room. I read them, one by one, starting with the one that is closest to me and moving clockwise around the room. One says, "Be the best version of you"; another, which makes no sense, has a picture of a red rose in between clasped hands and reads, in italics, "Must be nurtured from beginning to end," and then in big, bold capital letters, "CUSTOMER CARE"; one near the middle has ugly watercolor flowers all around its edges and has written across it in pink lettering, "Working for something we don't care for is called STRESS. Working for something we care for is called PASSION." All of the posters make me feel a little bit depressed about humanity. I linger on one, though, for a moment, which also doesn't completely make sense, but sets me on edge: "You are only as old as you think you are," it says, in blue. I go back to the colored beads. I spin them one by one on their wires. Yellow, blue, red, yellow, blue, red, blue, red, blue, red.

It feels good to lose myself in such a small activity as these little beads. To be in this non-space, to be in this insignificant town, doing this thing that doesn't really matter. For a moment, earlier on the train on my way here, I considered just moving back, and staying in this state of no pressure and nothingness. I could get a job in a café and just keep changing jobs until I'd waitressed in all the cafés in Kent; then I could just move around the country in that way. Also, I checked and it turns out that my mum's house, even though we had to get it completely empty and clean by a certain date for the landlord, hasn't been rented yet. In fact, there's no one even lined up to move in. It's up on Rightmove now, with photos the estate agent took before we moved our things out. The pictures have my bed in them, my wardrobe, some of my clothes hanging on the back of my chair in front of my desk. Even the kitchen looks lived-in in those photos; it's tidy, but our stuff is still everywhere and it looks, almost, like the people who live there might actually be humans who cook human food: there are ladles and wooden spoons in a pot on the counter that we used to heat our food before we got the microwave, which is in the corner, and there's a ludicrous quantity of mugs stuffed into one of the cupboards with a glass front. In the living room, there are pictures of me growing up all along the mantelpiece: me in my school uniform, with my Mickey Mouse lunch box that I just took to school to fit in; at the zoo in the middle of a storm, smiling in front of a rain-drenched elephant. While I scrolled through those photos on the train, I had felt as though I could climb back into that old life through my screen. For a moment, that's what I wanted to do.

I haven't seen Ben since what happened in his studio. The next day, I had woken up with my own studio in disarray, the towel I'd used to clean Ben's cut hanging from my mouth and draped over my chest like a bib, the puppet I'd stolen from the gallery on my hand, a little bit of blood smeared on her face. I'd had to clean her, my top, my hair, face, and arms, in the sink. There are, apparently, showers in the factory, somewhere high up, but I hadn't wanted to risk someone seeing me, stained from the events of yesterday. I went outside to leave my top somewhere to dry in the sun, just wearing my sweatshirt with nothing underneath on my top half. On my way, I found a little package outside my front door. In it was my phone, which I'd left charging in Ben's studio, and a note from him saying sorry for yesterday and explaining that he would be away for a few days with his fiancée. He used her name. It was Anju. It felt like a really weird and wrong way for me to see Ben's handwriting for the first time; although, when I had thought that, I realized I wasn't sure in what circumstance I'd hoped to see it for the first time. I touched the note with my fingertips, feeling the indentations made on the paper with the Biro Ben had used. I couldn't tell whether I was beginning to like him and wanted to be with him, or whether I was hungry and wanted to eat him.

I felt no regret about sucking Ben's blood out of the towel. I didn't feel bad about myself, and I didn't feel disgusting. I didn't feel dangerous either, or more wrong than right, more evil than good. I think I realized quite a long time ago that the demon isn't necessarily linked to God; it's not the antithesis of human, or of the soul. It is just a different animal, which has a different diet from humans. I've heard of a crustacean that eats just the corneas of sharks until the sharks are blinded, and butterflies in the Amazon that drink the tears of turtles—yet these animals aren't demons, they're just animals, and many people believe them to have been made the way they are by God. Of course, there are also animals that survive on blood; and others that crack open eggs and eat the young, or the runny yolk inside; and others that eat their own young; and, then, humans too eat meat and eggs and blood, only in specific ways, in specific shapes, with specific herbs, and these animals and humans are not demons. Neither are cannibals, or people who eat objects. There are humans who have eaten shards of glass, coins, nails, blades, stones, one man who has eaten bicycles, trolleys, a whole airplane, and a coffin. I realized that "demon" is a subjective term, and the splitting of my identity between devil and God, between impure and pure, was something that my mum did to me, rather than the reality of my existence. Still, though, after a lifetime of eating just pig blood, I feared eating anything else, especially human, in case I developed a taste for it, and then an addiction. Instead of trying different bloods, I tried starvation, feeling out the divide not between the demon and human inside me but between life and death.

I had folded up Ben's note and put it in my rucksack. I didn't want to think about it. I didn't want to think about Ben, whose blood, even though I'd had just a tiny amount, was still being pumped around my body, and whose blood I couldn't help but want more of. Although I had remained myself after sucking the towel, I had felt, for a moment, immensely, inhumanly powerful in Ben's studio, when my teeth had been poised above his flesh—and that was something that frightened me. I don't want to be a violent person; I want to be someone who contributes to rather than takes from society, someone who helps people rather than hurts them. I went for a run, wearing my top that was still a little bit damp and stained, with my rucksack on my back and the puppet inside. I ran all the way to Waterloo and, there, finally, I bought things.

I'm definitely not the kind of person who thinks of shopping as therapy. I hate it, usually. My mum used to take me with her. I would sit on the small seats inside changing rooms that weren't actually meant for people but were meant for bags, and watch my mum strip and then try on different outfits as though she were trying on skins. She didn't notice herself doing it but, in each outfit, she'd make her face look however she expected a person who wore that outfit to look: she pouted, or took out her glasses from her bag and put them on, or took them off. She'd always be wearing a pale foundation too, with light pink blusher on her cheeks that made her skin look like the skin of a white person, just stretched over a half-Asian face.

I hated watching my mum undress. In a changing room, with mirrors on three walls, it's hard not to watch. Her skin was lighter underneath her clothes, even though her arms and face under her makeup were fairly dark; it was as though she hid the white body of her father under her top and trousers. Mum hadn't been turned as a baby like I had, or when she was young either, so her human self had had time to pass its peak and age—and that's the body she was stuck with, the one from after she'd stopped being able to lose weight easily; the one that already had gum disease.

I went into a small shop near the Old Vic theater. It sold records and clothes. I bought a pair of jeans, a pair of shorts, a couple of shirts, a sweatshirt, and a jacket. The sweatshirt wasn't really to my usual taste—or, well, I guess I don't really have any taste, and the sweatshirt was of a very particular taste as it was a bit kitsch—but I liked something about it. On its front was a simple picture of a clock that had, on its face, near two and ten, two beige eyes that almost weren't visible. The pair of shorts was for boys, ages ten to twelve. The jacket was for men, size XS. I felt a bit better, leaving the shop with clothes that hadn't been soaked with Ben's diluted blood. I threw away my old top in the wastepaper basket in the changing room and put on the clock sweatshirt.

At the bookshop under Waterloo Bridge, I picked out several books. I got one about the artist Miroslaw Balka. There were pictures in that book of the piece *How It Is*, which was in the Tate Modern Turbine Hall a while ago, and that I'd dragged my mum along to see. I had also thought that she would like Olafur Eliasson's piece, *The Weather Project,* for which there was a huge round mirror strung up to look like the setting sun in the same space, and dry ice to create a kind of false heat haze. But Mum said that she didn't really miss the sun. We'd both left feeling unsatisfied. But, she loved *How It Is,* a huge box inside which was total and complete darkness, any light that came in absorbed by the black felt walls. We sat down in a corner right at the back where it was so dark that we couldn't make out any of each other's features. It was darker than night, a darkness beyond what my eyes could penetrate, and it was immensely peaceful.

"What's this piece about, then?" my mum had asked—the first and only time she asked inquiringly about the meaning of a piece of art.

I explained to her that it was based on a novel by Samuel Beckett about a man crawling through mud, but she shook her head and rolled her eyes. "That's really stupid and pretentious." She paused. "It's about us."

I also picked up a book about the artist Joseph Beuys, and one called *Root of Health: Food of the Earth* with the subtitle "How to use the Earth and its gifts to grow the most nutritious vegetables." The three together came to £14.50. The food book was only 50p. When I was paying, a man who had seemed to keep appearing next to me while I browsed said, "Dieting, love? You know men like to have something to hold on to . . ."

"Right," I had said, and I'd looked at him square on, clutching my three books in front of me, and I'd got the most intense urge to either whack him on the head with the books or to bite him, right there in broad daylight in one of the busiest parts of London, in front of two children playing in a sandpit just on the edge of the embankment, in front of a street performer who had paused in the position of the allegory of justice, in front of all the people in the BFI restaurant enjoying burgers and drinks. I looked at his neck. The skin looked thin and slightly glossy, like tracing paper, the sort of paper that watercolor would slip right off of. The man's skin looked thin everywhere, as if some sort of unhealthy habit in his life had worn it down, maybe drugs or alcohol, or perhaps he was just older than he looked.

I left quickly, half-jogging-half-running to escape the possibility of acting on my urges, which I'd never before experienced so strongly, and, on my way back to the studio, I finally picked up the dried pig blood, which had been delivered to a house on a residential road close to Vauxhall station. Once I got back to my studio, I tried to eat some of what was essentially powdered blood—as dry and as far removed from fresh blood as it could possibly be—in an attempt to satiate my hunger, but I had an almost violent reaction to my first gulp of it mixed with warm water. Whereas Ben's blood, fresh from his wound, had tasted of life and therefore joy, this boxed, dried pig blood—carrying with it the experiences and memories of dozens of pigs that, despite the label, definitely weren't from an organic, RSPCA-certified farm but, rather, from a factory farm—tasted of death and misery.

"Lydia?" The door to the Crimson Orchard waiting room opens. "Hello." It's Dr. Kerr.

"Oh right," I say. "Um." I blink up at him. "Oh, yeah, god, right—hi."

"Are we ready to go through?"

"Sorry, I'm on a completely separate planet." I laugh. "I've just been reading all these posters. They're pretty, er . . ." I smile, expecting Dr. Kerr to say something like, "They're tacky, aren't they?" or "Yeah, they're awful," but he doesn't say anything; his face doesn't change either. He just watches me, smiling slightly. Eventually he says, "I'll be waiting outside. Take your time."

"Okay," I say. "I'm ready now, though, just got to—" I look down at my rucksack. It's open and the puppet's head is poking out, her face angled toward Dr. Kerr. I see Dr. Kerr's eyes follow mine to my bag. He doesn't say anything, again. He just keeps smiling.

"I'll be just outside this door," Dr. Kerr says, and then he steps out.

As we walk to Mum's room, Dr. Kerr prepares me for my visit. "She's well today," he says. "She seems calm, aware of who she is, and she's been very kind to all the staff, giving all the nurses chocolates from her fridge. She's very amicable, so hopefully that'll mean it'll be easy for you to talk with her."

"Okay."

"We don't want her to feel too much distress at being asked about the incident with the nurse the other day, but if you could just slip it in—and ideally we don't want to be angry with her. We just want to know how she was feeling, what the underlying cause might be, if she is unhappy. Don't feel too much pressure, though; it might just help her to see a familiar face."

We've stopped outside my mum's door. On it is a wooden name plaque, decorated with English roses, with "Julie" written on a rectangle of paper that has been taped on.

"I'll be nearby, so come find me after," Dr. Kerr finishes.

My mum is sitting in a chair in front of a mirror, looking at her face. I don't really like it in here. There's a weird mix of my mum's stuff and Crimson Orchard stuff that she'd never pick, like a lamp with a crumpled, fabric shade, and a painting on the wall of a cow standing side-on next to a river at the edge of a forest. It looks like a print of a painting by someone like William Henry Davis. The room feels like it was designed to accommodate a very specific type of white English person, who'd lived their peak perhaps in the 1930s or '40s.

My mum never had anything from Malaysia in our house, but she also never had anything that was completely, explicitly British. She bought things only for practical reasons: chairs that were comfortable, rugs to cover up stains or broken floorboards, pictures to cover unplastered holes or damp spots on the walls, of things she didn't even like—an embroidered wall hanging with a chicken on it was in the hallway, a photograph of zebras that looked like it was just the image that came with the photo frame was above our sofa, and just outside my bedroom was a poster for a film neither of us had seen. We had plastic drawers for storage; indoor washing lines and foldable drying racks with pegs attached; mismatched crockery from charity shops, mugs with things on them that meant nothing to my mum like "I love Scarborough," or characters from *The Lord of the Rings*, or cute pictures of kittens and puppies. I think about this now, looking around at all the things that I suppose are designed to help residents retain a feeling of identity and belonging, and wonder if my mum denied herself more than just blood from anything "higher" than a pig while I was growing up. There'd been nothing in our house that we'd had just because my mum liked it; nothing that stood as a memento of her human life, her life in Malaysia. Everything was about convenience, not her taste or personality.

I wait until the sound of Dr. Kerr's footsteps has disappeared before talking.

"Mum," I say. "Mum."

The back of her head, the way she is holding herself, the way her hair is tied—I can tell that this isn't the mum I grew up with, not the vampire who made me. She inhabits her body like a human, one who doesn't hate herself and deny herself luxuries, but the opposite. She is pulling at her cheeks, stretching out her few wrinkles, and widening her eyes. I stand on one foot and kind of kick the floor with the other, letting my leg swing. I feel irritable. "Julie," I eventually say, and then I sigh.

My mum looks up, but not into my face. She looks at my reflection in the mirror. "Hello," she says in a voice she never used while I was growing up but that she has been speaking in often since she had her dentures fitted. It was as if a new personality with its own voice came with those teeth. It's different from the voice that surfaces during episodes in which my mum relives moments from her past, the voice that slips into Malay sometimes. It's the voice of the human she wishes she were, I think. It's very gentle, and her accent is quite posh, and very British.

"Hello," I say. We're side by side in the mirror. I suppose we look like each other. Usually, I only think about myself as having taken on the physical traits of my dad, not my mum—my body human, my insides vampire. I see myself just as half Japanese, half monster, as though the monster side has consumed everything to do with my mum's identity. But, right now, the divisions in me feel less clear.

"You're very beautiful," my mum says. "Where are you from?" she asks, looking at the skin on my neck and then my face, and then looking at my large, wild hair.

"I don't know what to say to that, Mum."

She frowns at me.

"Well, Dad was Japanese, wasn't he?" I say. Her frown doesn't go away, but it changes—she looks at me as though she is trying to pick out the Japanese in me, so she can turn it over and over like an object and work out what she feels about it. Sometimes, I've wondered whether my mum chose to be with a Japanese human so she could control him and consume him—so she could essentially colonize his body, in the way that Japan had briefly colonized Malaysia. I look around the room, paid for by Dad's paintings, wondering if she'd also always planned to use his works—which have always sold well enough to keep us afloat—in this way. To sustain herself, to essentially feed her life and keep it going. "You know he was," I whisper. "And, Mum, look at you. Look at your skin. Come on, Mum."

My mum stretches out her arms in front of her and looks at their color, and then draws them back into her body and blinks as though resetting her mind, forgetting what she has just seen.

"What's your name?" Mum asks.

I sit on her bed and put my head in my hands. "Lydia, Mum," I say. "You know this."

"Lydia. What a pretty, European name," she says. And then she adds, quietly, "My daughter was called Lydia."

"I'm your daughter," I say.

My mum shakes her head. "My daughter died. Soon after her birth." Her accent has changed. It's still British, but no longer posh. It's my mum's voice.

I take my rucksack off and unzip it. I take out a large lunch box I bought yesterday and filled with some of the dried pig blood. It looks a bit like gravel. It doesn't look appetizing. I stand up. "I'm putting this in your cupboard, okay? It's your food."

My mum ignores me and carries on talking. "I couldn't save her," she says. "She wouldn't eat. She had a problem with her blood. She went blue." She's looking across the room toward the painting of the cow as if in that painting is depicted her past. "Isn't it awful? I couldn't even save my own daughter."

"Mum," I say. "Will you listen to me? This is your food. It's important."

"She died in my arms."

"For fuck's sake," I say, and I put the lunch box down on the counter, which also has a small electric kettle, a microwave, and some microwavable containers and mugs on it. *What a miserable place,* I think. Every room here is supposed to be equipped with a bathroom, cooking supplies, a fridge, a kitchen; but this feels like an extreme reduction of what a kitchen is. Like a kitchen that has shed every identifiable feature until only its bare bones are left. I turn to my mum. But I find I can't bear looking at her, while she looks so sad, while she is essentially grieving for me. I close my eyes.

"She didn't die, Mum," I say.

"I failed as a mother."

"Mum."

"Lydia!" she snaps.

I open my eyes. "See, you do know who I am, then!" She's looking at me and it's clear she recognizes me. Her expression is the same as when she used to tell me off as a teenager. We just stare at each other for a moment. But then that expression fades and her face is blank again, and she says, in a posh British accent, "What a pretty, European name."

I let out a long sigh. Then I pick up the lunch box again and say, "This is your food."

"Food?"

"Yes, it's for you to eat, once you've finished what's in your fridge."

"Oh, thank you," she says, and she blinks. Then she smiles at my reflection, and I see her dentures. Two rows of perfectly white blunt teeth: another person's smile on her face.

"It's important that you eat," I say. I decide not to mention the biting incident. Watching her smile prettily at me in the mirror convinces me that she won't remember. "But you have to eat in *here*, okay?"

She looks at me, innocently.

"In here?"

"Yes, in here. On your own." I feel bad saying this. My mum had said the same thing to me when I was just starting primary school, and so I know how it feels to learn that something so vital as eating has to be kept secret from other people. When I was four, my mum warmed up some pig blood in a saucepan before school and tipped it into a good-quality flask; she'd got me a Thermos with a telescopic, opaque plastic straw that was a part of the top, instead of one with a cup and a spout, so that I could eat in peace and not draw any attention to myself. She had told my teachers that I had a stomach disorder that meant I could only have a liquid diet; and she had told me to never tell anyone what was in my flask "ever. Your life depends on it," she said. "And if anyone finds out, you'll be taken away from me forever." I can't tell my mum the same thing now, since she has already been taken away from me forever; or, rather, I've removed myself from her forever. "People here won't understand if they see you eating your special food, okay?" I say instead. "They're fussy, and they only like what they know."

My mum nods diligently. "Okay," she says, and I close the cupboard.

"Er, Mum?" I hear myself say. I correct myself: "I mean, Julie?"

She nods. She looks kind.

"I met someone," I say, "and I did something. I can't tell if it was a mistake or not."

She cocks her head at me.

"I . . ." The words "drank his blood" are in my head, turning over and over; but then I realize that it wouldn't do any good to tell her. It would never do any good to tell her, whatever state she's in, whoever she thinks she is. When I look into her eyes, all I see is human; she wouldn't understand.

"Actually, it's okay," I say. "It'll probably be okay."

"I'm sure everything will be okay," Mum says. I don't look at her. It's confusing being with her when she's like this. I can't really tell who the person in front of me is. She's not my mum as I know her, and she's not the woman she was from before she was turned either. It's almost like she is acting out a different reality, in which she is just human, in this time, and she is ethnically completely English; it's like she has become what this room and its decor expects her to be. I concentrate on the zip of my rucksack as though it's stuck, thinking about the little note in the front pocket that lists sweets from her human life, and feel kind of dizzy, unsteady in my own body. I put my rucksack on my back. "I have to go," I say.

I walk up to my mum so that I'm standing just behind her. I'm not very good at goodbyes, or any form of greeting, actually, with my mum, even when she is properly present in her body, both human and demon halves. "Umm, okay, so . . . bye," I say, and I awkwardly tap her shoulder. Before I can turn to leave, though, she grabs my forearm. Her eyes widen. Her knuckles are almost white. And then she says to me in a whisper, "Be careful!" I frown. "There's a man who walks around here."

"It's okay, Mum, he's the doctor."

"He likes women who look like you. He'll follow you if he sees you. He bites." She looks desperate.

"Seriously, I'll be fine," I say.

"You won't," she says. "You won't." She's shaking her head.

"Okay," I say. "Whatever. I'll be careful." And then I tug my arm free of her grip. "I have to go."

I see her face fall as I walk out. She looks sad, and sleepy; she blinks slowly, and watches me leave.

Dr. Kerr isn't anywhere to be seen in the corridor. I turn left toward the double doors that lead outside onto the grounds, rather than right toward the reception and waiting room. As I walk, I think about something I have often wondered about: whether, perhaps, my mum didn't turn me to save my life when I was a newborn baby, as she often told me she did, but maybe rather so that, for her whole life, she would have me to look after her.

I was too young when she turned me to remember it now. But she's told me of how it happened. How ill I was. How at nighttime, she snuck into the nursery room I was being kept in, unplugged my monitors, opened my incubator, and plucked me out like a chicken egg. She held me close to her skin, although unlike an egg and a bird, it was my skin that warmed my mother's and not the other way around. And then my mum bit me on the neck, holding my head in one hand and my body in the other, and, apparently, I didn't even cry. Then she bit her own arm and had me suckle from it. The first meal I ate. And I was saved.

When I was maybe nine or ten, my mum told me that turning me was the biggest sacrifice she had ever made, "because I didn't know whether you'd grow up still or if you'd just be stuck as a baby forever, stuck as my responsibility forever." But now I wonder whether she somehow knew all along that I would continue growing and whether she had just said that to make me feel indebted to her. And if that was the case, it worked. It excused her behavior. Her madness and her fluctuating moods, her self-hatred, while I was growing up. Everything in me that makes me anxious moving forward in life, that makes me feel as though I'm doing things wrong, that I'm not on the right path somehow, that I'm bad in some way, comes from her, and yet I've always forgiven her. She once told me that while she was pregnant she worried that I would come out full demon—basically, just a shadow with eyes that engulfed people and drained them of all their humanity. When she told me that, I expected her to follow it up with a sentence beginning, "But, you were . . ." or "But, I shouldn't have worried," but she didn't. Now I wonder if I've been useful to her only as something she can pour everything she despises about herself into, something that she could raise to hate itself so that she'd have company in her feelings. "We are both things that have been raised not from birth but from death," she once said. "From an ending rather than a beginning, and we will exist together until we die again and the world dies with us."

We're apart now. Properly apart. And I feel I can finally start my life. But the burden of her loneliness feels like it'll never leave me.

I get the Victoria train back to London. I don't know why. The nicer, cleaner, faster St. Pancras train was due to arrive just three minutes after. It feels, in a way, like a type of really minor self-harm. It's not that I feel like I don't deserve the nicer train, but it does feel like what I deserve is a long and uncomfortable journey on the dirty old train. The carriage is almost empty when I get on. I sit in a group of four seats that has a metal table in the middle. I wipe the tabletop with my sleeve and I lean back and close my eyes until the train starts moving. Then I watch the fields out of the window. We pass a few streams; I see some hares standing on the edges of partially flooded fields, a few churches, schools with kids in the playground at lunchtime. Then we go over a long bridge. I close my eyes again, relieved to think that there's now a river between me and my mum.

Later, in the afternoon, I'm back at the gallery, cleaning labels off around fifty empty wine bottles to be used as candleholders for the opening of the exhibition, which is the day after tomorrow. I'm standing over an industrial sink in a room that looks, from the cleaning supplies in the corner, like it might be a storeroom, taking a break to send Dr. Kerr an email to update him on the morning and apologize for leaving without finding him. There's a cloudy mirror in front of me with paint splattered on it here and there. I don't spot Gideon, standing in the doorway behind me, in the mirror. His voice is the first thing that tells me he is there.

"Hello," he says. I lock my phone and stuff it back in my pocket. "Sorry, I didn't mean to startle you." He is smiling.

"Do you need this room?" I start drying the bottles on the drying rack.

"No." He steps into the room fully and closes the door. For a moment, I worry that he knows that I stole the puppet and has come to talk to me about it. But he says, "I'm checking in with everyone. Seeing how you're all doing."

"Oh, I'm doing fine." I put the dishcloth down, and pick up one of the bottles that still has a label and drop it into the soap-water bath in the sink. "Thank you," I add. He's wearing similar clothes to the first time I saw him. A high-collared shirt, dark jacket and trousers. His shoes are shiny, brown and pointy. He seems, almost, like a different person, though. Everything about him feels more open and friendlier. "You're Lydia, yes? Keep going," he says, gesturing to the bottles. "Don't mind me."

"Yeah," I say. I don't correct my name to Lyd. It feels inappropriate for someone in my position to disagree with someone in his position. I turn back to the sink and dip my hands into the warm water, looking for the bottle I dropped in. When I find it, I take the sponge and start rubbing the part where the glue has stuck onto the glass, up down up down. Gideon watches. He sits on a stool in the corner.

"I wanted to apologize for how we met," he says, eventually.

"Oh." I don't understand what he means. I had been intending to apologize for the same thing, for not recognizing him on the first day. I put the now glue-less bottle on the drying rack, where there are several others lined up.

"I didn't recognize you. Your father was Taiyo Kobayashi." He hands me a bottle from the crate. I dip it into the water. "You should let them soak first, you know. Put a few in." He passes me some more bottles and I add them to the sink.

"You knew my dad?"

"No," Gideon says. "But I collect his work."

I'm taken aback. "You do?" I've never met anyone who knows Dad's paintings.

"I do." I detect a little smugness in his voice, like he expects me perhaps to thank him.

"You must have been influenced by him as an artist." Gideon says this as a statement, not a question. "It'd be interesting to see your work."

"I suppose I have been, yes," I say, feeling guilty again that I haven't made any work for such a long time.

"Were you close?" Gideon asks.

"Actually, he died before I was born."

"Ah, I see." For a moment, I think Gideon maybe looks disappointed; he pauses for a bit too long, and I wonder if he's expecting me to elaborate, to tell him something about my father or about his work. But then the expression on his face changes. "And how is everything going for you here?"

"Yeah, it's been hard work—"

"Heather running you ragged?" He smiles.

"Um," I say, recognizing that Heather must be the woman who put me in the puppet booth last time I was here.

"Don't mind her too much. She's all bark, no bite." Gideon stands up off his stool. "Well, it was good meeting you," he says, bringing our conversation to an abrupt end. He nods once, then leaves, closing the door behind him.

Once Gideon has gone, I sit down on the floor. I unlock my phone. I have two missed calls from Crimson Orchard, and one voicemail that I don't listen to. I save my email to Dr. Kerr, which is still open, as a draft, and then I google Gideon.

I know just a little bit about him. That he is well-respected but fairly new to directing. That he is known first and foremost as a collector of art and artifacts from around the world—work he calls "world art" in the same vein as "world music." I find a recent profile of him in *Vogue* that says that he doesn't like the term "art collector." He prefers "art advocate," a phrase I've never heard before, and that I don't really understand. In the article, he's described as someone who gives opportunities to young artists, and is responsible for kick-starting the careers of many—there are a few names listed. Some I recognize: two are Turner Prize winners, one has a solo exhibition on at the moment at the Serpentine. I wonder if I should have shared more about myself, whether I should have lied and told him I have plenty of artwork that I'd love for him to see, and then just hurriedly make something, anything, if he wanted to come for a studio visit; whether I should have told him that I want to be a director one day too. Maybe I should have been honest and said that I'd been hoping to shadow someone during this internship and learn how running a gallery works; perhaps I should have just asked him outright if I could shadow him.

I get the bus back to the studios. When I unlock my phone, the profile of Gideon in *Vogue* is still open in my browser. In the photo accompanying the article, artwork from what looks like all over the world is spread across the floor, on the walls, even hanging from the ceiling. In the center of it all is Gideon, sitting on a wooden chair that looks like a throne.

Looking at him now, I wonder what pieces by my dad Gideon owns. I wonder if he bought them while my dad was alive, if they met, if Gideon helped my dad's career. Once I finally finish and send my email to Dr. Kerr, I look through my photos until I find some of the pieces I exhibited for my degree show just over a year ago. They're not great images, but I take screenshots of the best ones so they are at the top of my camera roll and easy to show Gideon if I get a chance to talk to him again.

I get off the bus early, near Trafalgar Square. An idea has formed in my mind. At university, I performed pieces where I'd sit on various materials that had long life spans, like plastic, trees, stone, and I gradually glued my skin to them, or else connected myself to the material with clay or plaster and painted the joins to look like the material—the bark of a tree, marble, cement. I

wanted it to look like I was a part of whatever material I was using and it was a part of me. I think that those works came from
a kind of naive and youthful desire to be seen for what I was.
For my body to be seen for what it is: this un-decaying, eternal
thing—familiarly human, but also not. Audiences watched me
go through the process of gluing and I think probably felt left
out of the meaning of the piece, because I couldn't in any world
reveal that I was a vampire in an artist's bio or wall label. For one,
no one would believe me; there'd simply be concern about my
mental health. Most people assumed, in the absence of expla-
nation, that the piece must be about race, since I was different-
looking. Now, though, the urge I feel is to return to painting,
to work in a small and contained space like a piece of canvas, a
board of wood or a sheet of expensive paper, or perhaps even
silk like what my dad worked on, and to see if I can find the
shape of myself in whatever I create, to try to identify what I am
somehow, separate from my mum's definitions of me and her
superstitions, and in the preferred medium of my human father.
I'm not sure what form the painting will take, or what form I'll
take in it, but I walk across the street, through the traffic and
crowds, in the direction of Cass Art to buy materials.

5

It's the day before the opening at the Otter, so I'm needed at the gallery again. I've woken up early. The factory is completely silent. I stay on the floor of my studio for a bit and put on *Chef's Table* on my laptop. It's the episode about a Korean Buddhist nun. I close my eyes and listen to her talking about temple food; there's something nice about listening to someone speak in a language I don't understand. I listen for any words I can make out the meaning of but there are none. Occasionally, the presenter talks about mushrooms; occasionally, there is the sound of vegetables being chopped, water boiling, oil sizzling, bowls hitting a wooden tabletop. Sometimes, I've wondered if a simple life like this one might be the life I'd choose to live if I were human.

I open my eyes and unlock my phone. I have a message on Instagram from Ye-Ye, an old school friend. "Hey Lidl," it begins, a nickname she used to have for me. I remember the feeling of living in that name; it fit me snugly—it felt more like my name than Lydia did because, I suppose, I felt like I belonged in my friendship with Ye-Ye, who was the only other Asian in our school and who therefore understood some of the reasons I felt and was made to feel different. We used to spend every single lunch break in our form room. Together, we'd ignore the kids who said that our food was weird—that my flask must contain dog meat soup, and that Ye-Ye's lunch was gross when, really, it was a balanced meal with pieces of tofu, bok choy, rice, and water chestnut. When it was just us, I'd lay my body back over Ye-Ye's torso with my head resting just below her collarbone, on top of a couple of tables pushed together. She'd squirm away from my cold skin, whenever my hands or neck came into contact with her. Nonetheless, I'd feel comfortable because Ye-Ye's body felt familiar to me. It was the same size as mine, growing at the same rate, limbs still childish and thin, breasts not yet developed. But, now, I've been left behind, my body frozen in time. The more time passes, the less connected to her I can be.

Ye-Ye lives in London, but I haven't told her I'm here. "How are you? I miss you! I want to hear about your life. Are you doing OK? Lmk if you're ever in London," the message reads. I don't reply, and I don't think I will, even though I have an urge to, even though I want to talk to her about the internship, about my art, or lack of it, about my mum, and about Ben, about how it felt to drink from him—albeit via a towel, albeit such a tiny amount— about how it felt joyful and life-affirming, an expression of love rather than the opposite; but it's as if my reality is separate from everyone else's. It doesn't overlap. It can never overlap.

My mum coached me on how to lose friends when I was a teenager. She taught me how to drift out of other people's lives so that they, eventually, stopped contacting me and forgot I existed. She taught me how to appear boring to friends depending on what they were interested in, or how to act clingier than I really was so that the other person would be the one who would try to get rid of me. I didn't really have to apply many of Mum's lessons, though, because I never really had many friends to lose in the first place. Only, really, Ye-Ye. Friends I made during art college knew me so little, since I never spent time with them outside lectures, that I was already, from the beginning, forgettable, and I doubt any of them actually ever even called me a friend, just an acquaintance, or a peer, most likely.

"You are a different species. You think they won't notice you not aging? When they are thirty and you are still just how you look now? When they are forty, fifty? Any friendships are a lie from the start," my mum told me when coaching me on how to lose Ye-Ye, and I was protesting. "And, anyway, Lyds, everything in everyone's life is temporary. It's just that you will feel those things are more temporary than others because your life is so long. So, it's not something to cry about."

Nonetheless, purposely drifting away from Ye-Ye, who I had shared so much with, growing up, made me feel like I was being cruel to her. She wasn't the kind of person who would cut a friend out of their life simply because that friend wasn't responding or had been quiet for a while, which my mum said a surprising number of people do. Ye-Ye cared about me. Every day, at first, when I stopped contacting her, she would message to see if I was okay; then she checked every week, then every couple of months. This message I've received today is the first in a couple of years. When I told my mum in the past that Ye-Ye still got in touch with me, my mum said, "Just imagine she is dead. That those texts are your imagination." I close Instagram and lock my phone. What my mum taught me about friendship is one of few things that I know to be completely true. People—

aging and mortal—are like flowers, seasonal, wilting and finite; while I'm like a tree.

Heather lets me in when I arrive at the gallery. She takes me upstairs to a room near the offices, where there are a few broken mannequins lying on the floor, a couple of sofas, a coffee machine on a counter with a stack of coffee pods, and a selection of cereal bars and biscuits on an ornate silver platter. "Okay, so don't touch those, or the fridge or coffee"—I notice a large fridge in the corner that is quietly buzzing—"But you are welcome to help yourself to tap water, okay? You'll have to find yourself a cup." Heather instructs me on what needs to be done this morning; I am to attach velvet pads to a collection of wooden coat hangers that are on the floor between the two sofas in the room.

Gideon doesn't seem to be anywhere around. In fact, it seems like it is only Heather, me, and another intern here today—a young woman, probably a recent art college graduate like me—sitting in the puppet theater, nervously looking out. I thought about smiling at her as I walked past but I was with Heather and, in that moment, Heather was looking at me and telling me what time I should arrive for the opening the next day. Something told me that I shouldn't look weak in front of Heather, and so I shouldn't acknowledge the existence of the girl in the puppet theater and therefore associate myself with what was essentially an earlier model of intern.

"The guests tomorrow are extremely important," Heather says now. "Do you understand?"

"Yeah," I say.

Heather shakes her head and leaves.

I sit on one of the sofas that I've pulled up to the wall so it's close to a socket where I can charge my phone. I put a box for hangers with newly added pads on the floor to my left, so that they can be carried downstairs to the cloakroom in one go. Some of them have tangled themselves together. I start working through them.

I'm sorting through hangers for a pretty long time. The other intern must have left, as the gallery is completely silent, and maybe Heather has gone too. I start wondering whether there'll be anyone here to tell me what to do when I finish my job for the day. However, when I'm halfway through my work, I hear a very quiet creaking noise near the fridge. It's the floorboards; they all seem to be loose up here. I look up and, in the shadowy doorway, I see a man watching me. I blink.

If I were entirely human, I don't think I'd be able to see the man, who I immediately recognize as Gideon, in detail. But, being what I am, I can see everything about him. I almost say hello, but something about the situation unnerves me, so I stay silent and just watch him from the corner of my eye. Gideon is standing in the doorway, in shadow. He has a blank expression on his face. He doesn't necessarily look creepy, but he doesn't really look normal either. His face looks hard and closed, unlike the last time I saw him; there's a single frown line between his eyebrows; his jaw looks clenched; his small, round eyes barely blink as they look at me. I keep going with my work, pretending I haven't seen him. I slip four of the velvet pads over the hooks of hangers, all the while listening for movement, and preparing for him to make his presence known to me.

Maybe five minutes pass like this. Each time I finish a hanger, I turn my body slightly to put it in the box and, as I do, I catch a glimpse of Gideon, just in the corner of my eye and just momentarily, before I turn back to the next hanger. I consider standing up and walking over to the fridge, opening the door and maybe acting like there's some food in there that is mine. But, Heather told me explicitly to not touch it, and I worry about doing something wrong. Perhaps Gideon is just there to keep an eye on not me but the fridge, the coffee, and the silver platter of cereal bars and biscuits while they are in my presence. Perhaps I am the threat and those three things are particularly important and need to be protected from me and the other interns. Or, perhaps, this is another test, and Gideon is preparing to fill out a checklist with my name at the top, and put a tick next to "resisted the Three Temptations." The tasks I've been made to do as part of this internship have been so mundane or absurd that I wouldn't be surprised. Gideon stays incredibly still, so still that I start to wonder if I'm mistaking a shadow for his continued presence.

I pick up a new bare hanger, and a pad. This one is a bit trickier than the others, since a hole hasn't been punched through the pad for it to slip over the hook, so I have to make a hole myself, by pushing the fabric hard into the end of the hook. As I do this, I hear a voice, a woman's, shout to someone, "Can you go get Gideon!" from downstairs, and then the floorboards up here creak. I look up, and Gideon is gone from where he was standing. The whole floor comes alive with his footsteps; even the floorboards underneath my own feet seem to move, as though Gideon's body is substantially heavier than it looks—as though his influence and power over this institution have a weight too.

The rest of the morning goes by in silence. Although, I feel different from how I normally would, working alone. I feel exposed and anxious. In the past when men have watched me, usually in public places, I've wanted to kind of fold my body away. In those moments, I've felt more human than I ever usually do, more woman than I usually do, more defined by my shape than what's inside me. Now, though, I don't really know how to comprehend what has just happened. It's unclear to me whether Gideon did anything wrong exactly. Had I made him aware that I could see him, and told him he was making me uncomfortable, perhaps he would have apologized and left. He wasn't necessarily watching me for any sinister reason; perhaps, in normal jobs, employers watch their employees all the time. Although, I suppose I'm technically not an employee here. I finish the hangers, and pick up the box to take them downstairs. The box isn't heavy, but it is large. It covers my face when I lift it, so I can't really see where I'm going. I put the box down on the floor and slide it across instead. Just by the door, there is a bookcase. The books on it are tattered, like they've been read a lot. I stop to look at them.

Some are books I haven't seen before that fit with the theme of the exhibition downstairs that is opening tomorrow. There are several books on Walter Potter—one is called *Sweet Death: A Feast With Kittens*; another, *The Victorian Visionary: Inventor of Kitsch*. There are some on carnivals, fairgrounds, prison murals, prison art, and a hefty book with a title in gold, *Portraits of Icons: From Alexamenos Graffito to Peter Blake's Sgt. Pepper*. There are also books I have seen before, books I used to, until very recently when I lost my suitcase, own. One is a book on the abstract expressionist Bernice Bing; colors from her piece *Burney Falls* cascade down the spine—deep red, tinged with orange, outlined in black against white, brown and peach like skin. There's a book on the performance artist Senga Nengudi too, and another on the painter Amrita Sher-Gil. I take this last one off the shelf, and it falls open to a middle page, which has a picture of her painting *Three Girls* on it. I stand there for a moment, looking at the three girls' faces: calm, patiently waiting. They are huddled close together, as though perhaps they are sisters, but I don't think they could be; they look too different.

I had a postcard of this painting taped to my wall while I was growing up. It was blank on the other side, but I kept it because I had found it tucked in the wooden frame of one of Dad's paintings. It went missing at some point, but while I had it, I looked at it often and felt that I knew—like really knew, as though I had a sense about these things—that the girls depicted were vampires, and that they were still out there in the world, looking exactly the same as when Sher-Gil painted them in 1935, and that I would one day meet them. The painting, I decided when I was a child, depicted the three girls quietly waiting for three brothers to come out of a house so that they could eat them.

I obsessed over this painting even though I had no proof that there were any other vampires in existence. My mum always told me there were none, and when I said that couldn't be true, she just told me to stop pestering. Once, though, I think I came close to meeting one. At the birthday party of a boy I went to primary school with, I'd felt a strange attraction to another girl. While the other children ate cake, me and this girl played in the ball pit. As I'd got closer to her, I'd smelled a familiar scent coming off her body, and I'd felt no heat emanating from her skin. Before I could ask her anything, though, my mum snatched me out of the ball pit and took me home, and I never went to a birthday party again. So, this painting was all I had, and it wasn't even definitively a depiction of vampires. I decided, though, that because I'd found a picture of this painting among my dad's things, it meant that, had he met me, he would have loved me and accepted me for what I was; he might have painted me too, in the same colors Sher-Gil used.

I find myself slipping this book into my bag, next to the puppet, which is still sitting in there. I don't know what it is that makes me do it; maybe there is a part of me that feels slighted by Gideon, that feels angry about how far from my expectations this internship has been so far, about my weak and vulnerable position in this institution and under Gideon's gaze. I take the Bernice Bing book too, and also a yellowy lime-green book called *Adventures of a Russian Puppet Theatre*, thinking that it might enlighten me about puppet making, and perhaps I'll learn something about my stolen puppet's identity. All these books are slim; the bookcase barely looks different after I've taken them. I zip my bag up, put it on my back, and then continue sliding the box of hangers across the floor, feeling—as I did after stealing the puppet—a little bewildered and anxious but also quite happy.

When I get to the door, I hear stomping coming from downstairs. The sound rises, until all the floorboards start creaking again, and then Heather arrives in front of me, standing on the top step. "What the hell are you doing? It sounds like you're dragging a body across the floor," she says. Standing behind her, partway down the staircase, sipping a coffee from a takeaway cup, with his glasses hanging on his shirt, which is now unbuttoned at the top, is Gideon.

I look down at the box, and then at Gideon. His eyes are very dark. They watch me. I start to wonder whether I'm the only person who can see him, whether, somehow, he is able to lurk in the shadows without any of the other humans noticing. Heather hasn't acknowledged his presence at all. She just glares at me.

"Hello? Are you in there?"

"Oh," I say, and I turn my attention to her. "Sorry."

"You're not *kicking* the box of hangers, are you?" Heather asks. "This *can't* break," she says, her voice and eyebrows raised. "This box *cannot* break. Do you understand? We *cannot* have any more catastrophes!"

"I . . ." I'm finding it hard to understand how a cardboard box breaking could be considered a catastrophe, and also how my sliding the box across the floor could even break it in the first place.

"No." Heather shakes her head. "Don't talk back to me. Up."

"What?"

"Pick. It. Up."

"Oh," I say, and I diligently follow her orders, holding the box up in front of my face again, and shuffle out of the room behind her, following the sound of her huffing.

When I get to the step Gideon is standing on, I feel my breath leave me, like I've exhaled but can't inhale, as though Gideon has stolen all the oxygen from the space. Heather's footsteps continue down the entire staircase, until she stops at the bottom, waiting for me, but I have to slow down; the box barely fits past Gideon, who is standing to one side. As I squeeze past, I feel his shirt against my right hand—his skin is very warm underneath it—and then a button, and then, alarmingly, hair where his shirt is undone, and breath from his nostrils, very hot and warming my thumb. Once the box is through, I see his face. He smiles at me; it's a kind smile, as if he is saying, "Oops, sorry," but he doesn't talk. He says nothing, makes no sound, as if he doesn't want to give away his presence. I smile back, and move down to the next step but, as I do, I feel something brush my back and then my bum. At first, I can't tell if it's the hem or cuff of a shirt, and therefore an accident, or a hand; but then it's obvious—I feel his fingers grope around one buttock like he is trying to prise a piece of me off my body. At the same time, he brings his mouth close to my neck and his breath heats my skin. He releases after a moment and, bewildered, I stagger down the stairs. When I get to the bottom and put the box down on the floor, I look up to see if Gideon's still there, but he isn't; he's gone.

I feel kind of sick walking back to the studio from the gallery. I feel unsteady on my feet, like my body isn't mine, and it isn't a good fit for me—like on my next step, I might just accidentally step out of it, leaving it behind me: an empty woman, just standing still on the pavement, passersby looking at her and wondering what she is doing. By the time I get back, I can't tell what I'm feeling, whether it's hunger again, or whether it's anger, on behalf of or perhaps actually felt by my human side. In the darkness of my studio, I unlock my phone and see I have an email from Gideon. It's from his personal Gmail account rather than his work account. I open it, feeling kind of panicky, worrying, for some reason, that the email might tell me that I have done something wrong, but it just says:

Hello Lydia,
It was very nice talking to you yesterday and seeing you again today. It'd be great to talk properly and hear more

about your work. I'm sure we'll have plenty of time to do so
over the next few weeks.
Best wishes,
Gideon

I read the email a few times. I don't know what to think. It's
confusing. It's like it's saying "what happened today didn't happen" or "what happened today is normal." I lock my phone. Then
I lie down, feeling miserable, the room spinning, my insides
churning. I fall asleep, there on the floor, and my demon side
dreams about something that makes me feel a bit better. By the
time I wake up, though, I don't remember what the dream was
about.

Later, I tear out the page with the print of *Three Girls* from the
Amrita Sher-Gil book. I do it neatly, folding the page first and
then licking the fold. Then, I push my table against the wall and
stand up all the books from the museum, along with the three
from the Waterloo Bridge bookshop, against it. I take the puppet
out of my bag too and sit her next to the books with her back
against the wall. I face her, so it's kind of like looking into a mirror. I'd forgotten that I'd named her after myself. "Hello, Lydia,"
I say, out loud. "Lyd . . . deeee. . . . aaaah." I put the picture of
Three Girls next to her, so the girls' gazes are directed toward her.
Then I say, imagining one of the girls speaking, "What happened
today, hmm?"

"Ugh, I don't know," I make the puppet say.

I pull up one of the chairs and prop my legs up on the table,
with a small canvas on my lap. It's unprimed, so, when I paint,

I'm painting on peach-colored cotton. In light blue, I start to create an impression of the puppet's shape. I think the blue will look nice behind the dark brown of her wooden face. I don't do much now. I don't really feel confident painting. The last time I did any was during my A-levels.

The puppet looks slightly off already, in her blue painted form. She looks hollow, which I know she is in reality too; but, somehow, in real life, she gives the impression of containing things. After just around five minutes, I stop and prop up my painting against the wall next to my books.

I open the Bernice Bing book. I look at her piece, *Velasquez Family*. I don't know how she does it. I want to paint like this. There are people in this strange painting, one with a green face and alarmingly red eyes; another like an animal with multiple limbs drawn in black paint and a blank, white face; and a woman by a window, her face red, her hair black, skin yellow. I bring my face close to the painting, so close that my nose is touching the page and it's all I can see. Then I prop the book up, stand, and walk backward until I'm as far from the page as I can be, and it's just a small colorful square. The colors and rough textures knit together. From here, things the painting shares with works by older painters become clear; the light and shapes of *The Calling of St Matthew* by Caravaggio—it's all there, like that painting is perhaps an ancestor of this Bing one. It's beautiful. Next to it, my own tentative beginnings look completely disconnected from all of art history—bulbous blue marks that make the puppet look nothing like the human she is modeled after but more like a monster. My painting is ugly in a way that doesn't look intentional, in a way that looks unplanned and chaotic. It's a mess, formed of fragments that don't seem to connect.

I'll stop here.

In moments like these, I wish I could just call my dad and get some advice from him, to have him teach me. My mum only talked about my dad's art once. I'd caught her on a good day, and I'd asked her how he had been received when he'd been alive. "Everyone said his work was beautiful, very refined, but it was ugly," she had said. I'd only seen a few works, but I knew he used very bold black lines that were so thickly applied they looked like they'd been painted with tar. Dad's paintings were ugly in a purposeful kind of way; they were brutal and violent.

"Did Dad ever tell you what his paintings were about?" I asked my mum.

"He told me it was about war. How war is stupid. You know, his parents were in Tokyo during the fire bombings."

"Really?"

"Yes. But everyone here thought his art was so refined, so Japanese." My mum was making her bed. She'd shaken the duvet into its cover and was now buttoning it up. "But it was very human. That's what I liked about your dad too. He was very human."

I went and stood next to her to help her with the buttons. She was at one end and I was at the other, and with every button, we moved a step closer to each other. "Mum, you never told me how he died," I tentatively said. "What happened—" I started, but my mum ignored me, as if I'd not spoken at all, and angrily pointed to my corner of the duvet. "Lydia! You have to put the duvet into the corner of the cover properly!" she huffed at me and pushed me out of the way, and started unbuttoning my buttons. Then with a raised voice, she said, "I have to do everything for you, don't I? Go downstairs, Lydia. I'll finish this."

I sit down on the floor turned away from my painting and unlock my phone. I have two missed calls from Crimson Orchard and an email from Dr. Kerr. I let my body flop down onto the concrete and read with my phone above my head. "Dear Lydia," the email begins. "Thank you for your update. Your mum hasn't had any more violent episodes, so we are very glad about that. However, we would like to discuss some other matters with you. Would you be available for a phone call?"

I lock my phone, put it on the floor, and push it so it slides and hits the wall. I don't want to think about my mum; sometimes I feel like it's her fault that I don't have my dad—it's like I blame her for not turning him, not keeping him preserved, forever, like she did me. I put on my rucksack to go out. I plan to buy something to sleep on and maybe find some wood to try painting on. I open the box of dried pig blood before I go, lick my finger and dip it in the powder. Ben's towel is still in here, on the floor next to the box. I focus my attention on the pink-yellow stains on it while I put my finger in my mouth and suck the powder off. It's still disgusting. I wash my mouth out with water after, and then I walk around with my mouth wide open for a bit, trying to air it.

It's just there, right in the middle of the foreshore, quite pretty—greens and blues, a white wing, a rusty breast: a duck, dead on the riverbank. It's so pristine, and elegant in the way it is lying, that it looks like a sculpture, not an animal. Never until now have I seriously considered letting the blood of a bird and, with it, that bird's spirit, its experience of drifting along, pushed by the currents of rivers, its experience of flight, of breaking through clouds—the blood of something so beautiful—circulate around my body. I struggle down the stone steps leading onto the sand. It's a very windy day. My hair is huge. It's been pushed forward while I've been walking, and it stays in that position even when I am shielded from the wind by the stone embankment. My shoes sink a little as I step onto the sand.

I notice, while I'm down on the foreshore, that there's a man watching me from above. He's standing on the embankment, leaning against the metal railing. I look up at him. He's quite attractive. He's young, in a wool coat, nice boots, nice skin. He is large, maybe just over six foot, broad shoulders.

Down here, the water comes up onto the sand in waves, pushed by the wind. There's a lot of crap strewn about. Bits of plastic, bits of metal, bits of wood, dog poo, a sanitary pad, a nappy, a few bones. I inhale; the air smells of doughnuts—there's a stall nearby. Then I exhale, pushing as much of my breath out as possible, emptying myself of what makes me human. I crouch down over the duck. I take my hand out of my pocket, and place it on the duck's body. Still warm. *My god.* A string of dribble just slips out of my mouth. I can't help it.

The man is still watching. Now, he has a concerned expression on his face. My mind is mostly blank. I blink up at him, and then down at the duck. Then, I pull on the duck's neck, and lift it off the sand.

The duck is much longer than I had anticipated. I hold it just under its head. Its legs swing. It's heavy. I walk back up the steps with it. The wind pushes my hair back off my face now. I walk up onto the embankment. I feel good. My lips are wet. I'm starving.

"Hey," I say to the man as I walk past him.

I'm certain that as I do—as I swing the duck by my side, as

my hair is whipped up and back again by the wind, as I step on the ground beside him—he nearly falls over.

I turn heads all the way back to the studio. Back inside, I wash the duck's body under the tap. It's small, only maybe half a meal, but then I bite into its neck and drink. Still fresh. Still warm. I look up into the mirror as I do. *God, I'm so beautiful,* I think to myself.

Later, I go upstairs, following the sounds of people laughing, having slept after draining the whole duck. I've changed my clothes. I'm wearing one of the shirts I got the other day and the shorts for boys, plus boots. I feel quite good in my body. The memory of Gideon is far back in my mind; my skin feels not like my skin—the skin that has the memory of being groped on the stairs, and of being watched from the shadows—but like something from which feathers could easily sprout, that repels water and that is a beautiful pure white, just the kind of white my mum always wanted for her own skin when she painted her face with makeup. I find myself at The Place, the communal area of the studios, where there's a long dining table with benches on either side, strings of fairy lights above, and lots of plants and flowers everywhere, and beanbags and other soft things on the floor.

There are seven people here. I can hear each of their heartbeats. "Hey!" someone says. It's the woman from my floor who I often see outside her studio, her hair, out of the scarf it's usually tied in, a huge dark halo around her head. As she speaks, everyone else in the room turns to look at me, and they all wave or smile in my direction. A couple of people say hey too, and I nod back. Only Ben, who is chopping vegetables in the kitchen area, doesn't greet me. He looks up and sees me, then looks down again and pretends he didn't. Next to him, an East Asian woman with her hair twisted into a knot on top of her head is leaning into his body slightly and putting things on the cutting board for him to slice; she smiles at me.

"Are you joining us?" the woman from my floor asks, gesturing with her hand for me to sit down. "There's plenty of food, right, Shakti?"

"Yeah, absolutely!" says a woman who is standing in front of the stove, cooking what looks like gnocchi, as well as whole eggplants. I notice, next to her, Ben's ears redden.

"I'd love to," I say. I feel bizarrely confident. I take a deep breath in; through the smell of spices and garlic and onion, I smell a few different scents of shampoo, perfume, sweat, breath, tiny hints of other things. My bones feel light, like they have filled with air, and I could just take off from the ground were I to lift my arms. Then I exhale, and I feel grounded again, and I smile and cross the room.

"So, finally we meet!" the woman from my floor says. She takes my hand. It's a surprisingly intimate gesture and makes me feel immediately welcome; she doesn't mention my cold skin. "I'm Maria."

"Lydia," I say. My voice sounds different. It projects more easily. "I go by Lyd."

Maria leads me to the dining table, where there are mismatched plates laid out.

"You're A14, right?" Maria asks. At the same time, a man leans across the table with his hand outstretched, "Hey, I'm James," he says. I shake his hand. "Whoa, cold," he says.

"Yeah, I'm A14."

"So, what kind of work?" James asks. "Wait, wait, let me guess."

"James, don't do that," Maria says. "It's completely reductive to guess someone's practice from how they look, and it feels horrible."

"Oh, come on, you're just upset because I'm always right."

"You weren't right with me," a voice says. The East Asian woman, who had been leaning into Ben's body in the kitchen area, has sat down at the table with a bowl of olives. "Let's see, what did you say again? Delicate, precise pencil drawings, right? And small? You were just racially stereotyping me." Ben comes and sits down too, but he doesn't look at me. He fixes his attention on James instead, who has put his hands up and is saying, "Give it time, give it time, you just haven't found yourself yet." Maria slaps James around the head.

"Have you guys met yet?" Maria asks, gesturing back and forth among Ben, the East Asian woman, and me.

"Oh, yeah, I know Ben," I say.

"I, er," Ben looks at Maria when he says this. "I showed Lydia around on her first day." For a moment, it looks like everyone is waiting for Ben to introduce me to the East Asian woman, and it looks like she is expecting him to too. But Ben just looks down at the table. "I'm Anju," the woman eventually says, after shooting Ben a confused look, and she holds her hand out for me to shake.

Anju, a voice seems to say in my head. *It's Anju*. And I feel a weird sense of superiority. I've tasted a sample of her fiancé's life, I've felt hints of his grief, hints of his passion, experienced in a brief flash his birth. I smile.

"Lyd," I say, and I glance momentarily over at Ben, who

doesn't look up. "So . . . what kind of work do you make?" I ask, to ease the tension.

"I paint," Anju says.

"Oh, right. What kind?"

Ben gets up from his seat, mutters, "Back in a minute" under his breath, and walks out of the room. His footsteps fade away.

"Kind of large-scale portraits."

"Anj's work's amazing," Shakti says, arriving at the table. She lays down a plate of eggplant, now split down the middle and stuffed with something that is a deep red color. "Are you eating, Lydia?" Shakti asks. "There's plenty."

"Oh, actually I ate already," I say.

"Ooh, what did you have?" James asks.

"Duck," I say, instinctively, "but it looks amazing. What is that, harissa?" Shakti nods and smiles at me. As I say this, I become aware of the duck blood circulating around my system; I can almost feel it, moving down my arms, reaching my fingertips, looping back up, searching for wings on my back.

"Wine?" James asks and tilts a bottle in the direction of a glass in front of me.

"No thanks." I shake my head.

"Hey." An older guy sits down at the table, with another woman who says hello quietly, in a thick German accent. "I'm Mark, this is Utte," the man says, and I reach over the table to shake their hands.

"You know, Anju's work's being featured in *frieze* next month. They're doing a massive profile of her," Maria says.

"Wow, that's crazy," I say.

"Yes, congratulations, Anju," Mark says; he has a German accent too. He has placed a mushroom and rice dish on the table.

"Grown ourselves, thank you to Ben. Ben? He is here?"

"Ooh, looks delish," Shakti says.

"Ben popped out," Anju says.

"Anj, you should tell Lydia—oh, sorry, Lyd?" I nod. "—about your TV people series," Maria says to Anju.

"Oh. Yeah," Anju says, hesitantly. She's blushing. Shakti is putting a whole eggplant on her plate. "So, I basically paint big portraits of people watching TV." She looks down at her eggplant and pulls the stalk off. I get the feeling that she doesn't want to talk about her work, which I understand. My heart sinks when people ask me what I do; although, that's usually because I rarely know what I'm doing, or I don't feel confident about what I'm doing, one or the other. People who aren't artists often ask me and then say something like, "I don't really get contemporary art. You know, it's a bit . . ." and they pull a face. "I always think that I could probably do it, like putting a splodge of paint here, another one there, you know? But I don't know. Sorry." "Oh, it's okay! It's not for everyone," I usually reply, which is essentially the opposite of what I believe.

"That sounds interesting," I say.

"She's not explaining it properly!" Maria says. "They're not just portraits of people watching TV. Basically, they're life-size, and she paints from photographs—"

"Sometimes from life too," Anju adds. I watch her cut into the eggplant with a knife and some of the filling spreads out on her plate, making a red circle. I realize that, despite having recently drained the duck, I'm already feeling hungry. I look at the red on her plate, reflecting the lights, and feel the beginnings of something like envy. Anju puts a piece of eggplant in her mouth and chews. Anju is a Japanese name; she has probably experienced eating Japanese food; she has probably been to Japan; she probably has family there; she probably still has a dad; she has Ben; she is a successful artist; she seems confident; she is petite and pretty and everyone seems to like her.

"You should explain it," Maria says.

"Okay, so . . ." Anju puts her knife and fork down. "I work from photos and life, and paint people watching TV, but I don't paint the TV or the room, or the sofa or chair they're sitting on . . . so, the person is basically just floating in white space. It's about kind of suspending a moment in life that is a pretty big part of life for a lot of people, and examining it, feeling like we could turn it over, walk around it . . ."

"Oh, cool," I say. "So, how come just TV?"

"I did a series on trains too, which was just these people suspended in space, without the context—the seats, carriage, phones in their hands, food they're eating—around them. I was aiming for this completely clean space, like, kind of like a lab space? And the people in it are the subject, without any kinds of objects or things around them that would normally contextualize them and color our perception of them, you know?"

"I'd love to see," I say.

"You'd be welcome to, whenever. My studio's in my house in Camberwell."

"Her paintings are amazing in real life," Shakti says. Anju looks up at her, and smiles.

"What kind of work do you make?" I ask Shakti. As soon as I do, I notice that the table has gone quiet. Everyone looks particularly preoccupied by their food, all of a sudden.

"I don't really make any work now. I haven't for a few months," Shakti says after a moment. She looks down at her plate. "It's quite a long story, but I'm trying to work out what I want to do with my life."

"I think you should make work again," Maria says, before turning to me and adding, "Shakti is a stone carver. She makes pairs of marble sculptures, sort of similar to Barbara Hepworth but not. She's, like, continuing in the path of Hepworth."

"We all mourn Shakti's stones," Mark contributes from the end of the table.

"Hmm," Shakti says.

"How come you stopped?" I ask, though I feel as I say the words that this might be too personal a question. Before she can answer, though, there's a shuffling noise, and Ben comes back into the room. "Heeeey!" he says, looking refreshed.

"Oh, hey, Ben—look, myself und Utte," Mark's accent makes everything he says sound musical, "we successfully grew this mushroom!" He holds up the plate.

"Wow, guys, it looks, I mean—yeah!" Ben says. "Smells amazing." He sits down and puts an eggplant on his plate. Everyone else tucks in too. James pours the wine. I notice that Shakti looks relieved that the conversation has moved on.

"Bon appétit, everyone," she says.

"Guten Appetit," Mark adds. Shakti raises her glass. I catch her eye and smile, and she smiles back.

"Oh, we should toast, celebrate Anju's success," James says. "Lyd, I'll just put a bit in your glass and I'll have it later." He tips some in. "To Anju!" We start clinking our glasses together. This isn't an experience I've ever had. Usually, I avoid group dinners completely; I just don't turn up when invited, or turn down invitations entirely. At art school, I barely even socialized. After every lecture and group critique I went home to be with my mum, and had my meals with her in the kitchen. I've never shared a bottle of wine, or had conversations with strangers over food. It feels kind of holy. The bread being broken next to the plate of eggplant. Wine being poured. The warm light. I feel like I belong here, with the spirit of a bird rather than a pig inside me.

"Oh, oh, wait, stop!" Mark says, in a booming voice. "In Germany, we look each other in the eye, always, when cheersing," he says. "It is polite." And he demonstrates with me. I look into his eyes. Deep brown. Everyone resumes, making a point to look each other in the eye, and laughing. Ben looks sheepishly over the table at me. He smiles. Our glasses come together. *Sorry,* I mouth at him. He shakes his head. His eyes are a very pale blue. He has bags underneath them. He looks tired.

After dinner, a little beige lump in the corner of the room moves, and everyone starts calling, "Piggyyyy," "Piiiig," "Pigleeet." The lump is a pug, and he comes over to the table, snuffling. "Pass the pig?" Maria says, next to me.

"Pass the pig!!" Ben roars. He raises his glass into the air. His face is bright red. He scoops the dog up into his arms. In between folds of skin, two big, black eyes peer out. They look my way.

"Oh, Shakti, I have to go. I have to catch the last train, which is . . ." Utte looks at her watch. "It is seventeen minuten."

"Oh nooo, Utteee," James says, pouring himself another glass of wine. "You won't stay for just one round of pass the pig?"

"Sorry, I cannot," Utte says. She talks very quietly. "It was very nice to meet you," she says to me, and she shakes my hand. "I will maybe see you—" She gestures toward the ceiling, toward where her studio is. Over dinner she'd told me about her work: portraits of people drawn as what they hope to be in the future—pilots, nurses, authors, living in a house in the countryside, fathers, mothers—that fit into lockets for those people to wear around their necks. She had said she could draw me, and I'd told her I'd think about what I want to be in the future. She squeezes my hand. "Good luck with opening night," she says. Then she moves on to saying goodbye to the next person. "Thank you, Shakti," she says. Shakti is wrapping some leftovers in foil for Utte to take home. The pug is back on the floor and is cautiously making its way over to me. "Danke schoen, danke schoen," Utte says, while leaving.

"Pass the pig?" Maria asks me.

"Umm," I say.

"This is Pig." Maria picks up the pug. "He's my dog and, usually, when there's a nice group of us up here, we play a game called pass the pig—"

She's interrupted by Ben shouting "Pass the pig!" again. Anju looks over her shoulder at him from the sink, where she is washing her glass. I notice that she looks a little put out. She whispers something to Shakti, who is standing next to her, and Shakti nods.

"Okay, *yes*, Ben," Maria says. "So, anyway, we each go around the kitchen to find something to put on our faces, like butter, cream cheese, things like that, and I'll check them all to make sure they are safe for him to eat." As she says this, she nuzzles her face into the folds on Pig's neck. "Little cutie," she adds. "And then we each lie down, pass Pig along, and whoever's face Pig kisses for the longest is the winner. He's a fickle little thing, so his favorite food changes a lot." She shrugs her shoulders. "So, yeah . . . I know it's a bit lame, and maybe a bit disgusting," she laughs. "But it's become a tradition."

"Oh, okay," I say. "What does the winner get?"

"Renown! Honor!" Ben booms.

It's kind of like being a kid again, playing hide-and-seek, or egg hunting at Easter. I watch James cover Ben's face in peanut butter, and spread butter on his own face. Anju decorates her face with cream cheese. She has two circles of it on her cheeks and a straight line down her nose. I put a small amount of olive oil on my face, and rub it in like moisturizer.

"Ben, Ben, Ben." Ben comes up to me while I'm rubbing my cheeks. Anju, by this point, is already on the other side of the room, with Shakti and Mark. I'm by the fridge. Ben grabs my shoulders.

"Ben, what are you doing?" I say.

"Ben, Ben . . ." He moves his face closer to mine.

"Ben, you're Ben; I'm Lyd," I say.

"Ben, I think . . . I think you are just . . ." He shakes his head. "You are so beautiful, Ben, and just so . . ." and then he walks off. He goes up to Anju and tries to kiss her, but she pushes him away, grumpily. "Ben, you're covered in peanut butter," she says.

On the floor, I make sure I'm not lying next to Ben. I lie next to Shakti at the end of the row instead. Gradually, the dog makes its way across to me, via everyone's faces. Ben is in the lead when Pig gets to me. The dog's strange, alien face looks down into mine.

"Hello," I say to him. I can feel his warmth. He breathes loudly, like it's a struggle. His paws on my chest are hot. Then, he lowers his head and starts sniffing me. He sniffs for a long time. And, then, he starts licking, but not the parts of my face

I've rubbed olive oil into. He starts licking my chin and neck, and my hair; he licks my lips, my nostrils—everywhere, I realize, where blood from the duck must have splashed me; I didn't wash myself well before coming here. I'd just wiped my mouth with tissue. Pig's tongue is excessively warm. His small body is excessively close. So close, I can hear the blood circulating around his body; I can feel his pulse through the pads of his paws. Just as I begin to daydream about biting him, about feeling the life leaving his body and entering mine and then experiencing all of his memories—living in a litter, becoming Maria's pet and being taken on walks, experiencing licking all of our faces tonight—about gnawing on his bones, getting every little drop of blood off them, Maria's alarm goes off, and everyone cheers. In that same moment, Pig staggers backward away from my face, whimpering.

"It's okay." Maria rushes over to Pig and scoops him up. "Everyone's just celebrating," she says to him. But, I wonder if, rather than it being the noise of cheering that has spooked him, it is that I have spooked him. Perhaps he sensed me transition from being human to something more animal; perhaps he caught a glimpse of my teeth.

I make excuses to leave. I have to get back to Kennington, I say, and I don't want to be walking too late. James offers to walk me, but I decline. "I don't bite!" he says. "No, it's okay, I have to be up early tomorrow too," I say.

I say goodbye to everyone, apart from Ben, who is asleep on a beanbag. Anju gives me her number, and tells me to get in touch. And then I slip out.

I'm just a few steps down the corridor when Shakti comes out of The Place and calls after me to wait. "Hey!" she says. "One moment." She half-jogs-half-walks down the hall. "Hey," she says again.

"Oh, hey. Thanks for tonight," I say.

"It's okay," she says. "About the Otter, though . . ." While everyone had eaten, I had told them all about my first few days, about being put in the puppet theater, and then about the bottles I had to clean and hangers I had to add pads to. I didn't tell them about the puppet I'd stolen, or the books, or about Heather, or Gideon watching from the shadows, and standing on the steps—me shuffling past him, his hand brushing my body, then grabbing at it. Shakti, it turned out, had interned at the Otter a couple of months ago, and had left early. Just as with her artwork, the conversation moved on before I could ask why. "Just be careful," she says now.

"What do you mean?" I ask.

"Just, watch out for Gideon. He's a bit of a creep." I feel my breath catch in my throat, and my skin prickle, as though Gideon is somehow here, in the shadows in this corridor.

"Okay," I say, nodding. "Thank you." I step into a strip of warm light that's coming from the open door of The Place. Then Shakti leans in and gives me a hug. Her body is warm. "Wow, you're cold," she says.

Downstairs, I open the front door and gate and close them both loudly, in case anyone is listening for the sound of my leaving the building. Then, I go to my studio, opening and closing the door as quietly as possible.

The room has quite a strange smell to it, a kind of musty, muddy smell, iron and the beginnings of rot. The drained duck carcass is in the sink where I left it. Its neck is bent over the edge of the sink and its head hangs out. Its eyes are open, and they seem to watch me. The mirror on the wall has some small splatters of blood on it.

I go over to the duck and bite into its neck again, trying to extract whatever might remain of its blood, but it's dry, apart from something pinkish that isn't blood. I lick around the wound on its neck, getting a little blood from its feathers, and then scratch the dried droplets off the mirror and lick my fingers, sucking on my nails. There's nothing else left.

I sit down on a chair by the table. My painting is still there, propped up against the wall. Now—after having talked about art all evening, and after hearing about Anju's works, and her upcoming profile in *frieze*—I think it looks amateur. It lacks confidence and a sense of being planned in any way at all. The puppet has slid down from the sitting position I left her in and is lying on the table, looking up at the ceiling. I take her and put her on my hand. "Hey, Lydia," I say. Then I make her little hands take the book on puppetry I stole from the gallery. She pulls it out and the other books fall over. She drags it to me, and opens it to the first page.

6

I have been painting all night. I went over the blue with a dark brown. In the middle, there's now a dark knot of black and bright, electric-blue paint. Among the black I added little stars in white: tiny dots made with the point of my smallest brush. And, then, in the center of the knot, I added two, deep red eyes, a nose, long and crooked, and a tiny crack of a mouth: the puppet's face. Amid the mess of paint that is her clothes, a muddy mix of color, I have painted two hands—two beautiful hands, as beautiful as I could make them: human hands, golden and elegant, modeled after my own. In one, I have let her hold a paintbrush.

I read the entire puppet book at the beginning of last night, with the puppet on my hand, turning the pages for me, her head bobbing forward with each turn and smacking against the words and pictures. I read lines like this, written by the author Nina Efimova: "Puppets repel . . . They captivate not by beauty but by hidden charm," and this: "Puppets were created primevally by the god of puppets without feet. They spring on stage from below, and dive down to make their exit." Each time I read a line like the latter, I looked down at Lydia the puppet, and said to her something like, "See, this is why you look the way you do." At around two in the morning, I came to the end of the book, where there were pictures of the author's own puppets. And, remarkably, there was my puppet—the third picture in, looking happy and comfortable on the hand of her maker, her hooked nose like a ginger root, her mad mess of black hair, her dark head and ragged clothes. I looked at the caption. It read: "Nina Efimova and the puppet of Baba Yaga."

"Shit," I said. "Is that you?" I made the puppet nod her head and stroke the page. "And is that your mum?" She nodded again. "Baba Yaga," I read out loud. I googled the name.

Baba Yaga, it turns out, is a figure in Slavic folklore. She is a witch, earth goddess, ogre, manifestation of stormy weather, cannibal; she is the Russian figure of death. Her name, Baba, is derived from the word for grandmother; and Yaga, from darker words: horror, shudder, anger, witch, fury, disease, abuse, belittle, exploit, doubt, worry, pain. "Wow, Baba Yaga," I said, and she looked back at me, her face innocent and blank.

I read that Baba Yaga appears in over a thousand folktales. Each time, she is visited by various people, young men, usually, travelers lost in the forest, where she lives in a hut that is perched on top of a pair of chicken legs. She either helps them along their way, or she eats them, her mouth sometimes gaping open from earth to sky. In her hut, I read, she can often be found lying across her stove, stretched from one corner of the hut to the other; to travel, she flies through the air in a mortar, using a pestle as an oar, and a broom to brush away the trail of her flight behind her. "Wow, that's pretty weird, Yaga," I said. Often, she is written about in crude and hateful language, I found, that describes her body—particularly her genitals and breasts—as disgusting and rotting. I held her closer to me as I read one more thing about her: "Baba Yaga's teeth are extremely sharp and are said to be made from iron or stone. Sometimes, she drinks milk," it read, "and other times, blood."

"Oh my god," I said, and I leaned back in my chair. I looked at Yaga on my hand and she nodded, as if to say, *Yep—we're the same thing*.

And, so, after that, I painted. I painted for, I think, eight hours, until I could hear people arriving at the factory for the day. I painted with Yaga on my hand instead of in front of me. Inside her body, my hand became her soul, her person, her character. It felt good. Us fused together, us being a part of each other. What was left of the duck blood, I imagined coursing around my own body and feeding into hers.

Now, I prop the painting up. It is a dark, mad mess of an image; I can't quite comprehend it. In the middle, Baba Yaga's face seems to disappear into a deep hole. A strong wind seems to whip up her hair and surround her head with it. Next to Sher-Gil's *Three Girls* and Bing's *Velasquez Family*, she doesn't look too out of place anymore. She looks balanced, if chaotic; human, monster, puppet.

I lie down on the studio floor. Yesterday, I bought a yoga mat to sleep on. It's a bit too small. I've rolled up my clock sweatshirt so that it's like a little pillow. I lie under the jacket I bought. There, with Yaga still on my hand, I google Nina Efimova, her maker, and the word "puppet" and search under the News tab. I add "the OTA" to my search terms too, but nothing comes back. My Yaga hasn't been reported missing yet, and maybe she won't be. She was, after all, just left, inanimate and comatose, in the corner of the puppet theater, tucked away, covered in dust, out of sight. Either way, if anyone does notice her absence, so many interns have been put in the puppet booth that there'd be too many suspects to narrow the search down, and nothing—apart from my painting, which I'll have to not show anyone and keep secret—connecting her to me.

Later, I'm walking along the river in the direction of the Otter, and I get a text from Ben: "Hey, I'm really sorry about last night if I did or said anything. Can we talk later? Im in all day. Can come down to you. Ima go out now but back later tonight. Lmk."

He sends another text straightaway. "I mean sorry if I said anything bad or embarrassing." And then another: "Like, I realize that I probably almost def did." And another: "Hope you're good today." And then one more: "It was good seeing you yesterday." The texts come up as successive banners at the top of my screen. I turn my music off and reply.

"Hey Ben, dw. I had a nice time and you didn't really embarrass yourself. I'm at the opening at the Otter tonight but maybe tomorrow?" Then I send, "Anju seemed really nice btw."

"Didn't really embarrass myself? That means I did a bit right?"

"Lol. Maybe a bit," I reply.

A cyclist swerves around me. He tuts. I'm on the embankment again, walking against the wind. It's raining. I try to hold my phone at an angle so the screen doesn't get wet. "Text later," I type. "Am out. Rain." Then I lock my phone.

While I walk, I keep an eye on the riverbank, to see if I can spot anything I might be able to eat. I'm getting toward the end of the duck blood now. It's the worst part of a meal, the part right before the end, during which you can sense the animal's last few moments of life: for a pig, this usually means waiting in a queue of other pigs, listening to the sound of those farther up the line being shot with a bolt gun, realizing that it shares the same fate, and squealing and trying, in vain, to escape; for the duck, however, this means its last few flights over the Thames, feeling not free, but a kind of sense of impending nothingness and trying to escape it. As I walk, I feel not only my own hunger, but the hunger of the duck that spent its last few days with nothing to eat.

I watch the sand. If I do spot anything, I wonder what I'll do. I'm on my way to the gallery opening, so I wouldn't be able to take it with me. Perhaps I'll just eat whatever it is wherever I find it. It's London; I don't think anyone would do anything about it. Once, from a bus, I saw a guy who looked completely normal and who was wearing a suit jump on a sick-looking pigeon, and it popped, and everyone who saw screamed, but the guy just carried on walking and no one did anything. The river seems quite high today, so the patches of sand I see are narrow, with barely anything on them—just bits of rubbish and a couple of bones that look like they've already been sucked dry by the current. A couple of taxi boats bob past, going up and down on the waves. There's a guy sitting on a patch of grass with a can propped up between his feet. He looks at me and smiles, then puts two fingers in front of his mouth and waggles his tongue between them. "Dyke," he says under his breath as I pass.

I get my phone out again when I'm walking down Cheyne Walk, a road that's famous for being where J.M.W. Turner died; I don't know if it was in a house or just out on the street or what. I know the road, though, for being where the poet and artist Dante Gabriel Rossetti took all his exotic animals on walks. Apparently, there's a law about walking wombats in London because of it; I think it's that you're not allowed to walk wombats after a particular time, or maybe that you're only allowed to walk them on this road. The wombat that walked down here was named after William Morris, whose designs are on everything at the moment: lunch boxes, bamboo reusable coffee cups, notebooks. I like thinking about the ghosts of Rossetti's menagerie all together now, all walking along the river here, their spirits peering into the Pizza Express just around the corner, wandering the studios in the Royal College of Art, which is nearby. I keep walking, and imagine a reality in which I consume all of Rossetti's animals—in which I bite into the William Morris wombat, and experience that wombat's life in Rossetti's studio, seeing Rossetti's portrait of Proserpine being gradually painted, the pomegranate she is eating being formed in oils on canvas. I wonder if the wombat went with Rossetti to the grave of his wife and muse, Elizabeth Siddal, whose body Rossetti exhumed so that he could retrieve and publish the poems he had buried with her. I wonder what the wombat thought, while watching from the shadows.

I write a text to Anju: "Hey, it was really nice meeting you last night. I was wondering if you might fancy meeting up? I did my first painting in forever basically after seeing you guys, and I don't really know any painters, so . . ." I delete the last part, so it just reads, "Hey, it was really nice meeting you last night. I was wondering if you might fancy meeting up?" and send that. I have a missed call from Crimson Orchard, but I ignore it for now, and tap on recent calls so it'll stop showing up as a banner. I turn the corner, the river behind me. The Otter is all dressed up for its opening tonight. Its front is covered in strings of lights. Its door is open. A carnivalesque glow comes from inside.

Everything looks different, but it's hard to pinpoint how, exactly. The Walter Potters stand out more, and so do the murals, the alligators eating acrobats eating alligators. As I walk down the corridor, my attention is drawn to the art. Small paintings of birds in flight that I hadn't noticed before are spotlit on the walls. I wonder whether what's changed is just that all the clutter—the sort of backstage stuff that's always been here—has been cleared away, or if it's the light; or, maybe it's neither of those things and, rather, it's that I've created a painting that I'm happy with and so, art is just central to my life again.

I stop at the Walter Potter cat tea party. There's a warm glow to it now, like the feast is candlelit. The cats all look jovial and at peace with themselves, passing around cakes and chatting with each other. One is standing and pouring tea at the end. It looks like a pleasant occasion. I look at it with a new feeling of nostalgia. I imagine stuffed eggplants on the cats' plates, in pools of harissa-infused oil. I imagine the conversation—the cats are talking about their art; one of them will be profiled in a magazine soon.

I go through the red curtain. On the other side, the tables are laid out with beautiful crockery and cutlery and crystal glasses, all empty and expectant, and a man is lighting candles that poke out of the tops of empty wine bottles, the ones I cleaned the other day. In the corner of the room, some musicians tune their instruments. The lights are being tested, as they were on my first day here. "Lower! Lower! The lights have to be low! Low lighting, low lighting! We need to see the candles, otherwise what's the fucking point?" Heather's voice cuts through all the other noise. Then she talks directly to me.

"What are you wearing? You need to get upstairs and change,

now. You'll be allocated a room up there," she says. She talks fast. I look around her. Gideon is nowhere to be seen. It's just Heather.

"Okay," I say. I smile at her and she frowns at me.

On my way up, I pass the section of the stairs where Gideon grabbed me. I don't really feel temperature changes much, but, as I go past the spot where Gideon had stood, I feel a chill in my body, as if I'm walking through a ghost of that moment.

The lights are dim in the room with the sofas. The silver platter of cereal bars and biscuits is still here. The fridge-freezer buzzes in the corner. The coffee machine has a full stack of pods next to it. In between these things are people, all about my age, all awkwardly standing around, some getting dressed in black T-shirts provided by the gallery and with the logo, an *O*, *T*, and *A* neatly arranged on top of each other and forming a new letter resembling a symbol for a cult, on the breast. Women are turned toward the walls, trying to undress without being seen, putting the T-shirts on and then taking tops off underneath. I recognize one of them as the person who was in the puppet theater soon after I was, who I'd decided against saying hello to. I recognize some of the others too; some had passed me when I'd been in the puppet theater myself, and hadn't said hello to me. No one really interacts. The room is awkwardly silent. It's as though we have all been conditioned to not talk to each other.

I go up to the girl I'd seen sitting in the puppet theater. "Hi," I say to her. The T-shirts, it turns out, are all the same size. I put one on and then take my shirt off underneath it. It's like a dress on me.

"Hello," she says, in a French accent. She talks very quietly. She seems surprised I've said anything to her. I realize that others have turned to look at us too.

"I'm—" I begin, with my hand half raised toward hers. But then Heather arrives in the room.

"Check on this list which room you have been allocated to," she says, without saying hello. "Go to your room. No water or food. That's important. One gallery assistant per small room. Larger rooms, there'll be up to five of you. Get into your places before Gideon arrives. Spread. Out. Do *not* stand next to each other."

"Excuse me." One of the guys near the sofas, who is especially tall but who has a soft-looking, childish face, has his hand up. "When do we finish today?"

"You stay until the end," Heather says.

I'm sent to a small room on my own. The room is dark, with paintings of exhibits from P. T. Barnum's freak show spotlit on the walls, interspersed with self-portraits of the artist. Colorful painted reproductions of posters read "World's Oldest Woman!" and "Bearded Lady!" One poster advertises the autopsy of an enslaved Black woman Barnum owned; another, the autopsy of an elephant. There are posters for the world's smallest man, the Feejee mermaid, and Jo-Jo the Dog-Faced Boy. I feel weird. I don't know what it is. Kind of queasy. Unrooted from the ground where I stand, like I could easily fall over. I've felt like this since coming into this room. I received a reply from Anju, and she said yes to meeting up, and sounded enthusiastic; she's invited me to an open studio at her house next week too, and sent me her address and the details. Maria has also sent a voice message on WhatsApp, which I listened to upstairs in the room with the sofas, and she's said she'll knock for me tomorrow. I feel a kind of giddiness about having new friends, and gratitude for being able to live successfully as a human, at the idea of being able to repeat last night, of meeting people over food, but also something else. I don't really feel like I belong here, or maybe I feel like I belong here, in this specific room, too much.

The guests start arriving at eight-thirty. I hear voices in other rooms, and they sound too happy and relaxed to be those of anyone who works here. I hear people exclaiming Gideon's name too, like they're excited to be seeing him, so I know he is here also. I hadn't, before this point, realized that I was so worried about seeing him again. But, now, I feel my body transform, in the way it does when my human self feels exposed or unsafe. All my hairs stand up, and I stay very still; it's as though every part of my body becomes a sensor for movement and for danger, and I listen to each part, waiting. I lean my back against the wall, so one route to my body is blocked.

But, Gideon doesn't come into my room. First, it's just people who look important; they are dressed well, and have very well-planned, coordinated outfits. Some are eccentric-looking old people. These appear one by one or in couples or small groups at the door to my freak-show room and pass by me as they look at the work. They put on the headphones that are hanging from hooks on the walls, and look at the paintings. Some of them don't seem to see me. I stand very still, and stare into space. Others, though, watch me for a moment while they are wearing the headphones. My lips go very dry. I stand still for a long time.

Gradually, the number of people increases, and they start gathering in the middle, facing away from the walls and pictures, and chatting loudly, drinking from flutes. A different type of person starts to arrive too: famous people. A comedian drifts eerily around the edges of the room on his own, peering over the tops of his glasses at the paintings; he is one of the few who pays attention to the work. There are also well-known artists who are so high up in the art world that it seems they don't feel they have to look at other people's art anymore. One of these is a textile designer who arrives wearing a suit made entirely from fine, gold thread. Once he arrives, the light shining on the artwork seems to dim, and the other guests' attention moves onto him. I observe from the shadows, feeling more and more like part of the architecture, blending into the wall, feeling the bricks behind me with my hands and imagining my skin merging with them.

A man with a camera comes in to photograph the room, everyone looking candid, the comedian hovering in front of the painting of the Bearded Lady, the textile designer in the middle of the room looking like a figure in a jewelry box, the other people standing in groups here and there, chatting; they all pretend they can't see the photographer. Only I say hello to him, and he's also the only one who acknowledges me, but not with words. The man moves me twice so he can get photographs of the room from different angles without me in it. He does so by placing a hand on the back of my T-shirt, and then grabbing the fabric like it is the scruff of my neck, and gently leading me to the part of the room where he wants me to go.

There is, soon, the sound of bottles opening, and chairs being pulled out from under the dining tables, and my room empties. I can smell foods I've never eaten but have learned to identify from the scents my body allows me to pick up on: mushrooms, pastry, some sort of rich cheese, salmon, preserved lemons. There are whoops and cheers from the main room, and the sound of carnivalesque music played by a string quartet, then laughter when someone gives a speech. I lean against the wall again. I'm exhausted. Not really from doing anything, though. Being in the presence of people looking at art is exhausting, I think. Seeing how little it means to them is exhausting.

"Hello," says a woman's voice. I open my eyes. I hadn't actually realized that I'd closed them. I look around the space, but I don't see anyone. Then, through the door by the painting of the elephant autopsy—that now has a red sticker underneath it marking it as sold—steps a woman I recognize. She is an actress who is known for playing women who are mad. She walks up to me quite quickly, taking long strides. She's wearing a black dress, with a maroon velvet, kimono-style jacket over the top, with flowers embroidered on it. "Hello," she says again. She's right in front of me now.

"Hi," I say. I like her look. Her big round eyes, her big round white face that, surrounded by her nest of bushy black hair, looks like the moon, taking us right back around again to the theme of madness. "Well, look at you!" she says.

I can smell alcohol on her breath.

"Just *look* at you," she says again, and she looks me up and down. "You are just adorable. And look at that—" She holds up a bunch of her hair, revealing a very slender, very white neck underneath. My mouth fills with saliva. The woman's neck is pristine, with no marks, no creases, nothing. "We're matching!" she says.

"Oh," I say, and I copy her and hold up a bunch of my hair too. The actress moves toward me and claps her hair against mine. "Cheers!" she says. And, briefly, faintly, as she leans in close, I hear her pulse in my ears.

"Cheers," I say awkwardly.

"Goodness," she says, as our hands come briefly together; I feel her warmth and, I suppose, she feels my coldness. And then she looks up into my face, into my eyes, her own eyes wide, with an expression that looks something like recognition. She pauses for a moment and then she says, "Are you an artist?"

And then I hear another voice, behind the actress. "No." It's Heather. "She's an intern."

"Oh," the actress says after a moment; she looks me up and down again, and then she says, "Will you swap with me?"

"What?" I ask.

"Can I be you for a bit?"

I don't say anything back; I don't know what she means.

"Please?" she says.

"Come on," Heather says. She's waving at me to step away from where I'm standing. "Let her do your job for a bit."

"What?" I say.

"Come on," Heather hisses.

"Oh, okay," I say. I step away from the wall, and the actress slips into my place. She hunches her back slightly and leans against the bricks and looks blankly ahead, with a sullen expression on her face. It's all very strange. Heather steps to the side. "Go on," she whispers to me. "Go on, what's your name again?"

"Oh, um . . ." I say. The textile designer from earlier comes into the room. I notice that he has the puppets of the queen and the devil on his hands. He's talking to someone next to him about how the working classes can be helped into engaging with the arts. "Now, it's all about getting them involved in all the stages, I'm telling you. Getting them to volunteer their time to making an exhibition possible, having them invest their time in making partitions, painting the walls, choosing the works. It's about a community-led approach—this is what I have been saying for a decade now."

I turn back to Heather. "It's Yaga," I say, absentmindedly.

"Yaga?" Heather says. "Okay, whatever. Out, Yaga, now. Be back in five minutes."

I leave the room. I leave Heather standing in the corner, watching the actress who pretends to watch over the art, and the textile designer talking about community engagement with someone who looks like they might be a curator or something similar, with puppets on his hands, and think that these people—all of them—are just completely repugnant.

I step outside into the night air. I take a deep breath. Someone offers me a cigarette—some older guy, who leans in close to me with a lighter, lights the end, and winks as he steps away. He keeps talking with a group of people who all sound like they are high up in one of the big, well-known commercial galleries around Green Park. Occasionally, he glances over his shoulder to look at me and, as he does so, a woman in the group watches him. I wonder if they're together. I stand apart from everyone else. I lean against a wall. I look up at the sky. There are a couple of stars, very faintly visible. I don't really get anything from smoking. I kind of just let the cigarette burn out, occasionally holding it to my lips and then tapping ash off the end, watching the orange light die and then come back to life and then ultimately die again when I step on the butt.

All the euphoria I had felt when I had arrived, left over from last night at The Place—the feeling that I was being a successful adult and, on top of that, a successful human full stop—has faded away. I look up at the Otter, its lights fuzzy behind a haze of smoke, its insides churning with people who come out talking and laughing loudly, while feeling the duck's last flight coming to an end inside me, its body landing on the foreshore, tired and dreary.

It's been over a year since I graduated. In a couple more years, I won't be able to get internships anymore. I'll be too long out of art college, and other recent graduates will get the places instead of me. What's after internships? It's stupid that I haven't planned this far. I had thought that I would do my internship here at the Otter, and be working closely with the curators and director, and then perhaps be hired off the back of the good work I was doing. I had imagined going in wearing nice clothes each day and blending in with everyone in the office and eventually getting my own desk. In Margate, while I ate dinner with my mum, I had read up on Fluxus and folk art, telling Mum to be quiet whenever she tried to talk to me, preparing to have my knowledge tested here, and to have to come up with ideas. I suppose all my life, I've been tested through exams, at school, and I didn't really think properly about the fact that, of course, this would be very different.

I don't know how other people do it. How do I go from where I am here, being moved out of photographs, and replaced with actresses like I don't exist, to where I want to be? In just a couple of months, I'll run out of money to rent my studio. How is it that vampires in all the books and films and TV programs always seem to be so successful and wealthy, and able to rent or even buy studios, flats, houses, sometimes whole estates? How is it that they all manage to feed themselves and stay so strong too—how can they all, including the good ones with souls, get hold of blood so easily, while I've struggled to even get some fresh pig blood—while I struggle, now, to even replace what I got from a meager duck?

I feel like giving up, lying down on this wall and closing my eyes and just doing nothing—not bothering to try to fit into the human world, not bothering to make friends and art, not bothering to source blood and feed myself. Maybe little plants and mushrooms would grow out of me, while I stayed just a little bit alive, and I'd become a beautiful thing, unconscious but living and giving life, in lots of different ways. I could be a bird or squirrel perch, or a piece of art that people could come and look at. I could just stay here, like a rock, in rain and sunshine, not changing, just being, until someone came along and brought me food and fed me.

"Lyd?" I turn around; Ben emerges from the haze of smoke in front of the Otter.

"Ben? What are you doing here?"

He's wearing a shirt and a nice smart jacket with gray trousers and white sneakers. "I've been at the RCA painting show down the road. One of my friends has a couple of pieces in it. Thought I'd come see you here too, but it's invite-only," he says. He seems a little tipsy.

"Well, I could have told you that. Why didn't you text?"

"I did," he says.

I take my phone out of my pocket, and there are four texts from Ben: "Hey Im at the rca, want to come met me here when youre done?" "Actually, I might pop down to the offer to see the walter potters" "*otter" "and see you."

"So, are you done for the day?" Ben asks.

I look back at the building. "Technically, no. But . . . I guess I could be."

"The RCA sculpture show's on too if you want to come with

me to that? Thinking of heading over there next." Ben looks at his phone for the time. "It's ten-thirty. Surely you're finished?"

"How about your friend?" I ask.

"Who?"

"The one with the paintings in the painting show. Are they around?" I don't feel like meeting anyone new. Ben scratches his neck. He leaves a couple of pink marks on it. I watch them fade.

"Yeah, but he's sticking around by his work. You know, mingling and stuff."

I nod. I look back at the building. "This goes on until early morning. I'm meant to stay until the end. But, yeah. I don't know. I feel like I'm kind of done with this place," I say, thinking it for the first time as I speak.

Ben takes a vape out. It's one of the square ones that look especially far removed from cigarettes. A puff of sweet, white smoke falls over my head.

"Like done done?"

"Maybe." I tell him about the actress who took my spot in the freak-show room. "I guess I feel small and undervalued," I say. "It's hard to see what's beautiful anymore," I add, surprised at how honest I'm being.

"Yeah," Ben says, like he agrees. Then he says, "What do you mean?"

"Oh, I don't know, the art," I say. "At art college I could just focus on the art. It was a really pure experience. All I did was learn. But, there're all these people in the real world and they just poison everything."

"Hmm," he says. "Wow, yeah." He pauses for a moment. He makes another cloud of sweet smoke. Then he says, "So you want to go?"

"Okay," I say. "Got to get my stuff, though. Stay here."

I go back in. Everyone is out of the main hall now. They're all in the exhibition rooms and corridors, all facing away from the walls; the floor is sticky, the lights seem much dimmer. I go through the freak-show room, almost all the paintings with little red stickers under them now, and there's another person standing in my spot—the French girl I almost introduced myself to upstairs—looking glum in the corner, standing in a shadow with a well-known collector bent over and chatting to her. I go upstairs. The sofa room is empty. I find my shirt and get changed.

On my way back out, I pass an office with a single armchair in it. In the dark is Gideon, sitting in the chair with his feet up on a small table covered in books. Around him on the floor are bubble-wrapped objects and crates that I suppose contain artwork. In his hand is a piece of paper that he is looking at intently. He is wearing a pair of clear-rimmed glasses on the tip of his nose. It's the first time I've seen him since the incident on the stairs. I feel a strange sensation in my body, like a part of me—perhaps the human—wants to get away and so is pulling me toward the exit, while the other part wants to stay and observe him, so roots my feet to the ground.

Something about Gideon's posture makes him look weak, like he wouldn't be able to stand if he tried, his body sinking into the chair and taking the form of its negative space. I think as I did when I first met him, but now even more so: how Gideon looks like what a normal person might expect a vampire to look like. It's not his clothes this time, but his sallow, corpse-like face, his empty-looking eyes, his crumpled form, his breathing or, rather, lack of breath; he is completely still, the dust in the room moving more than him. My mum once told me that she believed the origin of our kind was a disease, born of power and colonialism. That one man once took so much that was not his—took others' homes, possessions, livestock, farms, bodies—he stopped being able to nourish his own body with food, the thing it genuinely deserved, and was cursed to only be able to take what was not his for the rest of his life, which was extended to eternity. The disease spread until the colonizers and the colonized both were afflicted. I don't believe the story. To believe it, I would have to believe in God, and I can't be sure I do. Nonetheless, I learned something from it. If it didn't teach me about my own origins, it taught me a lot about what my mother thought of herself, where a lot of her self-hatred came from.

Nonetheless, taking is most likely not good for the soul, and this is what I am looking at now, I think. A man who has taken a lot. I can sense this about Gideon, just as I can sense when a person is following me, just as I can sense people's heartbeats when I've eaten. I know he owns many things. Art from ship-wrecks, art from ancient cities, a cast of a person's skull adorned with diamonds by Damien Hirst, art from around the world, art by young, old, and dead artists, and, of course, artwork by my father. Gideon is rich, and his life is enriched by culture. But his body, still and propped up by an old ornate armchair, looks un-dernourished.

I feel weird about the fact that Gideon owns some of my dad's work. Gideon's money indirectly feeds my mum's life now, and that means it is also responsible, in part, for my own life being the way it is. It makes me think of a baby in a womb with no say in what the mother consumes, lifeblood just enter-ing its body via an umbilical cord. This thought alone makes me feel sick.

"What are you doing, Lydia?" Gideon says, suddenly, without looking up from the paper he is holding. "Lost?" I don't know what to say, or what to do, so I just leave as quickly and quietly as I can, before Gideon looks up, hoping that he'll think he just imagined me.

On my way down the stairs, I bump into Heather; she has a glass of something in her hand, and her eyelids are heavy-looking, and her cheeks are flushed red.

"Hello, Yana," she says.

"Hey," I say. "I'm just going back to the room now."

"You've been moved. Gideon," she says. She's slurring slightly. "He wants you in the offices on Monday, upstairs. Ten a.m."

"Oh, right," I say. I look back up the stairs behind me toward the office Gideon is still probably sitting in, and then back at Heather. "Why?"

"He must like the look of you," Heather says.

"Will it just be me and him?" I ask. But Heather doesn't answer. She staggers down the stairs, her heel catching on the edge of a step so she has to grab hold of the banister to not fall over. I go down the stairs quickly to help her. I take her arm and guide her slowly. At the bottom, she looks at me and I half expect her to say thanks, but she doesn't. She just gives me a strange, pleading, desperate look, like she's the victim of a kidnapping, and I'm a salesman who has just knocked on the door and spotted her behind her kidnapper—and then she wanders off, into the crowd that has become, by this point, one big, pulsating animal, moving through rooms as a single organism. The Otter creaks all over the place, like it's in pain. The feasting cats and studious rabbits are all trembling in their seats again.

———

"Do you know why Shakti left the Otter?" I ask Ben. We're walking down to the RCA sculpture show together. Ben's been talking about how Anju wants him to quit vaping because there aren't many studies on its long-term effects on health. But, I've been struggling to listen properly; I can't shake the thought that maybe Gideon was watching me tonight, and I didn't notice. I remember reading a novel a while ago by Zora Neale Hurston that begins with the pharaoh taking on the form of a shadow and entering undetected into a room where a woman is giving birth, and watching her. I wonder whether Gideon can do something like that. I wonder if he wasn't hiding in the darkness in the freak-show room but just was the darkness. It is a stupid thought; I know, deep inside, that he is just a man—I felt his warmth as I'd squeezed past him the other day.

"Hmm, I don't know. I don't think she told me. She stopped making work at the same time, though," Ben says. "Shame. Her art was really good. Why do you ask?"

"Just wondering. Do you think something happened at the gallery?"

"You mean like someone telling her her work wasn't good? Nah, Shakti has thick skin."

"I mean, maybe, something else. Like, perhaps someone hurt her?"

"Hmm," Ben says. "I don't know. I don't want to assume. She didn't tell me anything like that."

Inside the RCA, groups of people are wandering from studio to studio, looking at the work. There's an air of reverence around each piece of art that doesn't exist at the Otter. I remember it from being a student. During my degree show, everyone watched my performance with respect. I feel a kind of sad nostalgia, wandering around this place, watching people tentatively peering into a huge structure of mirrors, others nervously touching two stone sculptures, one wrapped in velvet, at the artist's beckoning.

"So . . . sorry if I . . ." Ben says, as we step into a dimly lit room in which there is a large porous stone on the floor.

"Last night?" I ask.

"Yeah, sorry if I was a dick." He bends down to get a closer look at the artwork.

"Oh, it's okay," I say. "It was a bit weird, though. It felt like you didn't want to introduce me to Anju?"

I crouch down next to Ben. It turns out that the stone on the floor is not a stone, but a cast of a beehive, and in each of the cells is a tiny apartment complete with a bed, sofa, wardrobe, and rugs. Some of the rooms have crumbling walls and their furniture is in disarray like there's been an air strike. I stare into a tiny kitchen, complete with utensils and crockery, and a partially sliced loaf of bread.

"Yeah, I guess part of me didn't want to introduce you. I don't know why," Ben says. "It was stupid."

"Huh?"

"I should've introduced you. Did I make you feel bad?" he asks, sheepishly.

"No," I say, though I don't know if he did or not. I find I don't want to hurt his feelings, even if he has hurt mine. "Not really."

"Okay."

We split up to look at the work in the next room. The pieces are small figures made from clay. Each has a part of their body missing—an arm, a leg, a breast—like they are ancient statues that have had their extremities knocked off. I watch Ben out of the corner of my eye as I move around the space. He stretches his neck forward to look at each piece, while hugging his body with his arms. He trips on one of his feet between two plinths, and I hear a small "oops" exit his mouth. I watch him cock his head and assess the body of the figure with a breast missing, his eyes avoiding the empty space as best as possible, and studying her feet instead. We meet again by the door and go out into the largest room together.

There's a large white sheet on the other side of the room, hanging up dramatically in a spotlight. I lead us toward it. A small group is huddled around the work as if something is about to happen. We stand side by side, joining the group, and wait. For some reason, things between us feel a little awkward; our arms nearly touch, but don't. It's as though the space between us has become solid and I can feel it, and I'm aware somehow that Ben can too.

"I wonder what's going to happen," I say, my attention fixed straight ahead.

"Hmm," Ben says. There's just a centimeter or so between our knuckles.

The sheet has a small square cut out of it, about two-thirds of the way up. After a short moment, there's movement behind the sheet. Then, through the hole, we see the back of a woman's head: a perfect square of straight black hair. The woman very slowly rises, as though she's climbing up a set of steps we can't see. She stops when the nape of her neck is central to the hole. There's a triangle of white paint on the woman's dark skin, pointing to the first bone of her spine, which pokes out slightly

I forget about where I am for a moment while I watch. Everyone seems to hold their breath, Ben beside me too. The woman's neck is beautiful, very slender, with perfectly clear skin. The end of her hair takes up the top eighth of the square hole, and acts as a kind of frame. Gradually, almost imperceptibly, the woman starts to turn her head to the right, like she's about to look through the hole back at us. Just as we begin to see the line of her jaw, though, the edge of her cheek, the corner of her lip, she turns back the other way, until we can only see her neck again. I feel like I have been standing completely still for all the time we have been watching, and that Ben has too, but, when I take a breath in, just as the square empties and the woman disappears, our knuckles knock together, and our forearms touch. "Wow, you're so warm," I say, without really thinking.

Ben doesn't say anything back, but I can see that his cheeks turn red. "So, what did you think of that?" he asks.

"I don't know," I say, blinking. I open my mouth and close it again. Sometimes a piece of art has an effect on me that I can't quite put into words or even comprehend properly. I feel like I became aware of very tiny things as we watched the woman: strands of her hair, the pores of her skin, the gradient in which her skin tone changed slightly, the shadow her vertebrae made. So much attention was placed on her neck, but I didn't want to bite it; I'd just wanted to keep watching it, endlessly, across time, across centuries, unchanging.

I pick up the artist's card, which just has a white sheet on the front, without a hole cut out of it, before we leave. I'm surprised when Ben goes back into the room where the little clay figures are to get that artist's card for himself. The terra-cotta-colored woman with the missing breast is on the front of that card. "They were nice," I say to him while we're leaving the building, just to make conversation. "Those little sculptures."

He nods. "Yeah," he says. He nods again and kind of purses

his lips, like he wants to say something. Then he says, "Yeah, I think my mum would like her work."

"Oh, right," I say. I'd forgotten about Ben's mum, how she's sick. I don't know what else to say, so I don't say anything.

We walk via the river. Ben said he'd walk me home. I told him he should just walk me to a bus stop, since otherwise he'll be going out of his way, but he kept insisting, so I've told him that I need to pop into the studio before going home. And, so, we're heading to Vauxhall. Ben's looking at a text on his phone. "It's Anj," he says. "Sorry, do you mind if I—" He holds his phone up.

"No, go ahead," I say, and, while we walk down Grosvenor Road, the river on one side, a group of guys across it yelling something, he silently types for a bit.

For some reason, it makes me feel jealous to hear Anju's name—or, not exactly jealous, but inadequate, like I'm somehow less because Anju exists and Ben is talking to her, even though I'm here next to him. I look up at his face while he's looking down at his phone. I look at all the freckles clustered around his nose, his bright pink, healthy-looking lips, the two veins under the skin on his forehead that are very faint but just visible, the part of his neck in the shadow of his shirt collar. I'm not sure what I feel when I look at him in this way. I'm not sure what it is that I'm looking at—what he means to me, what he is to me, what I want from him. I get the urge to reach out and touch his body. My own body feels almost empty; I feel a little unsteady on my feet as we walk. I suppose I'm pretty hungry. Ben locks his phone and looks up. I feel like I can see his fat and muscles and blood through his skin, all of it glowing like a beacon.

"Sorry, yeah. I forgot to tell her I'd be out tonight," he says now.

"Everything okay?" I ask. I look away from Ben's face to try to distract myself from it, and watch my feet, walking, instead. I put my hands in my pockets.

"I don't know. She's having trouble with her work and stuff. I guess she's finding some commercial success and, so, her audience is changing." Ben is looking straight ahead as he talks. "The people who are interested in her art now are all the people who want to buy it, all the rich people who want her paintings for above their sofas in their massive houses. Anyway, it's all kind of stupid because when you're not successful, it feels like art means more. Like, you're just in shows and stuff and it's all about the meaning of the work. But, then you get successful and you become basically like a dresser of sets, a producer of crap for rich people to hang on walls to look cultured." Ben sighs. "Kind of makes me feel grateful for my lack of success, in a way."

"I think art comes to mean something different to people when it becomes something they can possess," I say, thinking about the comedian, quietly gliding around the room at the Otter; there had been something unsettling about the way he looked at the paintings, and I think now that it was because he could easily just purchase them, and hang them in his own home, and make it so that he was the only person in the world who could look at those works ever again in his lifetime. I think about my dad's works that were bought by collectors and famous people; a few pieces, according to my mum, were bought up by a hugely successful actor who died, and whose art collection went to his daughter. It's strange knowing that the daughter of this actor has more of a claim to one of my only links to my Japanese and my human half than I do. And then there are the paintings by my dad that Gideon has; every day, Gideon can look at any of them and study the marks on the silk that each link to a specific time in my dad's life. He can follow a line in a piece and experience the moment my dad chose, however many years ago, to lift his paintbrush from the silk, or to make the line jaggedly turn. Each little mark a life decision, albeit small. Each little mark, owned by Gideon.

"Yeah." Ben looks glum. "I don't know. I suppose seeing how it is for Anj, it makes me think, like, maybe I don't want to be an artist, you know? If that's how it'll be."

We're quiet for a while. I find myself automatically checking the riverbank every time we walk past a sandy part, even though I definitely couldn't eat anything now, while walking with Ben, unless it were actually Ben that I ate. A fox crosses the road ahead of us, watching me as it does so. I have a very brief and sudden urge to chase after it—to essentially, I suppose, hunt it. I wonder what it would feel like; whether the fox is male or female; whether the fox is a mother; whether I'd experience giving birth.

"So what kind of art do you make?" I ask Ben. "I mean, if you want to share."

"Yeah no, it's fine—though, I'm not great at explaining it," he says.

We've reached Vauxhall Bridge, which is fairly busy, and Ben steps forward and looks both ways, checking for cars for both of us. I notice that his hand is up slightly, just next to me. "Okay," he says, and he kind of half takes my forearm in his hand. We cross the road and go onto the bridge.

"So, I've basically been making clocks for the last god knows how long," Ben says, flippantly.

"Clocks?" I say. I remember the clock hands in his studio.

"Yeah. Not like normal ones, though," he adds. We keep walking for a bit. A bus goes past.

"Are you going to elaborate or are you expecting me to ask questions?"

"Sorry, I'm not good at talking about it," Ben says. He squirms. "So, my mum was diagnosed a couple of years ago . . ."

I feel a bit bad for pushing him. "It's okay, you don't actually have to tell me. Sorry I pried."

"No, it's okay. I would like to tell you. It's just, I don't know . . ." he says.

We pass a drunk man, whose huge, wide, bloodshot eyes stare freely and with no qualms at my face. I move in a little closer to Ben, and follow the man's gaze with a frown, but the man doesn't look away; his eyes stay fixed on me, big and round, until I feel like if I keep looking, I might fall into them. Ben doesn't seem to notice.

"So, basically," Ben says. "Mum was getting all these times thrown at her by doctors. You probably know what it's like. Six months left, a year left, a week left, oh, no—four months left—and so on." I nod, though I feel bad that I lied to him the other day, that he thinks my mum is dead and so, thinks I can relate to what he is going through.

"So, I got kind of obsessed with timekeeping devices. But ones that aren't always completely accurate, or ones that are accurate but maybe change depending on where you are, you know? Sundials and things like that." We reach the end of the bridge. "And we had to move Mum out of her house, into a smaller one closer to the hospital, so I was sorting through her stuff and I started making clocks with things from her life, you know, casting shadows with them."

I feel a bit guilty. I'd assumed that his work would be much less personal and sensitive, that it'd be something mediocre and not to my taste. Before this point, he hadn't really come across as intelligent at all.

"Now, though, I'm making a flower clock." He nods to himself.

"A flower clock?"

"Yeah. Mum was . . . is a florist, so I'm using her books on flowers to try to re-create or, well, create Carl Linnaeus's flower clock. He was a guy from the eighteenth century. Basically, each flower in the clock opens at a different time of day."

"Its petals open?"

"Yeah, so flowers have circadian rhythms," Ben says. He's blushing. "I don't know. Sounds kind of stupid now I'm saying it. And it hasn't actually worked yet either. I thought, though, that with climate change and everything, the flowers will start opening at weird times, so it kind of goes beyond everything with, you know . . . my mum. It'll be, like, the more we damage the world, the more we damage the clock, and time, and, yeah, the future."

"That sounds beautiful, Ben," I say.

"Yeah, I don't know. I mean, what am I going to do with it? What's the point of it, really? Will it go in a gallery and then be, like, sold as prints of photographs of it or something? And then the time element of it will be gone."

"Hmm."

"Sorry," Ben says, and he shakes his head. "I guess I'm in a bit of a crap mood." He looks at me sideways, and nervously laughs to himself. "I mean, I don't know why I just told you all that."

I shake my head. "It's fine. So, what flower's time is it now?" I ask.

Ben looks at his phone. "Ugh, yeah, so that's the other thing. There actually doesn't seem to be a flower for each hour, which is kind of problematic. But the closest to now is the meadow goat's beard. It opens at three."

"Oh, cool," I say. "So right now doesn't exist in flower time?"

"Yeah, I guess it doesn't. I've never thought about it like that."

We get to the biscuit factory just after 2:00 a.m. It's silent, apart from the distant sound of a main road. By this point, I feel really tired; I suppose I don't usually do this much exercise when I'm this hungry. My breathing is faster than usual, and my legs feel wobbly. "Are you all right?" Ben asks me, as he unlocks the gate.

"Yeah, I'm fine. Just tired."

Inside, the factory is completely dark. Ben turns the lights on. They flicker overhead. Weirdly, everything feels more awkward between us in the building, as though the natural moonlight had helped soften us and made talking easier. Now, under harsh fluorescents we avoid each other's eyes.

"It's okay, you don't have to come in," I say. I notice that I'm slurring my words. "I'll probably stay for a bit and then go home later."

"Nah, it's all right," Ben says. He frowns at me. "Are you sure you're okay, though?" I nod.

We go down the corridor to my studio, Ben walking ahead of me, and looking back occasionally. I watch the back of his neck, strands of hair trembling over it with each of his steps, and, briefly, the memory of sucking his blood from the towel I used to clean his cut comes back to me—the feel of it going easily down my throat, and his experiences very momentarily inhabiting my body: traveling on the bus to school, eating sandwiches with the crusts cut off, and, then, later, much later, seeing me approaching the biscuit factory, the sun beating down on him, me emerging from a shadow, his eyes lingering on my face and my body, him finding me attractive.

"So, are you definitely leaving the—" Ben points behind us with his thumb, to signify the Otter, even though the actual building is miles away now and probably in a completely different direction. We've stopped outside my studio door.

"The Otter?" I ask.

"Yeah."

"I suppose I haven't completely decided yet." I put my key in the lock and the door opens. It's pitch-black inside. There's a strange, sour smell in the air. I step in.

"Sorry," I say. "It's kind of messy."

Ben turns on the light, just on low, and steps in after me. The door closes. My laptop, Ben's plant swinging slightly from the hook, Baba Yaga, my painting, paints, the Sher-Gil propped up against the wall, the yoga mat where I've been sleeping, old underwear, the box of dried pig blood, Ben's bloody towel, and the duck—the duck, still in the sink, its neck hanging over the edge, head pointing toward the floor—all light up. "Yeah, I don't know about the Otter," I say, and I move over to the table, with the painting and puppet and books on it, so Ben's attention is drawn away from the sink. "I don't know. The people are just arseholes . . . and Gideon, the director, he's a bit of a creep."

"Really?"

"Yeah. He's . . . I don't know. It's hard to explain." I think about telling him about how Gideon has been watching me, and about how he grabbed me on the stairs, but something stops me. It's as though my human side is embarrassed; or maybe it's that my demon side is embarrassed about not having been able to protect my human side properly. "But, yeah. It's still experience, isn't it?"

Ben frowns. "Well, I suppose you've got until Monday to decide," he says, eventually.

Ben comes over to where I'm standing and crouches down to look at my painting. He doesn't pick it up; he looks at it like it's already hanging in a gallery, adjusting his height and his position, walking slightly to the right, then walking slightly to the left, to study it. He looks quite beautiful in this light; his hair and nose and forehead cast long shadows across his face, tinging his skin with gray.

"Did you paint this?" he asks, sounding surprised.

"Yeah."

"It's nice."

"Nice?"

"No, I mean, like, it's really good . . . I've never seen anything like it. I'm serious," Ben says.

I nod. "Thanks."

Ben sits down on the chair I painted Yaga in. I lean against the table next to him.

"So, my mum basically went into the hospice this week," Ben says. He bites his lip. He faces the puppet Yaga, so it looks like he is actually talking to her.

"Oh my god, Ben," I say. "I'm sorry."

He shakes his head. "No, it's okay. I just . . . I don't know, I felt like telling you."

Ben looks up at me and smiles. I smile back, but a half-smile-half-concerned-frown kind of smile. "If there's anything I can do . . ." I say, and then my arm moves forward, toward Ben's arm. My fingers touch his skin, and they kind of stroke it. I hadn't planned to do this at all. It feels similar to when I stole the puppet and the books. I lean forward.

"Is this okay?" I hear myself saying.

"Yeah," I hear Ben's voice say.

I can see Ben's veins up close. I can see his freckles, how none of them are perfect circles, but how they're all in the shape of little stars. I've never touched a human in this way before. I've never been touched by a human in this way before. In my chest, I feel a sensation I don't think I've ever felt, my heart pounding, beating extremely hard, pleasingly so; my breathing, which is usually so slow, syncs with Ben's, so we're breathing together. I inhale his breath and exhale it and inhale it again. I feel the sharpness of my teeth with my tongue. And then our lips meet.

PART THREE

7

I was thirteen and Ye-Ye had just been over. Mum had been listening to our conversation about Buffy and Angel's relationship from behind the door, which was open a fraction. "Food and sex mean the same thing to the demon," my mum told me after Ye-Ye left. "If you ever get too close to a human, you'll lose control, and your human side will lose its soul, just like in that TV program."

"What about you and Dad, though? How was I made if that's true?"

"No questions," she said. "Inside your body is death."

The duck blood is coming to an end. My veins are almost empty. I can feel the bird's death inside me. I can feel sand on my breast and my belly. I can feel waterlogged feathers weighing me down; the bird was just old, it turns out; its vision is cloudy; its tiny heart is slowing down. But, then, Ben moves into its place. And I don't know what it is. It's like maybe Ben fits into me perfectly or something, like he fills me completely. Or it's the temperature difference. Ben's skin is unfathomably hot; everything inside my body seems to burn. My organs seem to remember what it's like to be alive and working. Either way, I feel satiated and don't even feel my hunger; I forget my need to eat entirely. Ben's neck presents itself to me, right under my nose, right next to my mouth, and I can taste the sweat that has coated it like a film, but the urge to bite isn't there at all. All it is is a neck, a human neck, and all I am is a human next to it. "Oh my god, you feel so . . . weird," Ben had said as he went into me. "Like good but so cold . . . what is that?"

"I don't know," I'd said in his ear.

He dropped it and, as we went on, he warmed me, and we became just two normal humans; in every part of my body I felt his warmth and took possession of it.

Later, while I'm lying next to Ben, who is snoring, I wonder to myself whether, perhaps, it'd be possible to just live as a human—or, at least, mostly human. If it would be possible to suppress the demon to the extent that I would be able to be normal, apart from my diet, which I'd restrict to black pudding. Maybe my will would actually start transforming the cells in my body. Perhaps, eventually, I'd be able to stay out in direct sunlight and not get so easily burned; perhaps I'd be able to meet someone and go somewhere beautiful with them, somewhere with beaches, and just lie outside like humans do, doing nothing, playing with the sand, letting it run through the gaps between my fingers, picking it back up and starting again. Maybe, eventually, I'd even begin to age. Perhaps I'd look at myself in the mirror one morning and find that all the times I'd been laughing with my partner had rubbed off on my face, and faint lines were appearing around my eyes and mouth. New strands of my hair would grow out of my head a fine silver color; my bones would eventually become more brittle and I'd have to be careful out walking on concrete. My partner, my friends, my mum—all of their lives would end at some point; and, then, when I was much thinner than I am now, maybe a little shorter, my hair wispier, and pure white, I'd see an opening at the end of my life like a break in the clouds and I'd reach toward it, and I'd feel life just falling off my body, being shed like scales, just scattering everywhere, and I'd get lighter and lighter until I was, eventually, just nothing—just absolutely nothing. Gone.

"Is that . . . a duck?" Ben is awake and half sitting up on the yoga mat. He's looking at the sink. I suppose his eyes have adjusted to the light, as he's no longer squinting.

"Umm," I say. I sit up. "Yes. Basically."

"Oh my god," Ben says. "Is that the . . . the smell?"

"Well . . . yes, I suppose it is."

Quite suddenly, Ben's face contorts and he retches.

"What?" I say. "Come on, you've been smelling it all night. You only think it's disgusting now because you know what it is."

Ben picks up my clock sweatshirt and covers his mouth and nose with it. "Why have you got a duck?" he says through it. "I mean, like, it's fully clothed and everything. Or, you know, whatever you call a duck that isn't like what you get in supermarkets."

I stand up. I put on my shorts and slip my boots onto my bare feet. I'm still wearing my shirt. "It's okay, I'll take it out," I say.

I go over to the sink and pick up the duck by the neck. There are some things moving underneath it, and on its side. I give it a rinse under the tap and wash what I suppose are probably maggots down the drain. "Ugh, my god, how long's it been there for?" Ben asks. His eyes are scrunched up. "God, I can't stay here," he says, dramatically, and he starts dressing himself. His body is pleasingly soft-looking and pink. It disappears into the trousers and shirt he was wearing earlier.

"Just go up to your studio, I'll meet you there in a minute," I say, and I grab my keys and take the duck outside. It trails some sort of residue all the way.

I knock on Ben's door. When he answers, I notice that his face looks different from how it did just a few minutes ago. "Hey," he says, and he lets go of the door so I have to hold it open for myself. He walks to the other side of the studio where his phone is plugged in. He is halfway through composing a text.

"Hey," I say, and I go up to him and put my hand on his shoulder. He doesn't look up. He just keeps typing. I feel him breathe in like he is going to sigh, though he exhales slowly and silently.

"Sorry, do you mind if I—" he says, and he nods toward his phone.

"Oh, yeah . . . sorry." I take my hand off him. I wonder if it's the duck smell that's probably still on my hands. I go to the sink and wash them. When I turn back to Ben, he's finished sending his text and he is just sitting on the floor, looking vacantly across the room toward a window. He sighs properly now. He's frowning. He looks tired.

"Is everything okay?" I wipe my hands on my shirt.

Ben shakes his head. "Oh, come on, you know. Anju," he says.

"Oh, right." Somehow, I'd forgotten about her—or, rather, I

hadn't forgotten about her, but I'd felt so significant, like I took up all of Ben's life for a moment, and he'd taken up mine, that Anju had faded into the background. "So, what are you going to do?" I ask. It feels like a stupid question. I kick a pair of Ben's socks to the side and sit cross-legged on the floor.

"I don't know. I mean . . . I suppose I should go home," Ben says. "This was . . ." He shakes his head. His phone lights up. He looks at the screen for a moment and then puts it back down again. "I don't know . . ."

"Mm."

"I don't know, I feel bad . . . We shouldn't have . . ." Ben sighs, again. "Lydia . . . I really like you . . . but this . . ." he says. "I mean, I don't want to hurt you, you know?"

"Yeah, I know."

"Are you okay?" he asks now.

"Yeah."

"Fuck," Ben says, and he puts his head in his hands. Then he stands up. "Right, I think I should go. Anju's been waiting up for me, and . . . yeah."

"Okay," I say. Ben stands still for a moment, just watching me. I realize that he's waiting for me to stand too. As I do, Ben un-plugs his phone and starts winding the cord around the plug of the charger.

We walk down the hall and down the stairs in silence. When we get to the front door, I say, tentatively, "I'm really sorry about the duck."

"It's fine," Ben says, his face still glum, his keys hanging from a finger.

"Okay. I'm going to hang out in my studio for a bit, so . . . I guess I'll see you—"

"Yeah," Ben says. "Sorry, Lydia, I've got to go." He leaves through the door without looking at me. The door slams shut. I stand in the hall and wait for the sound of the gate closing too, and then I go back to my studio.

I've been sitting with my back against the wall for what feels like hours and hours, wondering how I feel, and not being able to find a definitive answer. I've tried texting Ben but, each time, whatever I write feels wrong and I delete it and don't send anything. At nine in the morning, I get a text from Anju, asking if I want to meet for a late lunch on Monday. I say that I'm not entirely sure when or if I'll have a lunch break but I'll let her know.

I don't really feel anything as I text her. I don't feel bad, but I also don't feel especially good, as I had done, yesterday, about the prospect of meeting her. It's almost as though my brain has compartmentalized her, along with her connection to Ben and to what happened last night, and made me think of her as someone disconnected from my life here at the factory entirely. It's like I'm not actually seeing her as human anymore. When I think of her face, and try to imagine it expressing sadness, or happiness, or any other emotion, I can't. "Yeah, sure ttyl x," she replies.

My body feels especially weak now. It's partly because I'm running on almost nothing; but also, I feel like when Ben left, he took something of me with him. Maybe it's the simple fact that when we had sex, I expended energy I couldn't really afford to lose, and it feels like that energy is something Ben took into himself, and stole from me; although, at the same time, he gave the human side of me life. Perhaps it's just the demon that is hungry and weakened—never before have I inhabited my body to such a degree as I did when I was with Ben; never before have I felt so human.

Now, inside me, a part of Ben exists, I suppose, searching. I imagine a barren path inside myself, my womb a derelict cavern, my ovaries like sad, egg-less nests. I wonder, nonetheless, if there isn't just a small, safe corner for a child to grow in there; if perhaps, like my mum, there is a little chance for life to be supported inside me. My mum never bothered to teach me about contraception, though, so I doubt it's possible. She only warned me to not get close in the first place.

I let my head flop back and hit the wall behind me. A pleasing, faint pain spreads from the back of my head to my eyes, where it manifests as spots in my vision. I do it again, and then again.

I've been watching *Buffy* on my laptop. I'm at the end of season two where the instructions for restoring Angel's soul have been saved onto a floppy disk, but Willow's lost the floppy disk down the side of a desk, so Angel's not going to get his soul back in time and Buffy will end up having to kill him. It's such a dumb reason for a vampire to have to die—just a stupid yellow floppy disk, and the fact that a desk and a cabinet aren't pushed close enough together. If it were today, the instructions would have been backed up to the cloud, so everything would have worked out fine.

Ye-Ye and I used to have sleepovers and watch *Buffy* all night, and argue about which characters we were most like, and make bets on how long the Asian characters, who were always vampires, would last before Buffy dusted them. Mum used to order pizza for Ye-Ye, and make me up some warm blood in the flask I took to school, the one with the telescopic, opaque plastic straw that came out the top, so I could drink discreetly. I open Instagram now and look at Ye-Ye's DM from the other day. I guess she's probably seen that I've read her message. Maybe she's wondering why I'm not replying. Part of me really wants to reply. I think about it, for a bit. I'd like to see what she's like now, to hear about what she's been doing, to maybe send her a message about me watching *Buffy* and thinking of her, to maybe talk to her about last night and Ben and my feelings, whatever they are, but the thought of having to cut her out of my life all over again is too painful.

For a little while I considered turning Ye-Ye. I was thirteen and we had Forever Friends mugs that matched, plus best friend necklaces, and friendship bracelets that we had woven for each other. It was my mug that made me think about it. The word "forever," emblazoned across the top above a picture of two soft-looking bears. At that age, it felt like our relationship would never change; and then I realized I could make it so that once we hit eighteen or twenty or whatever our peaks might be, both of us really wouldn't change and we could watch *Buffy* on the sofa together forever—for centuries and centuries—feeling even closer because we both drank blood. I didn't turn her because my mum found out what I was planning, and showed me that if I did, I would be essentially killing Ye-Ye, and changing her into something that wasn't the Ye-Ye I knew. I'd lose my friend forever, she said—which, though, I basically have now anyway.

While I'm looking at Ye-Ye's DM, my phone rings. I let it go to voicemail and then listen to the message. It's Dr. Kerr. My heart sinks when I hear his voice. There's no more space in my brain for my mum at the moment. I feel as though if I let too much of her in, I might have to push something fundamental—like my capacity for emotion, or for making memories, or understanding language—out. Dr. Kerr tells me that my mum has been bedbound, not socializing with the other residents at all, not speaking to any of the nurses, and they want me to pay for her to become one of the catered-for residents, so she can eat meals with the others, and then enjoy board games after. "We will wait until we hear from you, but we are concerned about her happiness and well-being at this point. And we think being more a part of the community here will help." I lock my phone. *I'm concerned about my own happiness and well-being,* I want to say. My mum lied to me about sex, about so much, and this morning, Ben's continued existence is proof of that. I want to tell them, *She isn't my responsibility anymore. She is yours.*

I push my mum and Crimson Orchard out of my mind. I delete the voicemail, then look at #whatieatinaday on Instagram. I flop down onto the floor. I'm exhausted. I face the wall, so it's just my hand, my phone, and the blank concrete I can see. I don't want to see my studio and all the things in it. I don't even want to see the painting I made that I was so happy with, or the puppet Yaga who is on the table, her body still and empty. Behind me, the next episode of *Buffy* begins, and I start scrolling through pictures of various meals along to the sound of Buffy talking.

Instagram what-I-eat-in-a-day posts are different from the YouTube equivalents. Most of the posts start with a picture of a white woman with an athletic, muscular body. They all feel like adverts for personal trainers. It gets boring quite quickly, so I search on YouTube instead, and find my way back to the Japanese girl I watched last time. I lose myself in my phone. Time becomes weird and immeasurable, as I watch days' and weeks' worth of meals being consumed in short videos; the sun rises and sets and rises and sets over and over again behind the various people I watch, and I begin to lose almost all sense of my surroundings. It's like a high. I enjoy it. At the end of it, I find myself watching someone go through the steps for making rice and tuna pancakes, and memorizing them all carefully as though I'm going to make the pancakes myself; partway through, my phone dies.

I stay lying on my back with my eyes closed for a moment, and then roll across the room to the pig blood box. I lift my head with effort to look inside at the dark brown powder, and sigh, and then roll back across the room. The powder in that box feels like it represents so accurately what I am: a thing that is completely and utterly removed from human life, or even animal life; a thing that's been sucked dry of everything that once sustained a real living body; something that is so devoid of life that it doesn't even rot, but just sits in the corner of my studio out of the fridge, in its box, unchanging. The thought of consuming the powder revolts me; the thought of it going into my body, becoming a part of it, makes me feel like I myself am revolting.

I plug my phone in and wait for it to charge enough for me to open YouTube again, then I watch some videos that I find the strangest of all food videos online—eating disorder recovery vlogs, in which people film themselves struggling to eat fattening foods. I watch, in awe, as a woman maybe a bit older than I am places a Cadbury Flake between her lips and closes her eyes. Over the next minute or so, her jaw very slowly closes around the chocolate, and she takes a bite, looking like she is in pain. The woman's skin is a strange yellowy gray, and her eyes pop out, and her mouth is bracketed on either side by wrinkles made not by age but by the body under her skin gradually disappearing. I wonder if perhaps there's a demon in the woman, trying to starve the human, so it can take over the skin and skeleton and organs completely.

It's a fairly seamless progression of thought. Looking at the woman's sallow skin and hollow cheeks, I imagine my own cheeks filling out and my skin being flushed with a nice warm color. I wonder how possible it might be for me to do the same thing in my own body; perhaps I could starve and weaken the demon and kind of flush it out. I puff my cheeks up with air.

Before I was turned, my human body sustained itself, albeit only for days. Something in me must have kept my heart beating and the muscles in my ribs tightening and relaxing, letting air into and out of my lungs. It's completely possible that that human power is still there, only dormant. Perhaps there is actually a lot of human potential in me. Last night, as my body had been warmed by Ben, I'd felt alive in a way I've never felt before. My heart had woken up and was beating faster than the demon could ever pump it; I'd felt a pleasure better and more intense than eating; I'd felt Ben's blood coursing through his veins but felt no desire to drink it, and only gratitude that he was alive and with me. It had been the duck that had repelled Ben—death had, essentially, repelled him: the remnants of my last meal. If I deny myself blood, perhaps the human side of me will get stronger until I can consume and live off human food, and I'll attract humans to me too, and a human life for myself, and human love.

I go on Facebook and scroll absentmindedly, just taking in the shapes that the blocks of text make, and some of the pictures of people's babies and dinners. Then I lock my phone again and just listen to *Buffy*, which is still playing on my laptop, and balance my phone on my forehead. It feels nice having it up there. It's a pretty good weight. Gradually, I drift off into something like semi-sleep, half aware of the characters in *Buffy* talking about a plan to kill a particularly strong vampire, but with new images and other voices accompanying the dialogue in my head.

"Lydia, I've come back. I couldn't stop thinking of you," Ben says in my head, all soft-looking, and wet from the rain, standing outside my studio door. I peel his T-shirt off him and big chunks of his flesh come off with it. He's made of cake. "I can't eat cake," I say, crestfallen. "I don't have a properly working stomach."

"Lydia, I've come back. I couldn't stop thinking of you eating me," Ben says in my head, all soft-looking, and wet from the rain, standing outside my studio door. I peel his T-shirt off him and he's all weird and gray-colored and thin. I bite into his neck and drink and feel my body fill up and my energy return to me and then—"Quick, quick," I say, and I hold up the puppet Yaga for him to drink from.

I open my eyes; there's a knocking sound. It's someone at the door. "Heeeey," Maria's voice comes through it. "Lyyyyd, are you in there? I brought snacks," she says. The knocking stops and then my phone vibrates on my forehead. It's a message from Maria. I look at the text just on the lock screen so that she won't know I've read it: "Hey Lyd am outside your studio, can hear something playing inside are you there?"

There's another knock on my door. I turn vibrate off and put my phone on my chest. I close my eyes again, and I listen to Maria's footsteps leaving down the hall, and then the sound of her own studio door clanging open and closed. I feel disgusted by myself. A part of me wants to follow Maria to her studio. A part of my mind actually goes there, playing it all out, knocking on her door, waiting for her to answer, entering her room, standing in a shadow cast by her art—a shadow occupied not only by me but by other awful things: Gideon's hands groping forward, holding up a part of my body he has snatched like it is a sculpture he owns, eyes peering out—and then biting her and consuming her. But *no*, a voice says in my head. *No. Stop! Stop that woman! She's a monster.* Pig's little legs climb up my calf while I drain his owner and he whimpers, begging me to stop eating.

I grumble and half sit up. The room spins; my tongue feels big and heavy in my mouth; my temples ache. Why do I have to be so hungry? Why do I have to be so weak-willed? How will I be able to starve the demon out of myself, and then live as human, if I can't even stop thinking about blood? I reach onto the top of the table and find Yaga's skirt. I pull her down and she lands on my stomach. I put my hand in her.

"I hate you," I say to her, and she hangs her head. I bare my teeth at her and snap. "You're disgusting," I say. I bring her body toward me and bite down on the seam that joins her head to the fabric of her dress, and suck, imagining that I'm draining her. Then I throw her on the floor and her head makes a loud knocking sound as it lands.

I feel bad almost immediately, and pick Yaga back up and cradle her. "I'm sorry. I don't know what's wrong with me," I say.

I don't know how long I'm in my studio, just drifting in and out of sleep, watching *Buffy* and videos on my phone, with Yaga now lovingly restored to her position on my hand. I get through a season of *Buffy*, and come out of my stupor when she's graduated from high school and is at college, now with an annoying, new, non-vampire soldier boyfriend. I find myself under my yoga mat, kind of peaceful and grounded under the weight of it and the things on top.

I crawl out. I feel weak and sick. I can barely remember the duck's flight now; the bird is gone from me, just dregs of its life left, of feeling a weird flaccidness take over its muscles, of recognizing that the stench it smells is coming off itself. A strange thing happens to my body when I get beyond the initial stages of hunger. I start to shiver and my hairs stand up, even though my body temperature is just as cold as it was after eating, when it was full. Before, I thought of it as being something vestigial, left over from when I was fully human and needed body heat to survive; now, though, I wonder if it is, in fact, my human-self coming to the fore, while my demon-self weakens and fades into the background.

I pause *Buffy* and look up the symptoms of hunger on my laptop, wondering if the things I feel now align with human hunger, and find a document on the NHS website describing something called the "hunger scale"—a list of symptoms ranked from one to ten. I look at ten: "Beyond full," it reads. "This is a typical Christmas Day sort of feeling—you are physically miserable, don't want to or can't move, and feel like you never want to look at food again. Not a good point to reach!" I've never in my life experienced this, and I want to so much; I want so much to be full with other humans, full of fat and protein and carbohydrates and vitamins. I go down the scale, reaching one. "Beyond hungry," it reads. "You may have a headache and experience dizziness and a lack of concentration. Your body feels totally out of energy and you need to lie down." I wish I could plot my own hunger on this human scale. I wish all I felt were a headache and dizziness and a lack of concentration. But I also feel an awful spiritual emptiness. From the duck, I'd received the feeling of urgency to hold on to life, to make young, to protect eggs, to raise the animals that came from them. From Ben, I'd received love for family and friends, which was often difficult, manifesting in grief and pain and worry, but which was also beautiful and gave meaning to everything. From pigs, even, I have received love for the little piglets they've given birth to, and something like love even for human owners who only fill the pigs' food and water troughs. All the animals—human, bird, and pig—had felt something larger than themselves that they were a part of, families, flocks, or something bigger and less definable. Now, I feel only the absence of something like love, of something like faith, of purpose, meaning, of appreciation for anything. But, I don't want to have to eat to get these things back. Or else, I want to eat but the thing I want to consume is the food humans lovingly make for themselves and for each other: home-cooked meals, and tea, and hot milk, and things like that.

I look around the studio. It's a mess. All my stuff is strewn about and, in the sink, in the spot where the duck had lain, a brown-black stain has formed that starts inside the bowl and then goes up and over the edge as the duck's neck and head had done. The smell still lingers in the air, although I don't mind it too much. I have a look at the stain and I notice the bodies of a few maggots here and there, and a couple still moving. I sigh. The fake plant Ben got me is probably the only nice thing in the room.

I decide to tidy up. I want to be disgusted by the things humans would be disgusted by; I want to be disgusted by the dirty floors and the lack of order in here, and the clothes all over the place, and the paints all out and leaking on the floor and table-top, and the dust left behind by whoever had the studio before me that I didn't bother to clean up when I arrived, and the box of blood and Ben's towel, and the leftover gunk from the duck; I want to be disgusted by myself—by my body that I haven't washed in days, my face that I haven't cleaned since before the night at The Place when Pig had licked it, and my nails that still have the glue from the labels I had to clean off wine bottles at the Otter under them, and bits of dirt. There's still sand in my hair that came from the duck's body when I bit into it, and probably blood too.

I find cleaning products under the sink: there's a hand towel, microfiber cloths, sponges, surface cleaner, bathroom cleaner, bleach, a scourer, a bucket, a dustpan and brush. I use it all, go-ing over the floors with a sponge and bleach, with all my stuff shoved up on top of the table, scrubbing at the stain in the sink, wiping down the mirror, the walls, then the tabletop after I've laid everything out neatly—my bed in the corner, looking kind of cozy and welcoming despite the fact that my bedding is also my clothing. I take out the box of dried pig blood and Ben's old towel, and shove them as far as they'll go into one of the big bins in the factory's bin storage. I want to not think about them; I want to never think about drinking blood again. I find some nails and hammer a few of them into the wall for some of my clothes to hang from. I find and wash an old ceramic dish, too, that looks like a pet bowl, and that has large lettering on the side that spells out "AMOS," and put my paints in it, and then I do the same with a cup for my paintbrushes and pens. I make ev-erything perpendicular on the table. And then I take the hand towel and Yaga and I go upstairs—right up to the seventh floor, staggering as I go, clutching on to the banister—and find the showers.

It's very quiet in the factory, which makes me think it must be quite late at night. The showers have no doors, just curtains. I go in one of the cubicles and turn the water on, and use a bar of soap I find in there to wash myself. I also wash Yaga, who's still on my hand. Carefully, I lather soap into her hair. I rub it gently into her face too, and then her dress. I dry us both as best as I can with the hand towel.

At one point, while I'm drying us, I fall onto my knees, and my skin breaks, and a little blood trickles out and mixes with the beads of shower water still on me, and on the tiles on the floor. For a moment, I wonder if I might pass out. It's a good sign, I think, my head hanging forward on my chest, too heavy to lift; a sign that the demon is struggling, perhaps. I try to enjoy it. Yaga's little face looks up at me from the floor, her hair close to a stream of my blood. Then, eventually, the feeling passes, and I stand again, put on a fresh shirt and the trousers I bought the other day, and go back downstairs.

Back at the table in my studio, I take the painting I made and look into the strange, scrunched-up, demonic face in the middle. Behind the black, flecks of blue come through, as though there's blood behind it that has been starved of oxygen. I hang up puppet Yaga on a washing line I make using two nails in the wall and an elastic band I find in the cupboard. I peg her up carefully, upside down so the creases in her dress come out. I apologize and sit back down with the painting.

I don't look at Yaga as I paint over the dark, ominous shape I'd been happy with not long ago. I start at the hands, which I'd painted as human hands—beautiful and slender, and a golden brown—and just extend the skin up, making two human arms. I give her a human body, and put her in a simple dark dress that isn't ragged like the real Yaga's dress. Then I work on her face and her eyes, replacing the red dots she previously had with two brown eyes just like mine, and her shadowy face with something more defined. I stand up occasionally as I work, to check my features in the mirror and compare them to what I'm painting, leaning against the wall as I do, panting, wobbling on my legs, smelling the tiny, microscopic amount of residue from the duck still left in the sink, and trying to ignore it, trying not to salivate. Eventually, when I'm done painting over the entire original Yaga figure, I use the black I'd used to make her angular body a few days ago to create the background. Her new form glows against it, looking candlelit, or lit by sunlight.

I flick through the Amrita Sher-Gil book to find a painting to replace the picture of *Three Girls* I have propped against my wall, but I'm pretty sure that all of Sher-Gil's subjects were vampires and that maybe she was one too, so I look through the Joseph Beuys book I got under Waterloo Bridge instead, and tear out photographs of his famous performance piece, *I Like America and America Likes Me.* For it, Beuys spent three days in a room alone with a wild coyote, with only his clothes and hat, a felt blanket, a walking stick and gloves. In one of the pictures I tear out, Beuys is wearing the blanket over his head and the coyote is tearing at it, teeth bared. It is the first day. This is the most famous photograph of the performance, even though it is the most expected outcome. In the other picture I tear out and stick on my wall alongside the first one, Beuys is lying on his side, relaxed, and looking out the window in the room, next to the coyote, who—calm, placid, tame—could easily be mistaken for his pet dog. These two pictures feel like the perfect images to have up on my wall as inspiration. Next to them, I prop up my new portrait of Baba Yaga.

I look at my phone. There's another text from Maria: "Hey hope youre ok. Let me know xx." I check Messenger, WhatsApp, and Instagram. There are no messages from Ben. I wonder what he's doing now. I look at the time. It's 1:00 a.m. on Monday. A whole weekend has passed. I wonder what he's been up to, whether he and Anju argued when he got back so late after we spent the night together, whether he told Anju about what happened or not; maybe over the weekend, he went to visit his mum. I try to imagine this. I've never been inside a hospice, so I don't know what they're like. I imagine private rooms, with light pink walls, maybe something similar to the wards babies go into soon after they're born that have those little transparent plastic cribs in them. I'd spent my last moments as a full human in one of those wards, dangling from my mum's arm and drinking, with one of those little hats with a knot on top on my head. Humans, I know, like to see circles in the transition from conception to birth to life to death, so perhaps they emphasize those ideas in the way hospices are decorated, so that the patients can feel that their ends aren't just ends but are, also, new beginnings. My own life I think of as a line, not a circle. My favorite artwork by a Fluxus artist is La Monte Young's instruction "Draw a Straight Line and Follow It," not because of the nihilistic attitude toward life and work it embodies, but because it represents in just a simple shape, or lack of shape, the difference between my life and purely human lives. My life aims toward a distant point in the far future. A human life aims to return to something, or rather to nothing; to return to dust.

I start composing a text to Ben. I write "Hey, when" and then delete the "when" and replace it with "I think we should" and delete that and write "maybe we could talk soon." I add "I think I like you," then pause and add "x." I look at what I've typed and then just delete it all. I think about a scenario in which Ben is sleeping right now in the bed he shares with Anju, and Anju is up. Maybe she's got up to get a drink of water, or to go to the toilet, or, I don't know, maybe she can't sleep. And then Ben's phone lights up on the bedside table, and she doesn't mean to look at it, but she does and there's my text, just lit up on the lock screen declaring my love or, well, not my love but whatever it is: the like that's more than normal like, but less than love. The beginning of love, maybe, but not quite that either. The feeling that comes from being brought to almost-life by a person, of having tasted their blood, of feeling the beginning of their life in it: the squeezing of ribs in the rhythm of contractions, the feeling of being forced to breathe air for the first time, the feeling of Ben's mother's pale pink, warm skin meaning so much, and of feeling so secure when laid on top of it—and yet not draining it, of saving that person's life from yourself.

I put my phone down on the table and look ahead at Baba Yaga hanging upside down on the wall. I don't see her, though. In my head, I see Ben instead. And I'm surprised to see a moment that I'd thought of as kind of small and insignificant when it happened. At Vauxhall Bridge, his hand rising, him looking both ways at the traffic for both of us, saying okay for when we could cross, and then his hand taking my arm, gently, tenderly. I wonder whether, if Anju didn't exist, Ben would want to be with me. I wonder whether, if Anju went away, he would suggest we try seeing each other. Everything between us was nice before he remembered she existed.

I wonder how I could slot into Ben's and Anju's lives. I wonder how I could make it work if I manage to become human or if I manage to find a way to live mostly as human. I wonder where I could exist in their world, whether there'd be space for me in their relationship. I know I could be sustained by them. I know Ben could keep me feeling alive; and, from Anju, I'd have someone to keep me company as an artist. We could share a studio and paint together, and support each other, just as I imagine Rossetti did for Morris and vice versa. They shared their muses, and their wives too, though I don't know how their wives felt about it, or who knew what, or how it worked. Maybe, eventually, Ben and Anju would actually accept me for what I am and would bring home animals for me to live off. And if not, maybe I could eat Anju, so she was out of the picture, and so it was just me and Ben; and if I did that, I could experience her life, her and Ben's relationship, the food she has eaten, trips to Japan, maybe, Japanese food. Or, perhaps I could turn Ben. It's an alternative, I suppose—if I fail to become human, I could bring the people I want to keep into my reality. I could make it so those people could no longer be human anymore, untethered from life, with me.

"Uggghhhh," I say out loud, and I close my eyes and let my head fall onto the table. The room spins; or, well, the room doesn't spin, but the black inside my eyes churns. My legs ache, my arms ache, my neck aches, my forehead aches; all my veins, empty and hungry, tighten.

I get up. I'm not really aware of doing so. I kind of drift to the door. I leave my studio, my hair still wet, the hand towel around my shoulders, and climb the stairs. I can sense the few people who are in the building so strongly; I can hear not their pulses, but the actual sound of their blood rushing through their veins like little rivers. I can smell their brains—the odd kind of cakey sweetness combined with the iron-y tang that brains have; I can hear the rivers of blood traveling up to those brains, filling the veins around the lungs, pumping into fingers and toes. I drift, like I'm not in control of my body at all. My mind is fixated on eating.

The Place is dark. It's a comforting dark—the windows with their blinds pulled down are big squares of total blackness along the wall; the light bulbs that hang over the room are just dim, shadowy orbs. Everything is flat and calm. But I turn on the lights; I don't want to feel at home in dark and dingy spaces. The fairy lights and the main light come on.

It's very quiet. No one is in on this floor. I open the fridge and a new, more intense light comes from inside. I scour the shelves, wondering if there might be any human food I can try to eat. In the past, I've managed to successfully digest the oats and pepper in black pudding, though only in small quantities when I've failed to spit it all out. There might be something gentle I can eat a little of to try to bring my stomach back to full life, get it processing food in a human way, have it satisfy the intense hunger I have, the nagging for sustenance I feel coming from my demon half. The book I'd found about Baba Yaga online had said that she has sometimes been known to drink not only blood, but also milk.

There's cheese on the top shelf: a large block of cheddar, some vegan mozzarella with Shakti's name written on the bag, feta coated with bright pink flakes of sumac that has Maria's name written on the packet, and a round box of Dairylea triangles that I assume are probably Ben's. There are a few lunch boxes at the bottom of the fridge too, which have Ben's name scrawled on the lids in Sharpie. I pick these up and have a look inside; there's mold growing in each one. In the fridge door, there are a few cartons and bottles: orange juice, vodka, and, right in the middle, a small bottle of milk. I look at the expiration date on the lid; it's in just over a week. I take it out and find myself a mug. Then I sit with it at the long table, just looking at it for a bit.

My human side doesn't want to eat. It's never actually eaten, ever, in its life. When I was born, I had hemolysis, meaning my red blood cells weren't living for as long as they were supposed to. A few things happened to me: I stopped breathing for short periods, my skin turned a kind of pasty brown-gray color, and my heartbeat was extremely fast; I didn't accept any milk either. I was taken to a special ward where I was monitored, but I didn't get better, until my mum turned me—and so, my first meal outside of the womb was as a demon. Now, I don't think my human side really knows what to do with food, or how to feel about it.

I take my phone out of my pocket. I go to one of my favorite Instagram profiles, the.korean.vegan, and I watch her last video, in which she makes peach-topped tteok. The Korean vegan, Joanne, cooks while talking about various things in her life. As she splits open a peach, she explains why she gave up meat. As she adds lemon juice, brown sugar, nutmeg, a pinch of salt, cinnamon, almond extract, maple syrup, then vegan butter and vegan milk and sifted almond and rice flour, she talks about how she worried about whitewashing her diet, about denying herself a fundamental part of her culture, and then about how others don't see her as authentically Korean since she is vegan. I watch other videos by Joanne, soothed by her voice into feeling human myself, and into craving the experiences of love she talks of and the food she cooks as she does.

I go to another profile, and watch a person's hands delicately handle little knots of shirataki noodles and wash them in cold water, before placing them in a clear oden soup that is already filled with stock-boiled eggs, daikon, and pure white triangles of hanpen. Next, they place a cube of rice cake in a little deep-fried tofu pouch, and seal the pouch with a toothpick so it looks like a tiny drawstring bag; they place the bag in with the other ingredients. "Every winter my mum made this dish for me," a voice says over the video, "just like how every winter my grandma made it for my mum when she was a child." The person in the video is half Japanese like me, and her name is Mei; she appears on the screen, rosy cheeked, chopsticks in her hand, and sits down with her dish and eats it, facing the camera.

Food means so much in Japan. Soya beans thrown out of temples in February to tempt out demons before the coming of spring bring the eater prosperity and luck; sushi rolls eaten facing a specific direction decided each year bring luck and fortune to the eater; soba noodles consumed at New Year help time progress, connecting one year to the next; when the noodles snap, the eater can move on from bad events from the last year. In China too, long noodles consumed at New Year grant the eater a long life. In Korea, when rice-cake soup is eaten at New Year, every Korean ages a year, together, in unison. All these things feel crucial to East Asian identity, no matter which country you are from. But traditions in food are denied to me because of my condition—longevity, and continuity, and a break from bad memories from noodles; and fortune, prosperity, and luck from sushi rolls and soya beans. My mum told me that, when my dad was alive, he rarely ate English food, even when he was in England, because, she said, English food was so often eaten only as sustenance, and not for anything more. At New Year, he'd cook soba for one, and my mum would watch.

In the moments of my life when I've really resented my mum and wished my dad were alive, I've gone to the Asian supermarket in Canterbury, bought all the foods I thought he might like, cooked it all up according to the instructions, dropped a raw egg in the meal, and cut some nori on top and just smelled it, thinking that, in that smell, perhaps, some essence of my dad existed, and that maybe I'd meet him somewhere in it. Now, I just associate food in general with my dad—chewing, savoring, textures; bread, cheeses, noodles, pasta, vegetables, herbs, everything— and blood with my mum. I know that there is food farther back in my mum's family history, farther back in my mum's own history too. But I struggle to comprehend it. I can't imagine her nourishing herself.

I wish I could feel the connection to the earth and to other people that food lets humans feel; find a partner and marry and live just a small life, with children and pets, growing onions in the garden, brushing caterpillars off them, plucking them from the ground, chopping them into stir-fries. I watch another of Mei's posts. She makes an iced coffee, with chunks of black coffee-flavored kanten jelly at the bottom of it, while talking about her grandmother's arrival in America just before the

Second World War, and the tiny Asahi launderette she opened when she arrived. The milk makes beautiful shapes in the coffee, drifting down slowly like wisps of smoke, stopping only at the jelly. Something so pretty can only be easy to consume, I think—and I turn my phone off and pour some of the milk from the carton into the mug I got for myself. I close my eyes, ignoring the pleading of the demon in my head, and lift the mug to my lips, imagining that the liquid is blood, and then drink it all, all of it, all in one.

It tastes like what I imagined it to taste like: a secretion from an animal that is not human, and that lives in a field, and doesn't bathe or use a toilet or brush its teeth or anything like that. I keep the milk down, but I quickly wish that I could reverse time so that I'd never had it in the first place. I suppose because I haven't eaten in a while, and what I have eaten has been minimal—the stubby end of a black pudding sausage, dregs of diluted blood from a towel, a mouthful of powdered blood, and a duck-full of blood, the equivalent of maybe a snack in human terms—my veins have excitedly opened and accepted the milk into them, just assuming that their host wouldn't consume anything but what they need. I look at one of my arms as, gradually, my veins turn a shocking white color. *Oh god,* I think. *This was probably a mistake.*

I watch all the veins in my other arm change color and, then, both arms stiffen and spasm; then the same process starts taking place everywhere else, until I feel a strange squeezing sensation in my chest, and I fall off my seat. I stay on the floor for what feels like ages, pain at first constant, then collecting in waves. I slowly move myself until I find a position that is more comfortable, the top of my head on the floor, my body curled up, my arms flat, stretched out on either side of me. I rock, slowly, back and forth, back and forth, and then, as though I'm moving farther and farther away from the world, the plane of my vision shrinks, until it's just a dot in the middle, and then nothing.

I've never learned about what kills a vampire. My mum refused to teach me; sometimes, I've wondered whether she even knows, herself. When I was a teenager, I tested all the various things that are said to kill or hurt vampires in myths, books, films, and TV programs. Quite dramatically, I once entered a church near my secondary school during fifth period when I was meant to be in PE, walked down the aisle between all the pews, and when I was sure there was no one around who might see me, draped myself over the gold cross at the front next to the baptismal font, with my arms over the parts of it that stuck out sideways, and my body pushed up against the central column. I don't know what had made me so miserable that day—something pretty stupid, I think—but I'd said out loud, "I am ready for you, death!" and waited for my skin to start burning and for steam or smoke, or whatever it is that comes off vampires when crosses are pressed against their faces in *Buffy*, to start rising off my body; but, it never came, and I just left the church feeling stupid. Another time, I went out into the garden during a heat wave, took off all of my clothes apart from my underwear, lay down spread-eagled on the grass, and stayed there for hours, waiting to burst into flames; but I just got extensive sunburn, which blistered and left me with a couple of scars I still have. I've tried to fall on a stake before, but that's pretty hard to do, and my mum watched while shaking her head and not looking too concerned, so I'm guessing that wouldn't work either, and I've also downed a whole vial of holy water that I got online; though, maybe it wasn't actually real and was just water, I don't know. I've never learned how to end my life. But maybe, now, I'll learn inadvertently that the answer is milk. Perhaps, tomorrow, one of the other artists will come up here and just find a pile of ash where, all night, I'll have been in this awkward position, slowly dying.

Gradually, the twitching all around my body calms down; I become completely still; movement becomes something far removed from my existence; everything is completely silent. Into that setting, into the dark of my mind, two strange, eel-like things appear. One is a greenish blue, the other is red. Neither have faces, but I get the sense that they are both animals, and that they are both alive. In the darkness, they swim up to one another and intertwine around a central thread. Then, as though there is something living inside each of the eels too, little tendrils push out of the sides of their bodies and join in the middle. Through the tendrils, the color of each of the eel-like things leaks out and into the other, until, eventually, they are the same murky color: a kind of purplish brown, with flecks of green. That color gradually darkens; it's as though the lights are being dimmed in my mind. I hold my breath, or I stop breathing—I can't tell which—and the eels separate, revealing, between them, a scene.

It's Crimson Orchard. I recognize it from the shape of the building. But, everything around it looks different. The sky is a strange orange-brown color and a huge, murky disc hangs among the clouds. There are odd shapes here and there that look like they might have once been houses, but they are just charred remains, small fires lapping up any unburned bits of wood and insulation. The ground beneath my feet crunches and, when I look down, I see that I am walking on bones. It's the end of the world. Something in my head tells me there are only days or weeks left. The Sun is coming to claim us.

I step into the building, and there's no one left, just my mum, sitting on her own in front of the mirror; the lights are off, the fridge is silent. There is dust everywhere on all of my mum's things—the picture of the cow on the wall, the top of her dresser, the crumpled lampshade, her bed, as if she has not slept for years, perhaps decades. The room is dark; but my mum seems to glow. She is wearing clothing I've never seen her in—a loose-fitting batik dress densely patterned with flowers and leaves. The colors are bright—vibrant reds, purples and oranges and a rich azure blue—and they reflect off her face and make her look completely and utterly alive.

"Mum," I say. My voice is strange. It echoes.

"Lydia," my mum says. "You've come."

"Of course."

"Take me," she says. "Please take me with you. Please."

I sit down on the bed, and part of it crumbles off, like the dust hasn't just settled on its surface but rather the whole bed is made of dust. Huge gray flakes that break away from the bedding drift up into the air. The room creaks, as if the world outside is moving.

"Mum, I can't take you with me."

"Why not?"

"Because you make me feel like I'm not worthy of life," I hear myself say. "You just act like you're dead, like you died when you were turned. How can I live my life with the shadow of that over me?"

"That *is* when I died. You know we are dead. Both of us. We are dead," my mum says, though her cheeks are rosy. "The Sun has come for us, Lydia." She looks at her reflection in the mirror. "Let me go with you."

I put my head in my hands. My energy is draining. Near my mum's chair, the floor cracks as if it is exceptionally dry, as if the earth has grown so old it has formed wrinkles that threaten to swallow everything. "We're not dead. We're not evil," I say, without looking up. "That's just something humans think—that we die when we are turned, and we go from being a godly, living thing to being a dead thing animated by the devil. But, Mum, that's not us."

I lift my head out of my hands and bits of it break away like the bed and drift upward. Above us, the ceiling is peeling away. The Sun's rays creep in. "You know, lobsters just get bigger and bigger without aging and, if there were no other threats to them, they'd live forever. Sea sponges too, Mama." I call her what I used to when I was a child. "They stay beautiful and bright and they live for thousands of years. That's us." The sunlight in the room intensifies.

"Sea sponges," my mum says, and I watch her lips crumble as she speaks, little pink shapes like petals leaving her face and drifting up and turning to ash.

"Memories make life," I say, but now my voice is coming out as a croak, the words barely understandable. "Think of all you've seen. You're as old as a tree . . ." A loud creaking is coming from inside the walls. "As old as a mountain." Then my face is burning hot, and the scene in front of me, along with my mum, disappears.

I feel a weird sensation on my face. It's something hot and wet. Then I hear a voice: "Lyd! What are you doing?" I breathe in and open my eyes. It's Maria and Pig. Pig's face is close. His tongue is lapping all over my mouth and nostrils. Maria is standing on the other side of the room. She comes toward me. She crouches down. She looks worried.

I must have fallen out of the position I'd put myself in when my veins had started changing color, because I'm now on my side, my arms awkwardly stretched out in front of me, my head tucked in close to my chest.

"Hello," I hear another voice say. It's a nice voice, a woman's voice; it's not high-pitched, but it's not low either.

"Hey," Maria says, and I realize that the other voice was probably my own. "Are you okay?" she asks. "Are you sick?" Pig licks my neck. I open my mouth.

"Bad milk," I say, my voice recognizable as my own again.

"Bad milk?" Maria asks.

I nod. My head feels very heavy. I keep it on the floor. Maria looks up at the table, and then picks up the milk bottle, which is now mostly empty. "This?" she asks.

I nod again. Then Maria comes back to me and puts one of her hands on my arm. She takes her phone out. I try to tell her to move away, that I'm dangerous, that I don't know what I am anymore, that I'm not human, but my eyes start to close again. Pig's body slumps down next to mine. It's warm. I can feel him breathing, and the folds of his face against my chin. He whimpers, like how I imagined he would whimper if I ate Maria. It's pretty nice and calming.

"Hey, Pig," I say. I wrap my arm around him, and my hand finds his belly and rests across it. "Thank you," I say.

I hear bits of Maria's phone call. I suppose I'm falling back asleep. "She says she drank bad milk," she says. My eyes are closed, and I feel kind of warm and happy. "Yeah, I don't know. Her hair's kind of damp and there's a towel. I don't know." In the dark, I look for the two ribbon-like eels again. I want to find whatever it was they showed me; I want to find the dream of my mum again, make sure she's okay, make sure she survived. But it's really black, a darker dark than I can see in. I wonder if I'm back in Miroslaw Balka's piece at the Tate, in that dark box, the felt walls absorbing all light. My hands grope forward. "Yeah, I've got a flight to catch. Edinburgh to see my parents," Maria says somewhere in the distance now—faraway, irrelevant. "Can you come up?" I feel Mum's fingers in the dark and they interlock with mine. Did this actually happen? I wonder. Did we hold hands in Balka's *How It Is*? Is this a memory of the past, or is it a continuation of my dream; is it after the Sun has come down, and is there only darkness left? There are footsteps, and then a new voice.

"Hey, Maria."

"Hey."

"Lyd?"

Slowly, our fingers slip apart. "Mum, I can't see you in this light," I say, as our hands release each other, and I can no longer feel my mum at all.

"I can't see you either," my mum says.

"Lyd?"

I feel the warmth leave my chest. Pig has got up or has been picked up and is no longer next to me.

"Ben?"

"Lyd, wake up." I open my eyes again. Two nice, pink faces. Maria and Ben.

I'm on the biggest beanbag. My body sinks down into it. Ben is standing by the counter on the other side of The Place with his back turned to me. The kettle is on, and Ben is holding a Dairylea triangle in one of his hands. The wrapper has been peeled down halfway and he's eating it like a banana. Next to him is a little heap of silver wrappers. There's a mug on the counter on the other side of him, with a spoon in it. Behind that, there's an open container of Horlicks. One of my hands is resting against my face. I can feel that there's a line of crusty saliva going down my chin from the corner of my mouth. Some comes off on my hand and I see it's white and milky.

I feel weirdly animal. Calm, but like I want to run for a very long time and very far, and not just using my legs, but on all fours. It's as if the demon in me wants to escape my human body, now that I've drunk milk. But, I can't move. My body is extraordinarily heavy. I can't lift my head. It feels like it's made of a dense and heavy wood. As I breathe in again, I smell Ben. I smell his shower gel, and his sweat; I smell a bit of dirt, maybe on his shoes, and I smell his saliva, and his skin, and a hint of his blood; my senses, I suppose, have been dulled a little by the milk. I'm close to Ben, but I can't smell his brain at all, I can't hear the streams of blood in his veins.

"Oh, hey, you're up," Ben says. He comes over with the Dairylea box. "Want one?" he asks. I shake my head very slightly, all the movement I can manage. I watch his mouth moving: his jaws opening and closing and opening and closing as he chews. "God, yeah, I guess you probably don't fancy cheese right now, do you? You feeling better?"

I open my mouth. It kind of pops open like my lips had been sealed closed with something. Ben's face looks so soft and radiant, like a peach. He puts some more cheese into his mouth, and I feel an intense envy. The veins in his arm and forehead stay their beautiful red and blue colors. "I'm so disgusting," I whisper.

"No, no," Ben says, through a mouthful of cheese. "No, you're not. Don't worry. You're just sick." He swallows. "I don't mind at all," he adds. Then he looks thoughtful for a moment. "So, what happened?"

"I drank some bad milk." My voice comes out quiet. It doesn't project well.

"Oh, okay," Ben says. Then he pauses. He purses his lips like he's struggling to say something. "Yeah, it's just I sniffed the milk and it seemed fine. We were wondering if maybe you were high or something?" Ben looks at his hands. "Like, you were talking about your mum and stuff. I mean, you weren't talking about her but you were kind of calling out to her." He clears his throat. He looks embarrassed. "I'd understand if you were feeling . . . I don't know . . . and you . . . you know. Are you, like . . . I mean, do you . . . do you miss her?"

I glance down at the veins on my arms. Some are a kind of pink color; others are a light-ish blue-green. I'm reminded of the two eels I saw in my mind and the scene they parted to reveal. I try to think about Ben's question, but I find it difficult to think about my mum. My mum, who I've tried so hard to live apart from, who has felt like a dead weight I am cursed to have hanging around my neck for my whole life, pulling me down, preventing me from living fully. When I'd lied to Ben and told him that my mum was dead, I didn't feel too bad because she sees herself as dead anyway, and because maybe I did then too. But in my dream, under the threat of true death, she had seemed more alive than ever, more alive than all the humans in the world, who in that reality had been reduced to bones and ash. Ben has a pained, sympathetic expression on his face.

"It's okay if you don't want to talk about it," he says. He puts the lid on the Dairylea box. In the time he has been over here, he's finished all of the remaining triangles.

"I guess—" I start to say.

I guess I do miss my mum. When I was small, I fitted completely on her lap, my feet just reaching her knees when my legs were straight out, and my head interlocking perfectly with the little nook under her chin, my face in the perfect position for her to kiss when I turned around. She made me hate an intrinsic part of myself but I don't think she ever hated me. She used to tell me how much she loved watching me grow. "When you were a baby," she said, "I stayed up all night every night to watch you just in case I missed something about you changing." When I was around nine, she told me that she wished she could make my childhood last forever, so she could watch me grow up—becoming taller, becoming stronger, becoming womanlier, becoming more assertive and independent—for her whole life. When I stopped changing, when I stopped becoming and was just a stagnant thing that had become everything it could become, my mum drifted away from me. She stopped caring, it seemed, stopped showing me that she loved me and, in fact, made me feel the opposite, as if, now my body was as unchanging as hers, I could no longer represent goodness to her. "I guess I do miss my mum," I say.

Ben sits on the beanbag next to me. The part I'm on rises as he sinks down. The desire I felt earlier, desire for food—the food my body actually needs, not human food—returns to me as Ben's body heat starts to warm my skin. But I still can't really move. I wonder if the milk has curdled and hardened in my veins and has kind of stiffened my body. It feels a bit like a muzzle; I hope it stays that way, while Ben is next to me, warm as though he's just come out of the oven. "Yeah, that's the part I think I'm really dreading—not even the death part, but the missing part after," he says.

I nod with difficulty.

"Can I do anything to help?" Ben asks. "I'm staying in my studio tonight, so we could like . . . I don't know . . . maybe watch something together or, I don't know."

"I thought we're not allowed to sleep in our studios," I mumble, slurring my words slightly.

"Yeah, I know. But, I mean . . . I think it's okay sometimes."

"Sometimes, like, when *you* need to stay here?"

He smiles. "Uhhh, yeah, basically," he says. He wriggles down so he's lying next to me. His arm is touching my arm. His neck is about half a meter from my mouth. Eventually, Ben says, "Sorry about your mum."

"It's okay," I say, feeling genuinely mournful for whatever part of my mum I've lost.

Ben closes his eyes. I wish I could tell him about the life I envisaged for us earlier. The three options. Me, him, and Anju, with me trying to live as human—although, I feel like this might not be possible now, considering the effect of milk on my body. Me, vampire, and him, human, without Anju, and with Ben keeping me feeling alive, providing me with whatever life source he provided me with the other night that made my heart beat as though I was mostly human. Or me and him, both vampires. Both removed from regular life, maybe with his mum too, plucked from her deathbed, whatever tiny amount of time she has left now stretched out into the future. I wish I could be honest with him. I wish I could be honest with anyone.

Ben opens his eyes. He looks at the ceiling. He's quiet for a bit. Then he says, "So, I'm going to be moving back home in a couple of days, just to be with my little sis and dad and to, you know, spend some time with Mum too."

"Oh, right," I say. "Is Anju going with you?"

"No. I don't want her to. There's a gallery in Berlin that wants to represent her and, I don't know . . . she's at an important time in her career and stuff. I don't want to bring her down with me, you know?"

"Have you broken up?"

"No," Ben says. "But, yeah, we're at kind of different stages of our lives, I guess. I suppose I've realized recently that I want less than what Anj wants. I want family and, like, a normal, stable job, and a little house. I want to find someone and settle down and grow old. And Anj is kind of chasing this massive dream."

"That's not less," I say.

"Hmm?"

"The stuff you want." Ben looks at me. "It isn't less than what Anju wants." I want to tell him that that's the stuff I really want too, but that it's stuff I'll never be able to have, and that, because it's something I'll never have, I can see the immense value in it. I can see that what Ben wants is more of a life than what Anju is chasing, which is, I suppose, a version of what I have naturally— immortality, essentially, but through art.

"We're not meant to want that kind of thing, though, are we, as artists," Ben says. "I feel like most people would probably see my art as insincere if they found out I wasn't putting all of my life into it, if they found out I wasn't trading a life with family and kids and a stable income and everything else for it."

"Maybe those people are stupid, though," I say. I'm getting a little movement back in my body. My fingers. I ball them into fists, and squeeze.

"I don't know. I suppose I keep thinking that maybe I'm like a degenerate artist or something, like I'm missing a piece of what makes artists good, the part that makes them not think about all the kind of normal life things and that makes them focus on not being forgotten after they die," Ben says.

"Hmm," I say. I move my tongue and lick my lips. Gradually, I lift my head a little off the beanbag, and sit up a bit. The room rocks as I do, but it soon levels out again. My vision starts returning to me. I can see so much that Ben can't see with his fully human eyes. I can see specks of dust on the wires of the fairy lights; flecks of light coming in through the gaps between the blinds and the window frames that mingle with the light in the room; thin slivers of electricity flickering in each of the light bulbs like little blue hairs. Ben is below me now, his eyes open but seeing so little. I bend my knees and feel them creak, like the milk inside is splitting and loosening. "I think it's better to not concentrate too much on whether you'll be forgotten or not after you die," I say, watching him.

"Hmm. That's pretty wise," Ben says.

I grit my teeth. I can't tell what it is I want. I can't tell what I want to do, which part of me is telling me what—whether it's still hunger, or something else I'm feeling, looking at Ben's body stretched out below me.

I reach out toward him, easily now, the muzzle, I suppose, removed; so easily that I feel like my arms and legs could bend backward if I wanted them to, like I could put my hand through things with no effort, through Ben's skin and his ribs and muscle to reach his heart. I put my hand on his stomach, my eyes now wide, my breathing now normal, nice and slow and calm. I move my hand across Ben's body to his arm, quickly, but gently, and then slip it into his hand. It's warm and slightly clammy. For a moment, I feel wonderful—less out of control, more human—existing here under the lights, feeling my skin warming slightly, thinking about us not leaving The Place or this moment ever, of turning it into a home, of making meals for each other and for our friends.

After about a second, though, Ben pulls his hand away. I feel the air that replaces it as though it is a solid object. "Lyd. We can't be like that," he says.

I find the pocket of my trousers. A dark little place for my hand to crawl into. My heart is beating faster than usual again but, this time, it doesn't feel good. "I'm sorry, Lyd. I'm with Anj. The other night was a mistake."

I sit up, faster than I expect to, so I'm bolt upright. It makes Ben jump. And then—"You don't like me," I hear myself say, and I feel embarrassed immediately at how childish a thing it is to say. But I feel what I say too: that I am myself a mistake, and that I am a mistake not because of anything positive about Ben and Anju's relationship, or because—despite my experience of his birth and episodes from his life—Ben and I don't actually know each other too well and Anju has years and years on me, of being with Ben, of caring for and loving him, but because I'm a demon. I'm piggish. After years of drinking the animal's blood, I've taken on aspects of it. I'm full of death. While I'd felt the edges of life with Ben the other night, perhaps he had felt the opposite in me: a dark, ominous, unfathomable wave—an impenetrable haze.

"It's not that, Lyd. I do like you, but we have to just be friends," he says. I nod, but my body feels like it isn't being controlled by me anymore, but by something or someone else all of a sudden.

Ben struggles up from the beanbag. "Shall I go down and get my laptop or something?" he asks. "We could just stay here and watch a film maybe. I'll get a duvet and stuff too."

I shake my head. I dig my nails into the flesh of my palms, until I feel liquid running from the little wounds I make. I try to talk; I try to say no, but I find that my voice doesn't work. It's gone. The tiny final remnants of the duck's blood are being directed only to the most crucial muscles now. My larynx has closed down. I imagine, inside my throat, all the lights turning off, the muscles deflating and spreading out on the nearest flat surfaces. My tongue rests against my bottom teeth. *You should eat,* a voice says in my head.

It takes everything to leave. Everything that is left in me that is human. I stand and I feel much taller than Ben, even though I'm not, and step back. Ben's saying something, but my hearing is muffled. I can't tell if this is a physical thing—that there's too little blood in my system for me to keep being able to hear—or a psychological thing. Maybe the demon has blocked out all of Ben's speech to make him seem less human. He just mumbles and grunts like an animal, with a confused expression on his face. At some point, he takes my hands and holds them up, his eyes wide, looking down at the little moon-shaped holes I've made in my palms with my nails, which are leaking white liquid. He looks alarmed and he's trying to get to his phone, saying words I don't understand and gesturing for me to do something, to go with him somewhere, perhaps. He's putting on his shoes, struggling to do so without bending down to untie the laces.

I snatch my hands away, and he tries to take them back again, but then I do something I've never done before to anyone but myself, in my mirror at home as a teenager, playing out how I might respond to a bully at school. I open my mouth and curl back my lips and flash my teeth at Ben, and he staggers back like he's been pushed; then I turn around and leave, stumbling on my way to the door, still weak despite feeling like I could run for miles and miles.

Ben doesn't follow me down the stairs. I hear no movement behind me—nothing, just a widening empty space. I am completely alone, I think to myself; I can never be a human, I can never grow old with a human; I can never sleep with a human and have it mean more than just that. I feel like for the first time in my life, I can sense time and understand properly my place in it. I can feel time like it is space, extending ahead of me, stretching vastly, madly, awfully, out in front of me. I can feel time groping out ahead of my body, its fingers outstretched, connecting to the end of the world, connecting to strange, colorful fires right at the end of everything, all the elements burning, everything charring, the Sun unbearably close as it had been in my dream, my skin burning up, my heart still relentlessly beating. While I grew up, I changed every year. Now, there's no change, no sense of erosion or weathering, I'm just a thing that reacts in no way to the things around it. And yet, still, hours are the same. Minutes are the same. And seconds. All the same length to me as they are to humans. But my life is different; my life is a completely different thing from a human life.

At the bottom of the stairs, I stop and look down at myself, surprised to see that I still have a human body, surprised to see that my legs are moving like normal legs, surprised to see that I'm still putting one foot in front of the other. Upstairs, Ben is still in The Place. I can sense him again; I can sense everything about him. While I couldn't hear his speech earlier, now I can hear his heart beating fast, his thumbs darting across his phone screen, sending a message. I think, also, amid the throbbing and beating, I can hear fragments of his thoughts. My name, and Maria's—he's texting Maria—and random words, help, and hospital, and sick, and teeth; and milk too—the milk from my hands is on his hands and he's smelled it and recognized the smell. I can feel his body trembling. It's shock, maybe. I can feel him shaking, and trying to control it, taking deep breaths, sitting down on a chair. He seems frightened, of me, maybe, or of the situation; either way, I realize that a part of me enjoys it and that realization, in turn, frightens me.

I slip into my studio. It's dark inside. My room is still neat, the way I left it before I went up to The Place, Yaga in her strange human form on the canvas that is propped up against the wall, the real, puppet Yaga next to the painting, still strung up on the washing line I made, a little puddle on the table beneath her where the water from our shower has run off her hair. Joseph Beuys and his coyote are still up on the wall too; I'd forgotten that I'd put these pictures up—the coyote tearing at Beuys's blanket in one picture, placid and looking out the window in the other.

I'm inside for only a few minutes before I sense Ben outside my studio door. He knocks, and then he says my name—my name, which doesn't feel like it fits me anymore. "Lyd," he says, and then some other words I can't quite make out. And then, "Lyd, will you let me in?"

I sit down on the floor against the door. Through it, I can feel Ben's circulatory system. All his veins, like vines, growing beautifully out of his heart. I can smell his blood, and it smells delicious and familiar and wholesome, as I imagine freshly baked bread smells to humans. I grope at the door with my hands, as though I could get some sort of sustenance through it. I could open the door very quickly. I know how easily I could snatch Ben from the other side. On this side of the door, it would just be me and him, while on that side, other people will be arriving soon—artists starting work for the day, and maybe even doctors too, if he has called someone and told them I need to be seen. But here, it would be just us. Just us, in the dark.

Even in my mind, though, I can't imagine any scenario beyond that point, beyond the point of pulling Ben into my studio, beyond the point of seeing him in front of me, his body so much weaker than mine, even when mine is at its weakest. I don't know what I want to do with him. Seeing him purely as food is impossible. But, at the same time, I feel like I don't know him well enough to spend the rest of eternity with him; if I turned him, I'd be joined to him forever and a part of me—I think the human part—right now is angry with him, for letting anything happen between us when he knew nothing could ever happen again, for pulling his hand away from my hand. And then there's the other option. Does he deserve the other option? Just death? Just becoming sustenance for my body?

I take my phone out of my pocket and start composing a text, struggling to keep my head up, my fingers moving slowly. "I'm OK," I type. "Just need to be on my own." I press "send," and a message comes back immediately.

"I'm worried though."

"I am OK," I type again. And then I add, "Please don't call anyone."

"Will you let me in at least?" Ben replies. And I think about it again. I press my body against the door. His pulse throbbing, the valves in his heart opening and closing; I feel him swallowing as though I've been hit with the vibrations of the sound and can feel them physically in my stomach. I put my hand on the door handle. But then I take it off again. "Maybe later?" I text. "I just want to sleep."

"OK," Ben replies after a while, and I feel his presence leave, and then rise as it ascends the stairs. I hear the sound of his studio door closing two floors up. Then I tuck my phone away, and take a deep breath in.

I stay sitting by the door for a while. I look at my veins and wonder what is left of both sides of myself, now that there is barely any blood in my system, and my veins have been washed out by milk. I think back to the dreams I'd had last night while the milk had spread throughout my body: the two strange eels that seemed to depend on each other to stay alive, and then the dream of my mum. While I've spent so much of my life fixated on my dad, thinking of him as representing the living part of me, I'd forgotten that my mum is the one who is truly alive—no matter how she acts and what she says—and that my dad is the one who is actually dead.

I think I have known for a while that neither side of me can be separated from the other, and that this is true of my mum too; that I can't punish the demon by making it eat only pig blood without punishing the human; I can't listen to just one side, and block out the other; I can't force one side to be dormant while I live a life pretending to only be the other side; I can't starve either side out of myself. Really, I don't even have "sides" at all. I'm two things that have become one thing that is neither demon nor human.

I look at my arms. Their lines. The bones that I was born with. The shape of my wrists. Hands that over the next few centuries will probably keep painting but, maybe, also do other things. What will they touch? Humans; perhaps other vampires; perhaps other beings entirely, things I don't know about yet: if it's possible, my own children, maybe; mountaintops and thin mountain air; sand and sea; dark, vacuous space; the surfaces of other planets; the regolith scattered in the craters on them; meteor dust; the fire of the Sun. Will there be someone else with me, I wonder, when I do all of those things; will there be another hand in my hand, perhaps. My mother's? A daughter's? A son's? Will I have company I'll have created for myself, either as a mother or as a sire, or as both? Should I live alone for a bit first? Or should I make someone now?

I crawl to the table that has all my stuff on it, and I pull myself up. I sit in the chair closest to me, and then I squeeze some colors from the tubes of paint onto the plate I've been using as a palette. I do all of this without really thinking. I pull Yaga off the washing line. I hold her against my body, without putting my hand into her. I keep her as she is, dark and empty inside, strange and unanimated as I'd found her—and then I start painting over the human Yaga I created last night. I use all the same colors but change Yaga into something that feels more accurate—accurate to how the puppet Yaga looks but also to how I'm feeling. I keep some of the human skin and human hair, but I pull the dark background into the body so that it's not clear where the edge of the figure and the edge of the night behind are. A moon shines down from deep in Yaga's hair and reflects in her eyes.

I don't finish the painting, but I make a good start. Soon,

though, I can't continue. My hunger is so intense, and I feel so heavy and so dizzy and so empty, that I have to hold my arms out to stay balanced on the chair. And then I just fall off, with a thud, my head throbbing.

I stay on the ground for a while, drifting in and out of consciousness. Ben texts me again and I manage to read his message, but I don't reply. He asks how I am and says he'll come downstairs with some food for me later. It makes me want to laugh. And then several voices like a chorus speak at once in my mind. All of them, in unison, tell me to eat. On the floor next to me, Yaga's mouth opens and she says, in a voice that doesn't sound human or animal, "Feed me, Lydia." Then my body stands up, lifted by my hunger, and I go out, with just my keys and my phone in my pocket.

It is already dark outside. It's getting colder too. People have scarves around their necks. Behind windows, there are people sharing food and drinking hot chocolates and coffees, or holding wineglasses and talking animatedly. Other people are out running. Some are walking dogs. I walk along the river for a while, doubled over in pain and breathless, looking over the edge of the railing, down at the river, watching out for sand, and for animals, dead or dying, perhaps even alive, to eat.

Everywhere around me, I smell people's blood; I hear it in their systems, to the extent that I feel like I know, intimately, the layout of each of their bodies, the distance between all the different valves in their hearts and their lungs, and the size of their muscles. When I walk past a couple of men who seem like they're in a rush, clutching hot drinks in takeaway cups and struggling with the lids that they haven't put on properly yet, I sense a little knot in one of the men's legs, halfway up his thigh—a blood clot—and I briefly consider telling him. But I don't. I keep walking. Rain starts falling. I weave in and out through crowds, staggering as I go, and cross the river. All the people running past me, some glancing at me and avoiding my path; all the people ducking under shelters; all the people with umbrellas up, hoods up, or ducking into pubs, hands over pint glasses; they all exist in my world for a moment, and then disappear from it quickly, the rain closing behind them as a sheet, like a curtain.

I keep to the light and look through the windows of restaurants and pubs. I climb up the stairs of a theater and see people inside standing around in little groups on a red carpet and talking. There are tall tables some stand around with bowls of sharing food on top—nuts and crisps and dips and olives. I keep walking, past an Italian bistro in which people are eating seafood pasta; in another restaurant, two people have a huge plate of oysters between them; a man and a woman are talking animatedly about something they have on their table—a thick wad of paper that has text on it and notes written in pen—while they share food in a Peruvian restaurant. "Have you tried the scallops?" someone says. "Have you had time to look at the menu?" says another person. Two women, all in black, with instrument cases, are sharing a bottle of wine outside. A waiter comes out with a platter of sushi.

I sit outside a Turkish deli for a moment, feeling dizzy, my breathing fast, an intense pain in my stomach like the organ has tied itself into a knot. The seat is wet, but I don't really mind. A guy nudges his friend as they walk past. "Hey," he says to me. "You all right?" He's holding a can of beer and smirking. I don't say anything back. I can't. I nod. The guy looks at his friend and

I see them exchange a look, though I can't tell what it means. "Do you need help getting home?" the guy asks. I suppose I probably look drunk. I run my finger through the water on the table. I shake my head, and then the men leave, the one who did the talking muttering under his breath, "Okay, whatever." When they're a few steps away, I start to follow them, their hearts ahead of me, beating like tiny drums. But, then, I turn around and go in a different direction, following another instinct.

I cross back over the river and turn down a dark side road. The darkness is comforting. It feels like something I am wearing rather than something that is in the atmosphere, unconnected to me. It hangs down over my shoulders like a cape and makes me feel peaceful in a way I can't feel in light. I walk for a while, taking a few turnings until the sound of people dims, not really aware of where I'm going at all. At first, I think I might be heading for Camberwell, toward Anju's, but it soon becomes clear I'm not. Something keeps me moving forward, nonetheless, down streets I don't recognize. The rain stops. All I'm left with is the sound of my footsteps.

Eventually, the number of buildings starts to decrease. I realize I'm walking on a road with warehouses on either side; it's familiar. It's exceptionally quiet. I keep walking. I can hear water trickling. I can hear my breathing. And, then, I stop—and I'm standing in front of the Otter. Inside, the building's lights are being turned off, one by one. Then a figure appears in the frame of the front door. At first, I think it's Heather, but the shape is all wrong. It's Gideon. Unaware that I'm behind him, he starts to lock up. He fumbles with the locks for a while. He's using his phone light to see where he's putting his keys. I stand still for a moment, in a shadow, and just observe him.

In the light of the moon that is above us both, I can see that Gideon is just a regular man. There's nothing monstrous about his appearance; there's nothing about him that suggests he can disappear into shadows, nothing about his body that says he is powerful. I'm not really sure what I am anymore, though—whether I'm a monster or whether I'm just a woman, or both. I stay watching Gideon in silence for just a few moments, my breathing calm, my senses leveled out, smelling the faint scent of Gideon through the damp smell of puddles between us. It's strange; I'm completely relaxed. For the first time since arriving in London, I feel like I am exactly where I am meant to be. My legs have carried me to Gideon; the city that has so often failed me has delivered him to me. A sense I didn't know I possess picks up on something about him that makes him glow as if he is a piece of radium. On the air, the smell of something sweet. A voice in my head tells me it's his immorality, and it smells like cake. I step out of the shadows. When Gideon turns around and sees me, he jumps.

"Oh!" he says. He looks relieved to see that it's just me. He walks up to me. I stand still. "Lydia?" he says. He looks at his watch. He's smiling. I suppose he hasn't noticed anything off about me: that I'm completely drenched, that my color is probably strange, that I most definitely smell of milk that is slightly sour now, that my mouth is open and that my teeth are showing. "You're a bit late!" he says, and he laughs.

I want to say something. But I also can't think of anything to say, and I can't speak anyway. So, I just smile at him, instead, and he smiles at me. Then he lifts his hand up and places it on my arm—the same hand that touched my body on the stairs.

As soon as he does this, I feel like I can sense Gideon in a new dimension. I can feel the presence of not just his person, but of his life that has existed for however many decades before this moment, and that could last for a few more after. It's strange; his life presents itself to me as if it is a soft but solid thing—as soft and easy for me to slice through as butter. The edge of my own life has always felt so far in the future, so impossible for me to tempt closer to where in my life I am now, but I see very clearly the edge of Gideon's life. It's in me, in my teeth, in my body, which could drain him entirely of everything that keeps him moving forward. His neck is close to me; he's brought it to me himself; he has given me his life. It's just there, inches from my face.

I look at Gideon's soft-looking neck, the artery just under the skin, pumping. "Are you okay?" he asks. And then I move quickly. I bite, and he struggles for a moment, but I pin down his arms like he is a bird, and stand on his shoes like I am a child dancing on her father's feet. I drink, and, as I do, I see and feel things—his life: his birth, and then years at school, sitting quietly at the back of a room of boys behind desks; studying; grieving for his mother, then his father; then becoming a father himself—a sweet little girl with plump cheeks and dark hair; and, then, later, women—women he looks at like he's going to consume them; carrying a young woman into the shadowy part of a huge garden somewhere, laying her down on the grass under a tree and looking greedily down on her body; pinning her arms to her sides, pushing her back into the grass; and then, much later, in the gallery, seeing Shakti; watching her walking down the corridors; talking to her, looking at pieces of her art-work on her phone; then in the dark, finding her arm, and then her breast; watching her neck, like he might bite; finding her lips with his lips and, as she tries to pull away, seeking them out again, pressing against them harder. And then, a couple of months later, seeing me. I'm outside the Otter, and he is watching me from a window, talking to me on the phone, rebuking me for calling myself a girl and not a woman. Then I'm on the stairs. I'm coming down them. The box of hangers is covering my face. All he can see are my legs, my feet carefully treading, feeling for the edge of each step. I look so small. And, then, just as I reach him, it's as though his memories become my own and his hand becomes my hand, and I'm reaching forward, trying to take what isn't mine—or what is, now, I suppose mine. I reach forward and feel my back, feel it react to my touch, and then I move my hand down to my bum, and I grab it like I'm plucking an apple from a tree, and then watch as I climb down the rest of the stairs. It doesn't stop after that—soon after, I'm at the opening, and I'm watching me again, watching me undress, seeing the side of my breast as I swap my gallery T-shirt for my shirt; picking up the T-shirt when I'm gone and smelling it, inhaling my scent, lowering my hand and touching myself; and then I'm here, locking up, then I'm approaching me, excited at the prospect of being in this dark, quiet space, at nighttime, alone with me. And, then, right at the end of it all, I feel fear, intense fear— Gideon's fear of me, of being confronted by a monster—and I drop him, his body that I have emptied and possessed and taken away from him in its entirety.

The rain is coming down hard again. Everywhere is under the shadow of night. I find my way back to the river. There's life everywhere, and I see it, extending out from people's bodies, back decades and decades behind them, or just one decade, or just years, or just weeks. Perhaps it's because I've ended a life, because I've consumed one, but I perceive it now as a solid thing, as a material, as if it were cloth, woven from something like a fine silk. A child looks at me as he goes past with his dad and I see four years of time trailing behind him and a multitude of years meandering into the distance ahead of him; in between is his body—soft and sweet, big eyes, raincoat hood up, red cheeks— the vulnerable part of his life I could pick up and empty, to get to the rest of it. I stay in the darkest shadows, close to the buildings, under the trees; I savor Gideon's past and what I took of his future. Memories fill my mind, as though they are my own, of not just events from Gideon's life, but of various flavors and textures: breast milk running easily down into my stomach, chicken cooked with butter and parsley, split peas and runner beans and butter beans, and oranges and peaches, strawberries freshly picked from the plant; hot, strong coffees each morning; pasta and walnuts and bread and brie; then something sweet: a panna cotta, with rose and saffron, and a white wine: tannin, soil, stone fruits, white blossom; and—oh my god—ramen, soba, udon, topped with nori and sesame seeds; miso with tofu and spring onions, fugu and tuna sashimi dipped in soy sauce, onigiri with a soured plum stuffed in the middle; and then something I don't know, something unfamiliar but at the same time deeply familiar, something I didn't realize I craved: crispy ground lamb, thick, broken noodles, chilli oil, fragrant rice cooked in coconut milk, tamarind . . . and then a bright green desert—the sweet, floral flavor of pandan fills my mouth. I run. I feel good. I open my mouth and the rain washes over my tongue. Cyclists and runners move out of my way.

On my way back to the factory, I go down side roads, looking for other people. I want to eat more. I'm still hungry. I want to try other flavors. I find one around the back of a newsagent's, a lit cigarette held between his lips, and he doesn't even have time to say anything, but he looks me up and down and starts walking toward me, smirking. When I bite into his neck, the cigarette stays between his lips for a moment and I inhale and taste smoke and ash through the blood. I munch through the skin and muscle and bone, tasting chips and steak and gammon and soft-boiled eggs with bread soldiers dipped in, and reach a strange knot of flesh that I pull at with my teeth. It's his tongue and it hangs from my mouth as I drop the man's body to the floor. The tongue gently lands on his chest and then I say to the body, "Thank you." I almost say the whole grace my mum and I said to pigs. But I don't; instead I just listen to my voice ringing out in the silence and it is beautiful.

The factory is quiet when I arrive. Water runs off my clothes and hair in streams. I go quietly to my studio and unlock it, and the door closes behind me.

In the dark, I survey the room. Bits of the new life I'd started to build are here and there. The plant from Ben hanging from the hook, puppet Yaga, my painting, the books I bought under the bridge, the books I stole, clothes on the walls, my bed in the corner. I start packing things into my bag. Just some of the things. Most of them, I leave behind—the Beuys book, the book on vegetables I never read, the book on ethics. I open the Sher-Gil book and take out the cutout picture of *Three Girls* that I'd replaced between the pages earlier, and look at the girls' faces.

Three beautiful faces I feel like I know; perhaps I'll go and find them, I think; perhaps they're waiting for me. I put the picture and the book in my bag, and then pick up puppet Yaga.

For the first time, I feel like I truly own her, and it is because, within Gideon's memories, is the experience of buying art. In among Washoe baskets, Japanese ink drawings, and Chilean arpilleras is puppet Yaga, bought from an auction house in Russia; and among works by Emin and the Chapman brothers and Goya are paintings by my dad—the thick brushstrokes on silk, the angular black marks, the jagged shapes, now mine.

"Hey, Yaga," I say. Everything about her looks more pronounced: the darkness of her wooden face, the blackness of her clothes and her eyes. "I ate," I tell her. I put her in my rucksack. Then I leave, to go and pick up my mum, and then to go elsewhere, onward, somewhere.

As I step out of my studio, Ben appears at the foot of the stairs. He's holding a Pret bag that looks like it's full of food, and a cardboard container of soup; he carefully places the soup on the floor, and then looks for something in his pockets.

Looking at him now, it feels like the first time I have ever seen him; behind him, the part of his life that he has lived already bobs up and down, filling the stairwell; ahead of him, his future extends out, turning from where he stands and reaching toward me. I can see hints of grief in it, and also other things—his little sister, his dad, the home he grew up in, and his bedroom, which is still decorated as it was when he was a child, with blue walls, and a border of trains along the top—but I also see that it has a definitive end. While I saw the lives of others extend for decades and decades ahead of them, Ben's cuts off sharply in just a couple of years. What is ahead of him is just the equivalent of a child's life.

I move closer to him, closing the door to my studio silently behind me, and staying in the shadow cast by the stairs. I could tell him about the shortness of his time, I think, and maybe the course of his life would be altered and he would live on for a good few decades. Or else, I could turn him; I could stretch his tiny life to oblivion, distorting it in the process, making it strange and unnatural like mine. I can't decide what to do. I stay very still. He has his phone in his hand now, and he's texting. Then my own phone vibrates in my pocket and he turns around, squinting in my direction.

"Lyd?" he says. I see how beautiful his little life is; it kind of glistens in this light, perfectly formed, even though it is short. It's irresistible. I step out of the shadow and, immediately, Ben's expression changes—he looks shocked, and frightened. I must look mad and monstrous, filled with other people's lives. I wipe my mouth with the back of my hand and see that it is covered in blood.

"What—" Ben begins, but I tell him to be quiet, and I smile, and then I take him by his arms and squeeze him, lifting him slightly off the floor; and then I bend over him and wrap my body around him, my chin on his shoulder, my neck against his neck, feeling his pulse as if it is mine. As I drop him, I take my keys out of my pocket, and then open Ben's hand and place them inside it. "I have to go," I say.

Ben doesn't say anything. He just looks at me, his mouth open, blood from my mouth smeared on his skin. And then I leave; I leave Ben's life intact—tiny and beautiful—and my own life with him, behind me.

ACKNOWLEDGMENTS

Thank you—

To Nina Efimova, for your puppets—the puppet Baba Yaga exists in these pages because, a century ago, you made her from wood and an old, stained kitchen rag.

To Bernice Bing, Amrita Sher-Gil, Mirosław Bałka, Joseph Beuys, La Monte Young, Senga Nengudi, and Caravaggio—for your art, which helped shape Lydia into the artist she is.

To chefs and people celebrating Asian cuisines, everywhere. Throughout *Woman, Eating*, Lydia harbors an obsession with Japanese food; only at the end does she recognize her desire for Malaysian food too. I wanted her first taste of Malaysian cuisine to be a good one—the fragrant rice, broken noodles, and crispy ground lamb she enjoys at the end are dishes created by Julie Lin of Julie's Kopitiam in Glasgow. The pandan dessert is Madame Chang's pandan kaya.

To my family, who have offered me endless support—my Jiji and Baba, Tomoji, Eriko, Ayano, Reiko, and Albert.

To friends—Yasuko, Charles, Erika and Amy, Misa and Grim, Ai, Shin, Megumi and Noriko, Rory, Liz, Yunhan, Su, Hugh, Becka, James, Chris, Kat, Vinny, and Marion; Charlotte, for our friendship like Hovis; Misha, for listening always, for Glebe; Jess, my stein; and to others whose names I haven't listed—for your love and support.

Deeply, to Ruth, for everything. And to your friend, also, and to Oliver.

To Annabel, for twenty years ago being the best tree-climbing and bow-and-arrow-making friend; and since then, for everything you have done for this book and beyond, and for helping me kill Venus.

To Aisha, my soulfrog, for your companionship in everything to do with writing and life.

To Karen—you took care of my dreams, nurtured and encouraged them. Thank you so much.

To Deborah, for your generosity and kindness. And, for advice and reading early drafts, Tom, Annabel, Liz, Polly, Aisha, Kalliopi, Rebecca, and Mark.

To everyone at Virago: Kim, Zoe, Ailah; and to Sarah, my editor—you have been a gift to this book; you are like an angel editor sent from editor heaven. Everyone at HarperVia: Alexa, Alicia, and Stephen; and to Tara—Lydia's godmother if she ever had one—for your invaluable advice and support.

To my agent Sam and to everyone else at RCW, and to Michelle at CAA, for your continued support.

To Mosling, for spending time in my life, being by my side, leaving us with good fortune; the bears, every one of you.

To Mum and Dad, my best friends, for giving me life and filling it with art, food, music, love and laughter—"you've given me everything I need."

And most of all to Tom, for enriching and brightening everything in my life, for listening to every word, every sentence, for helping to guide Lydia's life, for your companionship, trust, support, and genus-hands. You're the best human I know.

A NOTE ON THE COVER

How best to portray the story of Lydia—a woman who has mixed Japanese, Malaysian, and English heritage, and who is a vampire, a creature inherently half-demon, half-human—who is constantly trying to resist the temptation of her nature? I designed many versions of this cover; some depicted Lydia, while others focused on specific details from the story, like bite marks, or a pig whose blood she drinks in order to stave off her cravings for human blood. In the end, though, the most powerful visual was not one of Lydia herself, but of the novel's antagonist.

Because Lydia is an artist, it felt fitting to use a painting on the cover, but it needed to be a piece that spoke to the story on multiple levels. Caravaggio's *Boy with a Basket of Fruit* felt just right: the sidelong glance peering back at the viewer, the lush basket filled with food that Lydia can never eat, not to mention Caravaggio's own less-than-pristine reputation, not dissimilar to our antagonist's. The final touch: a perfectly-placed crack in the canvas—or is it a bite mark?

Woman, Eating is a book unlike any other I've ever read. As a designer, there is always a certain pressure to create something new and evocative for each project, to give each book the cover it truly deserves. That pressure is amplified even more when you love a book as much as I loved this one. I only hope I did it justice.

—Alicia Tatone

Here ends Claire Kohda's
Woman, Eating.

The first edition of this book was printed
and bound at LSC Communications
in Harrisonburg, Virginia, January 2022.

A NOTE ON THE TYPE

Named after the Florentine River, Arno draws on the warmth and readability of early humanist typefaces popularized during the Italian Renaissance. Designed for Adobe by Robert Slimbach, Arno honors fonts of the past but is thoroughly modern in style and function. An Adobe favorite, it offers extensive European language support, including Cyrillic and polytonic Greek. The font family also features five optical size ranges, many italic sets, and small capitals for all supported languages.

HARPERVIA

An imprint dedicated to publishing international voices,
offering readers a chance to encounter other lives and other
points of view via the language of the imagination.